"Samotin casts a spell over the reader with this sensuous dark academia novel as dark and twisted as the stacks of an occult library."

S.T. Gibson, internationally bestselling author of *A Dowry of Blood*

"I'm the one haunted by this tender and gorgeous story. Laura R. Samotin tackles themes of atonement and duty—and how those things can be wielded as a form of abuse—in the nuanced way that her readers have come to expect, while expertly weaving in Jewish mysticism and casual queerness. Fans of dark fantasy, shining hope, and everlasting love, don't miss out on this one."

Kamilah Cole, *USA Today* & National Indie bestselling author of *An Arcane Inheritance*

"*The Way It Haunted Him* is a love letter to horror readers. A story steeped in folklore, queer love, and the harsh reality of grief, guilt, and the monsters we inherit. Laura R. Samotin, the master of a one-sitting read, has struck again."

Ben Alderson, author of *The Haunting of William Thorn*

"Laura Samotin stuns again. Her dark, entrancing prose and wonderfully complex characters will leave readers spellbound, as they delve with Michael Stein into the secrets of Schechter Institute. A powerful gothic tale that will have readers at the edge of their seats."

ADEN POLYDOROS, author of *The City Beautiful*

"Beautifully poignant and chillingly dark, *The Way it Haunted Him* is an examination of grief, obsession, trauma and above all, love. It grabbed me by the throat and refused to let go."

FRANCES WHITE, bestselling author of *Voyage of the Damned*

"An unsettling and wholly original exploration of grief, desire, and the strength of belief, *The Way It Haunted Him* will get under your skin and linger for a very, very long time. Also: one of the best cats in literature."

CLAIRE SCHULTZ, author of *Even Your Bones Would Do*

# the Way it Haunted Him

LAURA R. SAMOTIN

TITAN BOOKS

The Way It Haunted Him
Print edition ISBN: 9781835412312
E-book edition ISBN: 9781835412329

Published by Titan Books
A division of Titan Publishing Group Ltd
144 Southwark Street, London SE1 0UP
www.titanbooks.com

First edition: June 2026
10 9 8 7 6 5 4 3 2 1

This is a work of fiction. All of the characters, organizations, and events portrayed in this novel are either products of the author's imagination or are used fictitiously. Any resemblance to actual persons, living or dead (except for satirical purposes), is entirely coincidental.



A CIP catalogue record for this title is available from the British Library.

Designed and typeset in Bembo Book MT Std by Richard Mason.

EU RP (for authorities only)
eucomply OÜ, Pärnu mnt. 139b-14, 11317 Tallinn, Estonia
hello@eucompliancepartner.com, +3375690241

Printed and bound by CPI Group (UK) Ltd, Croydon, CR0 4YY.

# A Note to Readers

*The Way It Haunted Him* centers themes of guilt, grief, and toxic obsession. As such, it includes discussion of physical and emotional abuse by a romantic partner, as well as subsequent mental health struggles and suicidal ideation. Detailed content warnings are available on my author website.

*To those who find it hard to trust themselves.*
*One day I hope you, too, believe.*

# Chapter 1

Michael Stein wasn't a good person.

The incision across his ribs was dripping blood by the time he pulled into the archive's driveway. He'd spent the entire drive from the city picking at it through his shirt, sliding his thumbnail across the ridges of his ribs and into the valley of what should have turned, by now, to a faded scar, prying at the scab that had been trying valiantly to form for the last seven months.

Putting the rental car into park, Michael leaned back against the padding of the driver's seat, staring blankly at the building in front of him, trying to will himself to care that he was about to walk into a world-renowned archive and meet the exceedingly selective archivist while wearing a blood-soaked shirt and pretending that no, it wasn't painful at all to stand up straight. But, like every other time he'd attempted to summon concern in the time since the altercation, there was just… nothing.

A blank spot where his pride and his self-assurance had once been, clawed out by the guilt and the unending, all-encompassing grief.

Being here was a reminder of just how much repentance was impossible, and yet how desperate he was to try anyway. Even if nothing he could ever do would make things right, not anymore.

Now that he'd arrived at the archive, tension was gathering in his shoulders, sweat breaking out on his palms. Breathing in deep caused the burn plaguing the incision to worsen, but he did it anyway, blinking in the weak fall sunlight just fading behind the tops of the old-growth, autumn-hued trees, their branches just starting to go bare. He'd set out early in the morning, not wanting to miss any time in the archives. The curator had been incredibly specific in the terse emails he'd read off Nate's pilfered phone, taken out of a bag of personal belongings that the hospital had left with him, since he was Nate's emergency contact. There would be no admission to the archive before twilight, and once the sun was fully down, no new researchers would be booked in until the next day. Something about security, although Michael suspected it was one of those eccentricities that he'd learned over the last few years most academics tried hard to cultivate.

He held his breath, counting in his head until the burn in his lungs was too much, and breathed out through pursed lips. It was one of the few useful things that his therapist—who Sarah and his family were forcing him to see—had done for him over the last several months. Talking things over with his therapist, who legally couldn't tell anyone else what had happened, had allowed him to be truthful, but hadn't made him feel better in the least. At least the exercises did something to calm the frantic pace of his heart.

His heart hadn't stopped pounding like this since his boyfriend had died. Not since he'd had to reckon with what he'd done, and what he'd made his boyfriend do. The horrors that he'd inflicted on another person, so thorough and monstrous that he'd caused *this*, a situation that had trapped him in a prison of his own making. Lies upon lies upon lies, in order to conceal the truth. Choosing, at the end of it all, to keep being selfish.

Everyone who knew Nate thought he had died in a random, tragic accident. Only Michael knew the truth.

It was all his fault.

This was what he owed Nate. Finishing the work he'd been known for, so that even now that he was dead, something of him would live on. So that the world would have memories of him that persisted, a legacy that wasn't the one the media had cultivated for him, the obituary based on lies. So that Michael could think of Nate and remember something other than those last, desperate moments. It had always been Nate's dream to publish his work, and no matter Michael's feelings about his late boyfriend's research, he was going to leave his personal trauma and his own thoughts on the matter behind to finish this for Nate, to the best of his ability.

Michael opened the car door, the cold, crisp air causing him to blink rapidly and wish he'd put a coat on. A rough wind battered his cheeks the moment his skin met the air. The dry rustling of the leaves on the trees made him wince, so like the dry crackle of the absorbent pads laid down on his hospital bed when his persistent picking at his incision caused him to bleed on the sheets one too many times. He put one foot in front of the other, the gravel of the drive crunching underfoot, heading toward the imposing stone house in front of him. He fought back a groan and shifted his backpack to hang loose off his left shoulder, somewhat obscuring the rust-colored patch on his Henley.

He should have worn the red one. He'd learned over the last few months that it was easier to hide bloodstains if the color matched.

The wind sent his nose numb before he made it down the long, tree-lined drive and up the expansive stone steps leading to the front door, but that was alright because the rest of him was numb too. The building didn't look much like a synagogue anymore, save for the large rose window that had been set high into the front. Anything on the façade that may have indicated it was a place of worship had been removed, replaced with ivy creeping over the age-worn bricks. The bushes out front may once have been neatly clipped but had now been left to run somewhat wild. The only reason Michael didn't worry he was about to accidentally knock on the door of a very rich person with very poor gardening skills was the small brass plaque that read Schechter Institute for Judaic Studies.

Michael hesitated before raising his hand to knock at the door, rehearsing his speech in his mind. He hadn't disclosed to the archivist that he wasn't Nate—he'd heard far too much over the last months of Nate's life about how picky the archivist was to attempt to switch researchers on the old man. Eleazar Schechter was something of a legend among the comparative religion crowd studying Judaism, Nate had assured him, having amassed the largest private collection of Eastern European Jewish archival material pertaining to the folklore, magic, and traditions of the Pale of Settlement Jewry.

But two years ago, he'd stopped admitting researchers to the archives. The doors were shuttered and inquiries to visit the collection were met with increasingly terse emails—there were excuses first about water damage, and then delays because of renovations needed due to the water damage, and then there just hadn't been any excuses at all, only silence.

Nate's advisor's email to Schechter, begging to use the archives, had gone unanswered. But Nate's own email hadn't.

Michael shifted his backpack so he could pick at his scar more. The fabric of his shirt was wet and tacky under his fingers. He stared down at the blood under his nails, wondered if the archivist would think he was a serial killer, and then decided that he didn't care and rang the bell anyway.

Nothing happened for long enough that Michael took out his phone to check the time, tapping his thumb against the cracked screen to light it up and make sure the clock was right at 6:38 p.m., the time which his weather app had assured him was the official beginning of sundown. Sarah had been begging him to replace it—it had been broken in the accident—but he hadn't been able to. Just like the torn skin on his ribs, he needed to see the damage so that he wouldn't forget.

Not that that was likely. Every time he closed his eyes,

he saw Nate's convulsing body lying on the pavement. Every time he jerked awake, he started gagging at the memory of regaining consciousness in the hospital with a breathing tube down his throat. Every time he made the circuit of their apartment, he was plagued by memories of Nate sitting on the couch and reading a book, working on his dissertation at the table, lying in their bed. Memories that only he had, memories that only he would ever be able to dissect, because when the time had come to tell the truth he'd lied.

Just like the monster in every story he'd ever been told, he'd hidden the truth when it mattered. He'd obscured his own nature. He'd tricked everyone into thinking he wasn't at fault. And like the villain in so many stories, he'd gotten away with the lie. It had worked, even when he was silently begging someone to believe in the truth that he knew in his bones, so that he could be punished appropriately for what he'd done.

His only punishment was the way it haunted him, and that didn't feel like nearly enough, even as the agony of it all felt like a knife slipping between his ribs with every breath. He hoped it would never stop, that the guilt would never ease, because right now he deserved to be in pain for his role in everything.

He couldn't turn back time and stop the accident he'd caused, no matter how fervently he wished. So he was left to punish himself for what he'd so carelessly done. This trip was part of his repentance. He couldn't repair what he had done, but he could repent. Owning the harm that he'd caused was the first step.

Michael shifted on his feet, his ribs aching, and was

about to ring the bell again when the door swung open. But standing on the other side wasn't an old man who was apparently notorious for his loudly colored argyle sweaters.

No, this man was his age, and he was hauntingly beautiful.

"Nathanial Lieberman?" The man looked down at a printout of an email, slightly crumpled around the edges like it had been well-handled for some time. His eyes flicked back up to Michael. "You look nothing like your website photograph."

"Uh." Michael's palms were suddenly slick with sweat, and he didn't know if it was from the edge in the man's voice, or the fact that he could have walked right off the runway and into this archive. "That's because I'm not Nate."

The man's eyebrows shot up, and the way he cocked his head and narrowed his eyes was disconcerting. He was a few inches shorter than Michael and, from the sharpness of his cheekbones and the pale cast to his skin, he looked like he hadn't eaten in days. There were purple bags under his eyes, his skin was drawn, and he looked as depleted as Michael felt inside. Still, his body was lithely muscular, the planes of his chest evident though the thin cotton of his white button-up shirt, the muscles in his forearms ticking as he fiddled with the paper in his hands. And his eyes were preternaturally green, fringed with the darkest lashes Michael had ever seen on another man.

Michael realized that he was assessing the man standing in front of him like he could be another mindless hookup, and reminded himself that this was real life and not an app. That he was here to do something for Nate, not take yet another thing for himself. That he was supposed to be trying to tame the demon inside of him, not feed it.

"Who are you then?" The man crossed his arms. "This archive is by appointment only, and I'm expecting a Nate Lieberman."

"Well," Michael retorted, "I was expecting an Eleazar Schechter. He's eighty-six years old. You either aren't him or you *must* share your skincare routine."

The man's eyes widened and he looked more than a little taken aback. Michael winced. He hadn't used to be cuttingly nasty—far from it. But these days, everything came out of his mouth with venom. Like the grief he was keeping within was rotting him from the inside out.

But then, the man shook his head and extended a hand. "Touché. Jacob Schechter. Eleazer is—was—my grandfather. He passed on a year ago. I've only just gotten the place back up and running. It's been something of an ordeal."

His hand was warm and dry, his grip surprisingly firm for someone who looked like he could break with the lightest touch. Michael's mouth filled with saliva at the thought, nausea rising in his throat. He drew his hand back, putting careful distance between himself and Jacob. Michael was, after all, too good at breaking people.

"May his memory be a blessing." It took him a moment of swallowing hard to both remember his manners and make sure that he wouldn't vomit when he spoke. The idea of mourning a grandparent cut through him, the mess of emotions constricting his breathing. Would he manage to be sad when his grandparents died, or would their memories be yet another casualty of his inhumanity? "I'm sorry to confuse you. It's just that Nate…"

His voice petered out, leaving him staring at the stone steps. Jacob didn't try to fill in the silence, though, just waited for him to keep speaking. Eventually, he worked up the courage.

*Name what you did.*

"Nate was my boyfriend. He died in an… an accident over the summer." Michael swallowed hard, trying to clear the lump that formed in his throat. "I'm here to continue his research. His dissertation. The project on folktales illuminating very real, unexplained phenomena which were dismissed because of the religion of Eastern European Jews and the way they were seen as liars by larger society."

The last part came out in a rush. Michael was a translator, not a scholar, and so reciting an argument sat strangely on his tongue. His job was, and had always been, to faithfully convey the words and meanings of another person. It was what he'd gone to school for, what he'd won awards for, and how he'd made a decent enough living that the people in his life were proud of him.

"I'm sorry to hear that." Jacob was looking at Michael like he might collapse. His eyes kept flicking down to Michael's ribs, which Michael supposed was quite understandable given the fact that the gray fabric was stained in blood. "May his memory be a blessing."

"It's—it's from surgery." Michael gestured helplessly to his ribs. "I have an incision that won't heal. I'm sorry. I know it's disturbing."

*Because you keep picking at it,* Sarah's voice taunted him. She was his best friend, and had been since they'd been in the same master's program, which she apparently took as license to nag him about how the surgical scar—inflicted when his lung was reinflated and his shattered ribs repaired—wasn't some modern-day mark of Cain. He shifted on the stoop, dead leaves crunching under the heels of his sneakers.

Jacob just shrugged. "We all bleed. God knows I've seen enough blood in my life to be used to it by now. Come in."

He stepped aside and gestured for Michael to enter, which he did. "I know it's not kind for me to show up basically unannounced, but I didn't want to risk losing the spot."

"Are you still here to do the research that was discussed in the correspondence?" Jacob closed the door behind him, and the rush of warmth from stepping inside made Michael's cheeks tingle in a faintly unpleasant way. "Because those are the materials that I've sequestered for you. It hasn't been easy getting the archive back up and running, so I'm afraid I won't be able to help you if there are other materials that you need."

"No, no." Michael looked around at the entryway, which had been decorated with items that were clearly from the building's use as a synagogue: cases full of decorative pointers for reading Torah, embroidered clothes hanging on the wall in varying states of decay that likely once covered the Holy Ark in some far-flung synagogue. The lighting and the carpet were clearly modern, but with the huge oak staircase dominating the entryway, and the way the walls had been turned into part of an archive, Michael couldn't help but feel that he had stepped back in time. The smell of old books—musty, slowly decaying paper, a smell that still managed to be comforting—permeated the air, along with something sharper. "It's my fault that I've surprised you, and I'm really just here to continue Nate's research. I'm going to finish his dissertation. For him."

Jacob leaned against the wall, perilously close to a beautifully crafted menorah balanced on a small table. The lights in the entryway were low, as though they'd been put on a dimmer turned all the way down, and in the soft, warm glow, Jacob was gaunt but still undeniably beautiful. "That's very kind of you. Did you work on the same thing, or is this a tribute to him?"

Michael couldn't help but give a grim laugh at that. "I'm not a scholar. Nate and I met—" He broke off, because this was the first time that he could remember telling anyone about his relationship with Nate since he'd died.

But now was time for confession. Jacob Schechter didn't know anything about what had happened seven months ago, in a city hours and hours away. And something magnetic in Jacob's eyes was coaxing part of the truth out of him, like a fisherman reeling in his catch. "Nate and I met when he hired me to complete a translation project. I was looking over documents he'd collected on a research trip to Poland and he was giving me the context for his work. Nate was arguing in his dissertation that folktales were illustrating a real phenomenon, and that household demons actually were plaguing Ashkenazi households. Me, I… didn't. I don't. We started arguing about it, and we were talking so long that we ended up going to dinner to keep up the discussion, and that was it."

"So you don't believe in demons?" Jacob brushed a lock of dark hair out of his eyes. It was shorn close on the sides, but left long on top, a trendier haircut of the kind Nate would have gotten. "Not even the small household ones?"

"No." Michael shifted his backpack. Its weight was making his ribs twinge, and this was veering uncomfortably close to conversations—arguments—he'd had over and over with Nate. He didn't know why the archivist was so interested in this. "I don't. Demons are just ways that people without access to science or resources tried to explain the world around them when things got frightening. We know better, now, and besides—until I've seen irrefutable proof with my own eyes, I'm going to believe in things like gravity and sanitation instead of things like demons. And, well, I think it's all bullshit."

"Too bad." Jacob smirked. "Because this place? It's full of them."

Michael froze. Every muscle in his body tensed at once, the way his parents' cat would go stock-still if she thought there was a threat. "Demons aren't real."

It was the one thing that he knew to be true, that he'd argue for, even if in every other sense he'd roll over and show his stomach if someone disagreed with him strongly enough. Because those folktales were stories that scared people told themselves in the dark. Michael hated feeling out of touch with reality—he'd been on SSRIs ever since a spate of anxiety-induced paranoid delusions when he was in grad school—and believing in creatures from the beyond that would punish you for leaving your water out overnight by poisoning it felt a bit too much like that form of losing your mind for his comfort.

Jacob's answering laugh and the gleam in his eye went straight to Michael's gut in a way nothing had since… a long time ago. Sometime in between being approached about the wildly well-funded project that would have sent him to Lithuania for a year to translate an entire recently discovered archive into English, and now. "Tell that to the mazzekin who crawl all over this place. They're mostly harmless, I promise. But when your notes go missing or your pen caps end up lodged somewhere they shouldn't be, that's what's happening. The best thing is simply to learn how to live with them. They coexisted very peacefully with Eleazar."

Jacob looked serious and not like he was trying to pull one over on him. And how hard could Michael argue for the idea that there was no such thing as household demons which created minor annoyances when he was, in fact, here to do research to prove that such a thing was true?

The tension made his stomach ache.

*Nate would have loved this*, his treacherous brain supplied. And then his equally treacherous eyes began to water, and his traitor of a throat began to close. Because he could see it, the way Nate would have been giddy to meet the archivist who had household demons inhabiting his shelves. A research trip and a practicum, all in one. He would have gotten so excited that he wouldn't even notice his glasses sliding down his nose or that he was close to knocking something over with his massive six-foot-three bulk, a mere four inches taller than Michael but so much sturdier. And just like always, Michael would have delighted in the way that his boyfriend was so intelligent, so passionate, and so alive with the desire to learn, even if he disagreed with the subject.

"Are you alright?"

The question brought Michael back to himself and he swallowed painfully, realizing there were actual tears running down his cheeks. Fuck, he hadn't started crying in public since his first trip to Whole Foods after he was allowed to leave the house again, when he saw Nate's favorite brand of coffee on the shelf and started to sob in the dry goods aisle, all his buried grief coming to the surface.

"Yes." He wiped his cheeks with the backs of his hands. "I'm so sorry. I'm fine."

"I was going to offer you the spare bedroom, but if you're that distressed by the thought of household demons, perhaps that wouldn't be wise?" Jacob stared down at the ground, his cheeks a bit flushed.

Michael bit his lip to hide the fact that he was taken aback. He hadn't known that the archive had a guest room—he'd never heard of such a thing, and his contract translation projects had sent him to archives all around the world—but he supposed it made sense, with the place being a former synagogue instead of a purpose-built archive like most of the modern ones. Plenty of rooms probably meant that they could be used for other things.

"I mean,"-Michael's voice came out scratchy again, and he swallowed past the gradually receding lump in his throat, "I booked an Airbnb in town for the next two weeks, but I'm on a tight budget. I wouldn't say no to free lodging. That's very kind of you."

He was self-funding this trip, and he'd had to push back or forgo three different projects in order to do it. Combined with not having been able to work reliably for the last several months, his bank account was suffering.

The funder of the large Lithuania gig had told him that the project was still waiting for him, that he'd have as long as he needed to recover from the accident after he'd emailed her from the hospital, and that the archive wasn't going anywhere. But until he was able to travel internationally to take that on, he was left watching his bank account slowly deplete. Unlike Nate, he wasn't loaded.

"Of course." Jacob nodded, crossing over the foyer to gently pry Michael's bag away from his shoulder. When the back of his knuckles ghosted over Michael's bicep, he felt that gut-punch sensation again. He couldn't help but notice that Jacob smelled like books and pachouli and the slightest hint of woodsmoke, an altogether intoxicating combination. "Here, let me take this from you. I can show you to the room. You may wish to get cleaned up before I introduce you to the archive."

"Thanks," Michael managed to get out. "I appreciate it."

"Of course." Jacob paused with Michael's bag over his shoulder, one foot on the bottom stair. "And I should have said, like Eleazer always did—welcome to the Schechter Institute. May you find truth here."

The hair on the back of Michael's neck pricked and his eyes locked with Jacob's, a sense of something like foreboding running through him.

He wondered if he would find truth; and if he did, what it would be, and what it would mean for him when he found it.

# Chapter 2

The guest bedroom was up two flights of stairs, just enough to leave Michael wheezing audibly even though he tried to hide it. He hadn't been able to take a proper deep breath since the surgery, although he wasn't sure if it was something still wrong with his body, or the vise his own mind had fastened around his chest. Jacob was pretending not to be concerned, but Michael supposed it was hard when the person who'd shown up at your door was leaning against the wall, dizzy and with blood dripping down his ribs, after climbing up a mere thirty-two stairs. Gone were his days of being able to pull off two-hour yoga classes followed by a run back home.

At least Jacob had taken his duffel bag from him after the first flight, probably out of concern as much as out of a sense of ingrained politeness.

"It's not much," Jacob said. "But it's free, and it's right here. So that you won't have to travel from town. Your materials will all be prepared by the time you wake up. I keep unusual hours, but I make sure that the archive is ready for researchers at a normal time. I'll stay out of your way until it's time to pack up the materials for the night—and anyway, this time of year I mostly wake up at five in the evening. Start by eight or nine and you'll get your full day in."

He turned the handle of a plain wooden door, revealing a small but well-kept room with a large bed and a desk by the window. Jacob deposited Michael's backpack on a chair, before pointing out where he could put his clothes, and the small adjoining bathroom.

It was honestly better than what Michael was expecting from the six-hundred-dollar-a-week rented room in town. "Thank you again. I really appreciate it."

Jacob smiled at him, far kinder than anyone had looked at him since the accident. It felt like everyone, after that, had been looking at him like he was about to break. And he couldn't blame them. His family had taken to sending him statistics about how safe the city really was, trying to get him back out into the world, even as they were also grieving the fact that Nate—who they had adored—was dead. Sarah, the only friend who'd put up with his long months of self-imposed isolation, had tiptoed around him as if she wasn't sure whether her next words would hurt or help.

The expression softened the sharp lines of Jacob's face, and it made Michael's heart lurch. "It's lonely here, especially at night. I could use the company. It's just been me here since Eleazer passed away. Just me, and the mazzekin, and the books."

Michael winced. "It's—really? You genuinely believe that stuff? It's not a schtick? Because the only people I've met who actually think that demons walk the earth and turn your milk sour and all that bullshit have about seven decades on you, and come from the Old Country." His grandparents believed in superstitions like that, and he'd always rolled his eyes at how old-fashioned it was.

"Ah." Jacob tapped his lower lip with a finger. "You clearly haven't met the right people, then. I'll have to convert you. I'm sure they'll do their part as well. And how do you know I *didn't* come from the Old Country?"

An ungainly snort escaped from Michael before he could stop it. "Because you don't seem like you spit three times into the fire to stop demons from stealing your cows."

"Hey," Jacob said, raising an eyebrow. "Don't knock it if you don't know for sure it's useless." His eyes crinkled up again. "I promise the mazzekin aren't all that awful. I got them to like me quickly. I bribed them with bread, salt, and honey when I officially moved in. After that, the rats in the basement were miraculously all taken care of, and the grinding noises the pipes used to make stopped... for the most part."

It was strange, meeting another person seemingly his age who apparently believed in all this stuff, just like Nate had, but seemed to be taking it even more seriously. At least with Nate, Michael had been able to rationalize it as being simply the product of academic infatuation.

For Jacob, this seemed like just a part of his life.

"Did your grandfather teach that to you?" Michael sank down onto the bed, leaning against the headboard, panting a bit. He hated being so weak, but it was unavoidable. It was probably better that he sat down than collapsed. "That's an old Ashkenazi custom for blessing a new dwelling."

"Eleazer taught me many things, but that was something that I learned from personal experience." Michael ran a finger around the rolled-up cuff of his shirt, tugging at it. "He was less inclined to those kinds of rituals, actually. He just grumbled at the mazzekin and they grumbled back, and they all coexisted in old-person harmony. He'd been here so long he was practically part of the synagogue. They accepted him after a while, bribes or no."

"Where did you grow up?" Michael let his head flop back against the plaster of the wall. "If you only came here recently."

Jacob shrugged. "Here and there. I came to the Institute at the end of Eleazar's life. It was just him and me. We were all the other had."

Jacob shifted from foot to foot, a muscle in his jaw ticking as he stared out the window. The setting sun was painting pink light over his face, and he looked more vibrant for it. But his eyes were sad in a way that Michael recognized, the kind of hollow pain that came from watching the people in your world leave one by one. The pain of being the only one left, because of death or distance or losing people due to who you were.

"It must be lonely here," he ventured softly. "I'm sorry again for your loss."

An audible swallow followed a shrug. "It's nice, being here with these things. It fills the void, access to all this knowledge. Still, I can't imagine I'll be here forever. I'm looking for a way to move on. It's just that for now, I feel quite trapped by his legacy."

"I'm here to work on the dissertation of someone who passed on," Michael responded wryly. It was still strange to be able to talk about Nate out loud, and something about it felt surprisingly good. "I know how it feels to have the past hanging around your neck like a noose. And grief strangling you."

"That too," Jacob said softly. Then he shook his head, the melancholy expression melting off his face as he visibly recentered himself. "Why don't I introduce you to the archive, and then you can spend a bit of time there before we eat dinner? If you'd like to eat with me, that is. You could also go into town."

The ghosts of a hundred solitary, sad cups of instant noodles waved themselves in front of Michael's face, and he had to fight not to jump on the offer in a way that made him seem like he was so devoid of company that he'd salivate like an excited dog to have dinner with a stranger. So, he took a deep breath before he replied, "That would be lovely, thank you."

Jacob cracked a tiny grin and jerked his thumb over his shoulder. "This way, then."

The hallways on the third level of the old synagogue were plain and somewhat institutional, as if they hadn't been decorated before and no one had bothered to remedy that since. Jacob pointed out a few other rooms—"Eleazer said these used to be classrooms for the Hebrew school, and he turned them into storage rooms and work rooms for processing materials"—and then led them back down to the second level. The other side of the second floor, opposite from Michael's guest room, was a small, snug office paneled in dark wood that Jacob indicated had belonged to the rabbi, and a set of meeting rooms that were now full of wire shelves bearing hundreds of archival boxes.

The wide wooden planks of the stairs creaked under their feet as Jacob led the way back down to the ground floor. "You've already been here, in the foyer. Eleazer used it as something of a museum. There's a sitting room to the left, and then behind us is the original sanctuary. It's what was turned into the main room of the archive. I think you'll like it."

When his right foot hit the boards of the first floor, Jacob wobbled a bit, like he was unsteady on his feet. He grabbed for the handrail, and Michael watched as he gripped it so hard that his knuckles blanched. Every one of the blue-green veins on the back of his hand was visible through his skin.

"Are you okay?" Michael scooted around him as Jacob stepped fully off the stair. If the other man was going to fall, Michael wanted to catch him, even though that would likely send the two of them tumbling into each other in a very injured heap. "Did you hurt yourself?"

Jacob shook his head, his expression clearing. He let go of the handrail and flexed his fingers, then put his hands into the pockets of his slacks. "I've never had the best feet. Sometimes I step weirdly and they hurt. That's all."

"Ah." Michael nodded. "Well, let me know if I can do anything to help."

"I assure you," Jacob replied with a staccato exhalation that could have been either pain or amusement, "there's nothing you can do, at least not right now. But I appreciate the offer."

A very brief tour of the first floor to the right of the central staircase revealed a kitchen big enough that it could have been used to cook communal meals, and a large, attached dining room with what must have been the original table, pockmarked from a hundred years of dinners and big enough to seat thirty. Jacob showed him the aforementioned sitting room, a cozy space with a large fireplace and a huge leather sofa strewn with blankets, a book left open on the coffee table that someone—he assumed Jacob—had been reading. There was a window seat that looked comfortable enough to fall asleep in, and Michael could envision spending hours in the room reading, if he lived here.

"What's on the fourth floor?" Michael tilted his head up when they returned to the foyer, looking at the hollow core of the staircase, extending up to the windows inset into the roof. There was a level above the third, clearly, and while he didn't know if he had the energy to go up there to explore, he was curious.

Jacob bit his lip. "It's not accessible, because it hasn't been restored and Eleazer was never sure if it was actually safe to be up there. It was the women's section of the synagogue, where they held their meetings. It's got a mikveh, an unusual placement on the uppermost level, and it caused some water damage."

Michael mentally flipped through the years' worth of emails he'd seen on Nate's phone, the ones claiming water damage. It made sense, if there was a ritual pool at the top of the synagogue. Any water damage could have trickled down to the bottom floor where the archive was kept.

Jacob rolled his shoulders and then walked around the staircase to one of the two pairs of double doors set into either side of the staircase along the back wall of the foyer. Michael could envision the way they'd be open during the period before services, admitting worshippers, filling the place with life. When Jacob unlocked the door using a key he pulled from his pocket and ushered Michael through, it felt oddly empty. Like there was never supposed to be just two men in the whole of this place, rattling around.

It made Michael's hair stand on end, the eeriness of it. How what this place had been—a center for a community, a place for communal life—clashed with what it was now: a place for the ultimate in solitary research, documents that could only be handled by one person at a time.

"Welcome to the Schechter Institute," Jacob half-whispered, flicking on the lights. They flickered to life one by one, as if the electricity couldn't support them all turning on at once, eventually illuminating the entirety of the room.

Michael made his way into the archive-cum-sanctuary. It was a massive room with exceptionally tall ceilings. Where there would have been benches to seat the congregation, there were now towering, freestanding bookcases made of dark wood. They were packed to the brim with books, arranged in no apparent order to Michael's immediate observation, old prayer books mixed in with what looked like Yiddish novels. The first shelves of the archive, it seemed, must have been stuffed with the congregation's old collection. When he turned back, to what was the front of the building, he was greeted by a view of the enormous rose window. He took a minute to appreciate the massive stained-glass design, a swirling blue scattered through with golden stars.

"Come on." Jacob beckoned to him, leading a wide-eyed Michael through the rows and rows of shelves.

The altar where the Torah would have been kept was still standing. Instead of the podium where the rabbi would have stood, there was now a long, solitary table. In front of it was a single chair, and nothing else. On the table was a single archival box, the kind with thick Velcro closures and hard sides that held sheaves of delicate documents. Michael's fingers began to twitch, the way they did when he was close to something he desperately wanted to touch. Being so close to knowledge could sometimes physically hurt, the same way as it felt after being punched in the stomach. A low ache that radiated out to everything else, making its presence known.

"Given your profession, I assume you know the standard procedures of any archive. Mine are no different. You're allowed six boxes a day." Jacob ascended the steps to the altar, the motion pulling his slacks taut against the curve of his ass. The sight made Michael ache in a completely different kind of way.

His fingers twitched again.

"I have to restrict it because many of the documents are delicate, and I want to limit scholars so they don't flip through the pages too quickly. You're here for a whole two weeks, which means you'll be able to cover the entirety of what I've sequestered for you. I'm not sure if you knew this when you came, but we have the largest collection of primary source material on your topic in the United States, although we don't touch the breadth and depth of the Lithuanian archives at the site of the former Grand Synagogue."

That soured Michael's attitude, and he winced. "I know. I was supposed to go. Before. For my own work as a translator, a contract project."

Jacob pivoted on his heel, standing above Michael and looking down on him, the lights casting shadows across his face. "So why didn't you?"

"He—" Michael swallowed, and then decided to divulge a tiny shard of the truth, given that Jacob had already been honest with him about his own fraught past. "He didn't want me to. So after— It felt like too much of an insult to his memory to do research there. This felt right."

"Ah." Jacob's tongue darted out to lick his lips. "Well, in any event, I'm glad you're here. Domestic collections offer a cost-effective way to explore research ideas. Maybe after this, you'll go abroad."

"Maybe," Michael answered limply, the contract sitting in his email inbox flashing before his eyes.

Jacob walked him through more of the archive's procedures—very much the usual: handling documents with gloves and the help of foam supports, only touching one piece of paper at a time, respecting the order of documents and making sure they were boxed back up the same way they'd been before. "Will you be photographing?"

"Yes." Michael had a small digital camera and a tripod that he used for archival work, but most of the time he defaulted to just using his phone. "If that's alright."

"Of course." Jacob shrugged. "The mazzekin don't like cameras, though. Your pictures may come out blurry."

"That's—" Michael was about to say *not real* when there was a long, loud creaking noise to his left. Jacob moved faster than Michael thought possible, dashing to the bookcase standing on Michael's left. He caught a shelf just before it slid out of its hardware, nearly dumping a dozen books onto the floor.

"Please don't insult them in here, of all places." Jacob's face was strained as he slid the wooden plank back into its brackets. "This is where they live, mostly, and they're very sensitive to insults. They're liable to make a mess if they get upset."

"I'm not so sure it can't simply be explained by odd airflow around an old building, or the foundation settling, or any of those things." Michael studiously looked anywhere but at Jacob, which was good, because then he didn't have to reckon with the disappointment and distress that he saw written all over the other man's face.

"It's not," Jacob said tersely. "It's real. You'll see."

Michael really hated the wounded look that Jacob wore, but every bone in his body told him that Jacob was wrong and he was right, and he clung to that. Michael knew his mind was fallible on a lot of things, but this wasn't one of them. Monsters weren't real. They were made up by people who wanted to hide the fact that they were monsters themselves, or too powerless to stop the monsters around them. "There really isn't anything you can do to change my mind on this."

He stared at Michael flatly, a hunted look crossing his face as his shoulders hunched a little. "It's all I have of my past. My family. These stories are as much a part of me as my bones or my blood. They're part of what made me who I am. These things that you rebel against? They're the fabric of me."

Michael didn't reply—couldn't reply—just looked away and to the rose window. But the light must have faded entirely in the time they'd been talking, because instead of seeing stars, all he got was a hollow, black void.

# Chapter 3

The bedroom, luckily, felt like a safe place to be. Michael was able to let out a breath and relax his shoulders enough that he felt less like he was about to imminently have a stress-induced heart attack. After rolling his shoulders a few times, he set about the uncomfortable task of changing out of his stained shirt and inspecting the bandage around his ribs.

It was bloodstained enough that he would have to change it completely. Despite his doctors insisting on several increasingly elaborate bandaging mechanisms, from simple gauze and surgical tape to an elastic bandage wrap that his surgeon had personally sewn padding into and then begged Michael to wear, he couldn't stop picking at the wound. Eventually, he determined that it was a compulsive, subconscious habit that he was unlikely to break, and so he gave in to the impulse and reverted to just sticking a piece of gauze on top and ignoring when his questing fingers meant that it detached and fell out of his shirt.

He left the bloody shirt on the bed—he would do well to try to wash it, but he couldn't bear to summon the will to—and made his way into the small bathroom with his toiletry bag. Its sole inspiring feature was the huge claw-foot tub, which Michael imagined would be nice to soak in after days of hunching over dusty archival documents. The tile was white and plain, like someone had done the most utilitarian bathroom renovation possible, and the pedestal sink didn't give him much room to lay out toiletries. Still, the accommodation was free, and it would work.

Looking at himself in the mirror was hard. It was always hard these days, which hurt because once, Michael hadn't minded his reflection. He'd been proud of his body, honed through running and yoga and the occasional weightlifting session, and he'd been told enough by other people that he was conventionally handsome that he believed it—olive skin and a sculpted jaw, dark brown eyes and sandy blond hair in a reasonably symmetrical face.

Nate had always told him that he was beautiful. It had been followed by a *but* more often than not —*but your attitude really sucks, but you're too controlling, but you use your looks to attract other men on purpose to make me jealous*—but it had still always been a compliment that Michael had greedily hoarded. Evidence that he was desirable, that he was something worth loving.

The dozens of people he'd been with after getting out of the hospital had rarely said anything. And Michael wasn't sure if it was because they were all anonymous hookups from the apps meant for the sole purpose of taking away his pain for a moment, or because he looked like a corpse with a huge wound in his side, or if it was because he wasn't really able to smile anymore after Nate was gone.

Maybe it was all those things at once. He prodded the incision after peeling away the soaked gauze and saw that two more of the recent stitches had popped. He pulled another butterfly bandage out of his bag and slapped it on next to the others, and took an iodine swab to the cut, hissing through the pain of the astringent.

The pain was fine. It was his penance. The least he could bear for Nate, who wouldn't ever have the luxury of feeling pain again.

Michael felt his teeth grinding together at the thought of what the last year had inflicted, and almost wished he could start sobbing. He was sure, if he could, that it would release something in him, at least part of whatever was causing the psychosomatic vise around his lungs. But there hadn't really been many tears since Nate's death, at least not of the cleansing type that would truly wash him clean. Whatever part of him would have grieved like that, open and raw, had been hollowed out and numbed.

Michael sighed and finished cleaning the wound before turning on the faucet and splashing water on his face. He was exhausted from the drive—the archive had been a good six and a half hours away from the city, given the traffic, and his stamina had been shot since the surgery. These days, it was all he could do to remain upright until the end of his still-abbreviated workdays, and he'd fallen asleep in front of his computer after only an hour of squinting at digitized documents more often than he could count. He prodded the bags underneath his eyes, wishing they would go away so that his eyes wouldn't be bruised as well as a muddy brown. Raking his hands through his hair failed to regain some semblance of a hairstyle instead of the dirty blond strands resembling a bird's nest, so Michael sighed, gave up, cracked his neck, and turned back to the bedroom.

This was the worst, any empty moment when the air felt dead and Michael had nothing to distract him. He could keep up a plausible semblance of normalcy when he was doing something, when his mind was occupied, but it became a struggle every time he lost momentum. Every time he allowed his body to just be present, breathing, *existing*, he remembered that he deserved nothing. That he wasn't worth the space he took up in the world, not now that he had proven so spectacularly monstrous.

After Nate's death, it started with the anonymous sex. In the time since he'd left his parents' house to go to college, up until he'd met Nate, he'd dated three women and slept with no one else, a serial monogamist to his core. He'd seriously contemplated proposing marriage to all of them before the relationships ended for one reason or another.

And then there was Nate Lieberman.

When Nate had died, it felt wrong to have his body be *his* again. So he let others use it, in ways that sometimes felt good but mostly felt bad, and which always gutted him when he woke up in the morning after the long, miserable subway rides back to his own apartment so he could sleep with Nate's ghost.

It was a good form of punishment, until he started getting used to it—and then, even worse, *enjoying* it—and so he'd stopped. He didn't deserve to feel good again. And he certainly didn't deserve the men and women messaging him on apps the night after, wanting a repeat performance, wanting to take him to dinner, wanting to catch a movie. None of them knew him, not really. And he didn't want them to, because moving on meant dishonoring Nate, and his guilt at that felt like a living thing sometimes, trying to devour him.

When sleeping around no longer scratched the itch, Michael googled until he found the magic combination of words to say to psychiatrists to get prescriptions for Xanax, Ativan, Valium, Klonopin, Versed. He went to five different doctors, most of whom were sketchy enough to see patients at residential addresses that definitely didn't seem like places a doctor would work, and asked for the prescriptions he wanted by name. Somehow, his insurance company had let him keep filling them, and while he spent most of his time in a dull haze, at least he wasn't lying in bed, staring at the ceiling and replaying the accident over and over and over in his mind until he couldn't help but scream into the pillow.

He'd become a different person, which his family and best friend Sarah hadn't hesitated to remind him of at every turn. Of course, they had a different reason for believing that he was broken and bruised beyond all comprehension.

Sometimes, Michael thought he wanted to die, but he didn't have the courage to kill himself because he still believed in the sanctity of God and life, even if he couldn't go on living this way. Therapy helped in the way the butterfly bandages holding together the gaping wound that led to his left lung helped. He wasn't dumping his organs on the sidewalk, but it wasn't as if anything was healing, either.

At a loss for what to do next, Michael did what he'd become accustomed to doing the past several months. He rooted around in his bag for the bottle of pills he'd gotten from doctor number two and took one, lay down on the bed, and closed his eyes to pray for blissful oblivion.

Michael was so blissfully out of it that he barely woke up to the sound of a polite yet firm knock at the door. He peeled himself off the pillow that had adhered itself to his cheek, reflexively ran a hand across the fresh bandage on his ribs to worry at the incision, and got up. He had to fight dizziness when he changed position, but by now he was used to blinking away spots in his vision.

It took him a few wobbly steps to get to the door, which he pulled open. Jacob was leaning against the doorframe, a smile playing around his mouth. "Sleepy, were we?"

And then his eyes trailed all the way down Michael's very bare chest, which he had neglected to cover with a shirt.

Michael flushed, even as the sedatives in his system dulled the embarrassment. The smell of crushed rose petals wafted off Jacob, over something darker and yet intoxicating, like wet dirt, or a fall night. He grabbed the doorframe to stop himself from leaning forward and burying his face in the crook of Jacob's neck, from inhaling that smell until it made him dizzy. But Jacob was still looking him over in a way that he was very familiar with, from having gone clubbing more than a few times with the intention of definitely not going home alone.

That kind of look usually meant one thing only.

Jacob seemed to acknowledge that, because he looked down at Michael's belt line, and winked. *That* was unmistakable.

"I, uh…" Michael licked his lips, the words refusing to come out in the way he intended them to. He swallowed and tried again. "I was taking a nap, yeah. It's been something of a long day for me. Driving always kind of stresses me out. I'm still finding it hard to be upright…"

He let his eyes words trail off as he moved his gaze suggestively to the bed. Arousal was curling in his stomach at the way Jacob's face flushed a delicious, delicate shade of pink, making him look far more alive than he had previously.

Michael stepped back and Jacob stepped forward, his pupils blown wide, like they were connected by a magnetic field, an invisible string.

This was what Michael craved more than anything now, a moment where he could forget about Nate and focus the entirety of his frazzled attention on some other person, let himself be used by someone else in whatever way they chose. He didn't even need to know their name. All they had to be was someone who looked nothing like Nate, and willing to take charge. That was enough.

If he were to talk this over with Sarah, or his therapist, he'd get horrified reactions. He'd be told this was just another manifestation of his self-destructive streak, which had appeared in the wake of Nate's death. It was a terrible idea.

Michael would stare at them dead-eyed, agree, and then do it anyway. Because bad things and terrible consequences were what he deserved. After all, he'd proven that he was in no fit state to ever be in a relationship with anyone ever again, and so this was what he got, now. This was his purgatory, a thousand empty hookups in dingy bathrooms and other people's apartments, in the stacks of the library or in the back of an alley.

All of that vanished when Jacob reached forward with a tentative hand and wove it around the back of Michael's neck.

"I've been alone," he said quietly, "for what feels like a very, very long time."

The skin of his palm burned against Michael's neck, his long fingers sliding through Michael's hair. Jacob licked his lips. Michael was lost in his gaze.

He surrendered to the moment, thanked God that apparently he was here for two weeks with someone who had no trouble using him and was able to take from Michael exactly what he wanted, and stepped forward to tip Jacob's mouth up and claim it in a kiss.

It wasn't elegant—*brutal* might have been a better descriptor. That was how Michael liked it, rough and unforgiving; that was the best way for it not to feel like those tender moments in bed with Nate. Slow, languid kisses, the sun streaming through the windows of their apartment on lazy Sunday mornings when neither of them could be bothered to get up, not even to go to the farmers' market. They'd just lie there, and kiss, and then make love because there was nothing more important than being lost in each other.

It was so hard to remember the good times. Those hurt the most. They cut bone deep.

Jacob moaned into his mouth, his lips parting eagerly and his chest molding against Michael's. The hand around the back of his neck tightened, Jacob's nails digging roughly into the tender skin and clawing at it. Jacob's other hand crept up Michael's chest and then dragged downward again, raking at his skin, catching on the bandage that covered his incision.

It hurt. Michael moaned at the perfection of it.

Jacob pulled away slightly, shifting his hips forward to show that yes, he was quite interested in the proceedings. He looked downward, to the incision, and then met Michael's gaze once more as he took his thumb and dug it directly into the wound.

It was so surprising that Michael couldn't stop the shout from escaping, curling forward instinctively. He panted, shaking, but relishing the way that the pain—not self-inflicted, for once—had finally, for a brief second, scrubbed his mind clean of everything.

It felt like punishment, and punishment fed the monster that was his guilt. It was perfect and felt so needed that Michael could have thanked him.

He dove forward again and kissed Jacob roughly, anchoring his hands on the other man's slim hips so that he could walk them both backward, pressing Jacob against the wall next to the door before flipping them so that Jacob was the one trapping Michael. Through Jacob's shirt, Michael could feel each and every one of his ribs, standing out like finger bones on a skeletal fist.

Jacob fumbled between the both of them and found the buckle of Michael's belt. It was easy from there to cant his hips into Jacob's questing hand, letting him know that he could take what he needed, that Michael was his to use in whatever way he saw fit.

Fingernails scraped down his length, drawing the same pleasure-pain from deep in Michael's core. When Jacob wrapped a hand around him and started up a steady rhythm, Michael's head fell back as he groaned.

"Wait," he said, panting. Jacob's hand immediately stilled. "What do you want?"

Jacob grinned wickedly, shoving one surprisingly muscled thigh in between Michael's legs, forcing him to widen his stance. "For now? I want to take you apart."

Michael looked down. His incision was dripping blood, and it was smeared on Jacob's hand. The other man didn't seem to mind, grabbing Michael's hair with his free hand and pulling sharply, causing Michael to bare his throat to Jacob.

When Jacob bit down on the crook of his neck, Michael's release was fast and relentless, fueled by the white-hot pain still rippling from the incision in his side where Jacob's finger had been, and the sharp sting of his teeth.

When his vision cleared, Jacob walked three steps back until his thighs hit the bed, and when he sank down with his legs spread and a smirk on his devilishly handsome face, Michael's knees hit the wooden floorboards faster than he could blink.

Jacob was unforgiving, as if he could tell exactly what Michael wanted and needed in that moment, a hand in his hair guiding Michael up and down, not even stopping when Michael started to choke. His hands fisted into the pillows as Jacob used him exactly as he wanted to be used, and when Jacob came it was with a groan that went straight to Michael's gut.

Michael sat back on his heels, looking at Jacob, flushed and rumpled with the zipper of his slacks hanging open, and thought for a moment that the man was truly beautiful before he chastised himself and remembered that, beautiful or not, he wasn't supposed to be having these kinds of thoughts about another person anymore.

He retreated to the bathroom to wash his hands and forced himself to look at his reddened lips in the mirror, the new blood on his side, reminding himself that he was a vessel for other people's pleasure and nothing more than that. This was his penance. Confronting the shitty person that he was inside, letting other people use him until he remembered that he wasn't responsible enough to have his body be his own, not when he'd been responsible for such terrible things.

So, it came as a shock when warm hands wrapped around the planes of his stomach, coming to rest one on top of the other, holding him, the sharp jab of a chin into his shoulder making him jump.

"I take it you're not the cuddling type," Jacob said into his skin. The heat of his breath on bare flesh made Michael's skin rise into goosebumps. "That's okay. I'm not usually, either. For some reason, people don't like sharing a bed with me. Something about the way I take up too much space."

Michael stepped to the side, breaking Jacob's hold, and

took him in. He looked perfectly composed despite having been blown two minutes before. There wasn't a hair out of place on his head, and his cheeks had no hint of a flush to them. "I'm sorry. We—I shouldn't have done that. It was unprofessional of me."

Jacob looked at him askance, then laughed, sharp and dry. "Of all the things you could worry about, having just choked on my cock, you're worried about your professionalism?" He sat down on the rim of the bathtub, perching on it with one ankle propped up on a knee. "Most people would be worrying about whether they were any good. Or whether the other person wanted to do it again."

That made Michael flush harder, from embarrassment this time. "Are you saying I wasn't any good?" Humiliation wasn't something he'd been accustomed to since Nate's death, and the ill feeling of it unsettled him. Even though it was perfect, Jacob putting him in his place.

"No," Jacob retorted. "In fact, I'd like to see what else you're good at. But not if you're going to get weird every time we fuck." He gave a shrug, all casual elegance that Michael would never manage to copy. "But that's obviously not going to happen if you need to guilt trip yourself every time for, what, being human?"

Michael had no answer. Instead, he just stared down at his feet, feeling faintly nauseous.

"Humans are great." Jacob got up and snagged Michael's hand in his. His skin was burning. "Don't apologize for being one."

Michael allowed himself to be towed out of the bathroom, still mired in shame and not even able to let himself enjoy it, now that Jacob was here. Usually, all the people he slept with were gone, after. He had nothing to interrupt his self-flagellation.

"You look sad." Jacob prodded him in the shoulder with a still-bloody hand when they made it out into the hall. "Let's have dinner."

Michael sighed, food the last thing on his mind. But he had already done enough to screw this up, and so he wasn't about to ruin this too. So he let himself be led.

# Chapter 4

"I'm very good at cooking frozen things." Jacob stood in front of the large fridge, the left-hand door open and the chilled air spilling out. There was, indeed, a very large assortment of frozen food items on display. "Do you like frozen French fries? Frozen chicken nuggets? Frozen lasagna?"

Michael leaned awkwardly against the counter on the opposite side of the kitchen and licked his lips. "Anything sounds fine. I'm starving."

He was, which was a change for him. Usually, the thought of food was repulsive and he had a hard time keeping anything down. He'd blamed it on the surgery for a while, but now he suspected it was more due to the guilt, his body punishing him for what his mind couldn't cope with.

Maybe it was being here, in a different place, that was responsible for the change. He hadn't left the city since

Nate's death, grief keeping him pinned down like he was a dead butterfly on display. But here, there were no lingering memories, no misplaced items of Nate's that he kept finding in drawers and tucked in between the cushions of the couch. Nothing to prod at the wound in sudden, unexpected ways.

In a way, even though he was here for Nate, he felt farther away from him than ever. And there was something about that which felt like relief. Michael immediately loathed himself for the thought. Because he didn't deserve relief, or comfort, or ease. He didn't deserve anything at all. That wasn't why he was here, and if those kinds of thoughts kept creeping up on him, he'd lose sight of all the ways in which he'd failed to be a good person.

"Frozen vegetarian pad Thai?" Jacob turned around, holding up a box that looked like it contained pad Thai for a hundred people. Michael managed a small smile.

"Fine." At least it sounded somewhat healthy. Michael would have to drive into town when he got a chance to buy actual groceries—manners that his family had burned into him surfaced, and he certainly wasn't going to stay in Jacob's house and eat his food without providing at least a few meals in return.

Jacob closed the freezer and started to meticulously open the box with a fingernail. "I never learned how to cook. I very much eat to live—it's one of my least favorite parts of the day, needing to consume something to survive."

Sympathy twisted Michael's gut; he knew how that felt. Except for him, it hadn't always been this way. There had been years of discovering tiny ethnic restaurants on side streets that had food so delicious Michael could have died and gone to heaven, years of standing hip-to-hip with Nate in their tiny kitchen as they laughed their way through trying new recipes. Michael had memories of cooking with his grandmother and aunts, them teaching him how to make the recipes he'd eaten all the way through his childhood, the ones with no actual measurements because everything was done through sight and feel and intuition. He'd cooked for himself when he was frustrated or sad or anxious, because making something soothed him. He'd cooked for others, elaborate meals to celebrate birthdays and professional accomplishments and engagements.

But he hadn't cooked in a while. He hadn't wanted to. He didn't feel like he was worthy of creating something, not when so much had been destroyed. But looking at Jacob, carefully reading the directions on the back of the box, something within him twisted. That sick, possessive part of him that saw another person who looked at him half-kindly and wanted to make them his, to make a life with them, to start imagining from the first glance what it would be like to stay with them forever.

"I could teach you."

Jacob's eyes snapped up. "Teach me what?"

"How to cook." Michael shrugged, hating himself for the offer. Here he was, falling into the same old pattern.

It was very much like him to take something and fuck it all to hell. But Jacob didn't see the danger, and just smiled back in a way that made Michael's heart flip.

"Ah." Jacob bit his lip. "I would appreciate that. I haven't ever stayed in one place for long, and by the time I came here, I spent most of my time taking care of Eleazer, in my way. And it wasn't as though I had much incentive to learn how to cook on my own after he passed."

"It's not hard." Michael immediately felt the need to retract the offer, to save himself from the growing horror that no, this wasn't a pattern he was ever going to be able to break himself out of. But there was no way to do that without being unaccountably rude, so all he could do was watch helplessly as Jacob inserted the tray into the microwave and pressed some buttons to start it. He turned around to mirror Michael's posture, leaning against the counter on the opposite side of the kitchen, the cotton of his button-down shirt straining against his chest as he leaned back on his forearms. His profile reflected in the pitch-darkness of the window, which was giving off an eerie creaking noise, like tree branches or finger bones were being dragged along the glass.

Jacob cocked his head. "It's a core skill, being able to provide for yourself in that way. And it's something I never mastered."

"I'm sure you're good at many other things." Michael couldn't break Jacob's gaze, the green of his eyes piercing in the low light of the kitchen. Just the look of him was making Michael forget everything he'd sworn to himself, all the distance he'd promised to put between himself and others, for their own safety and the sake of Nate's memory. It was like Jacob had put him under a spell. He was slightly dizzy, and a little bit flushed. "You seem like the type."

Jacob chuckled. "I'm not sure what gives you that impression. I feel less than competent these days. I have more goals that I've failed to achieve in my time on earth than I can count. And I'm working on a big project now which is going nowhere."

The disappointment that tinged Jacob's voice was noticeable, even to someone who had just met the man. Michael wasn't about to stick his nose where it didn't belong, but he wanted so badly to ask Jacob what he was working on, whether he needed help with it. That same old compulsion to connect himself to other people, whether it was the right thing to do or not.

So much of Michael had always been about helping. About making other people feel better, doing things for them so that they felt good. And while that part of him had been stripped away over the last several months, while his confidence in his ability to fix anything at all had been shaken, Michael suspected he would never be able to completely shake the impulse to *try*. Even if all he was good for now was letting himself be used.

The microwave dinged, and Jacob turned to open it, his shoulders hunched. Michael could tell it was a sore spot, whatever this project was, and he wasn't about to pry. People tended to spy wounds and want to dig into them, and not in the gratifying way that Jacob just had. And given that Michael knew how shitty that felt, he wasn't about to do it to another person.

"If you ever want help, I'm here for the next few weeks," he offered gently while Jacob's back was turned. "If it's something I can assist with, and you want another set of eyes on the problem, please just let me know. I'm not an academic. I'm just a translator. But I work with enough of them that I'm pretty well versed in academic logic."

Jacob's lips were pursed as he turned around, but as he

placed the tray on the island in the middle of the kitchen, steam pouring out of the hole he'd made in the plastic film, he sighed. "I've resisted asking for help until now, and I don't think I'm ready to do so quite yet. But it's a research problem, you're right. So maybe, in a few days, if you're open to it, I'll share what I'm looking for."

"Of course." He turned when Jacob pointed at the cabinet behind him, and he opened it to find stacks of plates. He took out two, along with two glasses which he filled with water from the sink. Jacob rounded the island to take the plates from him, their arms brushing and the heat from his body sending a shiver through Michael.

Jacob divided the pad Thai into two perfectly even portions which he shaped into precise circles. Michael admired the attention to detail as he followed Jacob into the dining room.

It was wood paneled, the last dregs of twilight filtering through the windows, framed with rose-colored velvet curtains. The massive dining table was polished to a dark sheen, clearly cared for lovingly over the decades even as it boasted the dents and scratches of a hundred years' worth of communal meals. A worn carpet had been laid on the floor, and Michael eyed it with surprise as Jacob set the plates down at the end of the table.

"The rug is Moroccan." Michael used his foot to trace the border, done in bright colors which contrasted with the navy of the carpet's interior. "Was it imported, or did your grandfather bring it here after traveling?"

"I don't know." Jacob sat down and motioned for Michael to do the same. Michael set down the cups he'd been carrying and pulled out the chair. Jacob had positioned them on either side of the table's corner, and when Michael sat, their knees touched.

Jacob didn't pull away. Michael didn't either, the warmth of the connection creeping through his veins. He hated every second of it, and hated it more that he couldn't move away.

"I don't know much about Eleazer's life, between when he was born and when he died. As I said, I lived elsewhere. But I do know he traveled extensively, especially to areas with Jewish communities. It was part of how he collected things for the Institute. Those boxes that you saw upstairs are mostly full of ritual objects that he collected over the course of his life. They're just as valuable as sources of learning for researchers, but they're much harder to display." Jacob stuck his fork into the pad Thai and twirled it around. Michael's stomach rumbled and he took a forkful and chewed it mechanically.

"The rug is interesting," he said once he had swallowed. "The diamonds on the borders are representations of the evil eye, to scare away evil spirits and curses. The zigzags mean long life. It's not Jewish, but I always found it interesting how so many different cultures have the same symbolism." He'd purchased a rug of his own on a trip to Morocco with Nate, and it was still on the floor under their dining room table. "Of course, it's not like the rug works, is it?"

Jacob's eyes flicked up from his plate and he frowned. "What makes you say that?"

The wariness in his voice made Michael wonder if Jacob was still upset at him for the earlier run-in with the mazzekin in the archive room. "Oh," he said, injecting false levity into his voice, "it's just that you said the building is full of household demons. If the rug worked, there wouldn't be any."

"Ah." Jacob said. "You know, I don't think I've ever had an incident with them in this room. Perhaps that's the cause. But I don't put great stock in symbols as a way to counter spirits or the like. I think it has much more to do with ritual and intent and the magic of it all."

"Magic?" Michael speared a piece of tofu. "You mean like mysticism?"

That, at least, was safer territory. Michael had translated a bunch of kabbalistic texts for a wealthy businessman a few years back, and they hadn't given him the same creeping sense of annoyance that stuff related to demons and superstition did.

"Whatever you want to call it." Jacob was still twirling the pad Thai around on his fork and hadn't yet put any of it in his mouth. He was wan again, or maybe it was the fact that the lighting in the dining room was dim, cast from small bulbs in a single antique-looking chandelier; but either way, the longer they sat, the quieter Jacob got.

Michael didn't want to interrupt the silence, so he concentrated on eating, watching Jacob out of the corner of his eye. The other man was slumping down into his chair, one elbow on the table and his chin in his hand.

"Are you—are you okay?" He didn't know how to phrase it, but Jacob's face was all sharp planes, and his eyes were growing glassy. Michael knew just how pain or grief could make eating torture. He wasn't here to get involved with someone—exactly the opposite. But he wasn't so callous yet as to watch someone suffering in front of him and not try to help, even if he was quite certain that he wasn't the best person to do the helping.

It wasn't like Jacob had anyone else on offer here to help.

Jacob's throat bobbed. "Yes." He pursed his lips and delicately speared a piece of tofu from the plate, inserting it into his mouth slowly. He chewed like doing so hurt his mouth. His hand massaged his Adam's apple as he swallowed, and his slim fingers encircled his neck, resting there for a moment, his gaze going distant. "I apologize. I find I'm not very hungry these days."

"Grief does that to you. It eats you up inside and leaves you hollow." And that was the truth of it that he'd discovered: that mourning someone could consume all of what you were. Like the biblical plague of locusts, swarming in and then leaving fields bare and people starving. Cutting through swaths of crops and devastating them, so it would be years before anything else would grow.

Jacob sighed but didn't reply. He put one piece of broccoli into his mouth and chewed it contemplatively, closing his eyes.

"Do you want me to maybe leave you alone?" Maybe it was the fact that Jacob was used to being alone, and here he'd had to interact with Michael for the entire afternoon. Maybe he was worn down and just needed time to himself, and he didn't have any polite way to tell Michael to leave him be. Maybe he'd realized that Michael was nothing but danger and was too kind to say it. Maybe he'd figured Michael out and wanted him to leave. "I don't mean to impose if you need time to yourself."

A breath of air left Jacob and he shook his head. "My

apologies. It's—things sometimes remind me of life… before, without me expecting them to. And that's hard."

"Eating with another person?" Michael guessed, since them sitting down had been the trigger for a change in Jacob's mood. "Is this the first time you have, since—"

He cut himself off at Jacob's strained nod. Michael wanted to reach across the table and smooth the furrow from Jacob's brow with his thumb. He wanted to kiss him, to make him smile the way he had earlier in the afternoon. The part of Michael that always wanted to fix, the side of him that had been born to mend and nurture, was aching to escape. He couldn't let it.

That wasn't what Michael was good at. No matter how much he wanted to care for someone else, his caring had only ever caused pain. He didn't deserve to fulfill that side of him, not when he had so clearly failed to care for Nate.

It wasn't something that Michael should ever attempt to do again.

"It's the oddest things that get me." Jacob placed his fork down onto his plate with a *clink* as the metal met porcelain, and leaned back into the dining room chair. He drew his feet up, curling his forearms around his shins. "I'm usually fine. I go about my day. I work with the archive and on my research project. I repair the house and I walk around. I'm fine, and I'm fine, and then I smell something, or I see a flash out of the corner of my eye, and all of a sudden it's like my heart is no longer able to beat."

Michael's stomach clenched in sympathy. "I know what you mean. I'm the same way."

"Your boyfriend." Jacob rested his chin on his knees. Michael watched the muscles in his forearms jump as he shifted position. "Is that how grief came for you after he died?"

Exhaling, Michael wondered if he was going to be able to talk about this without breaking down. It might be nice, he thought, to talk about it with someone who could know the whole truth, and who also wasn't being paid to try to fix his head and make him feel better. His therapist asked question after question, and after their sessions he was scraped raw and felt no closer to answers. His parents tiptoed around his grief because they thought he was broken in a way that couldn't be fixed. Sarah, on the other hand, was like a battering ram, trying to get him to see everything in a way that would absolve him of the guilt. Jacob didn't seem the type to try to bulldoze over someone else's emotions. Maybe Jacob would understand. Maybe that would mean something.

"Yes." Michael licked his lips. "The—accident. It left me in the hospital afterward, for a long time. I didn't know what happened at first because I had been through emergency surgery, and then I caught an infection, and they had me on so many drugs for the pain that I didn't know where I was."

The memory of foggy days blending into foggy nights made him blink hard. The unending monotony of a hospital room, the rotating cast of his parents, grandparents, aunts, uncles, and cousins that sat by his bedside and prodded the nurses every time they came in, wanting to know when Michael would be able to leave.

The friends from work and yoga and a decade living in the city that had visited him. His mother, crying, who had been the one to tell him that Nate was dead when he finally asked. Sarah, who held him as he was paralyzed with shock, asking for details about the accident, crying onto the shoulder of his best friend in the world.

"I—" Michael swallowed. "It was different, for me, than it is for you. The accident—I was recovering from that and processing my role in it and also mourning Nate. I was totally hollow for weeks and weeks, and the Oxy they gave me didn't help me feel anything, either. When I finally came out of it, the first time I was allowed to really leave the house on my own after the surgery, I saw Nate's favorite brand of coffee in the grocery store and started to sob out of nowhere. I hadn't cried since it happened. It all came out at once."

"Did you feel better afterward?" Jacob's voice was a near-whisper. His eyes gleamed in the light from the chandelier. "Was that cleansing?"

"No." The answer sprang from Michael's lips and he didn't even have to think about it. "It wasn't. Because I didn't feel like I had the right to mourn him, not after what happened. Not after what I had done. And it felt like my body trying to move on from him without my permission, and I knew I didn't deserve that."

He stopped before he got too honest, because Jacob wasn't going to want him to stay, once he realized what he had done.

"Why don't you deserve that?"

The question was too quiet, too gentle, too *kind*. And Michael couldn't stand it.

So he got up from the table and left without another word.

# Chapter 5

Michael Stein was a coward, and he hated himself for it.

It was just another thing on the long list of things he hated about himself, but this one was particularly raw. Jacob had been compassionate, and he'd been dealing with grief of his own, and Michael had abandoned him and been unforgivably rude at the same time.

He wondered if he could shrivel up and die if he tried hard enough. But when he'd laid in bed for an hour, staring at the ceiling, and was unfortunately still breathing, Michael conceded defeat. He'd have to make it through yet another day.

The fall mornings here out in the countryside were chilly, cold, gray. Weak sunlight filtered through the window across from the bed, since Michael hadn't bothered to draw the curtains last night. There was a skeletal tree whose mostly bare branches extended nearly to the window itself. Michael got up and stared at it for a minute, his feet frigid against the cold wooden floorboards, and wondered what it would be like to shed all your leaves but know they'd grow back in a few months' time.

It would be nice if he could do that, instead of remaining permanently dead inside.

The water in the bathroom was hot when he turned on the shower over the tub. He turned the knob until it was scalding and winced as he got under the spray. The burn hurt enough that something within him loosened, the part of him that was happiest when he was being punished. Michael ran his hand over the raised ridge of his incision, flicking at the scab with a nail. It was struggling to form and dislodged easily. The water getting into the wound caused an almost unbearable sting, and it was glorious.

The memory of a thumb in the incision made his breath catch in his throat.

When the water started to cool, he washed himself off and got out of the shower, the chilled air making goosebumps spring up across his skin. He used a tissue to soak up the blood running down his stomach—he wasn't about to get bodily fluids on the towels that Jacob had provided—and then dried himself off.

Rebandaging the incision took him another few minutes, and then Michael dressed and ate one of the granola bars he'd brought with him, and finally there was nothing left for him to do but leave the room, which he did with no small amount of trepidation.

He crept down the stairs as quietly as he could, realizing that Jacob hadn't pointed out where his own room was the night before. The last thing he wanted to do was wake the other man, who it seemed kept very strange hours. Michael had once dated a girl who had a condition called delayed sleep phase onset syndrome, which had caused her to become mostly nocturnal. It was probably what Jacob had, and Michael wasn't about to throw a wrench in his usual routine by stomping around like a bull in a china shop.

The first floor was quiet when he reached the landing, the sunlight streaming in through the windows and illuminating the collection of artifacts hung on the walls. There was a soft scuffling sound from one of the corners, and Michael shuddered—it sounded like mice in the walls, which he wasn't at all a fan of. Living in the city meant dealing with pests, and Michael knew from growing up that it could be just as bad in rural areas like this, but that didn't mean that he wanted to deal with trapping rodents and carrying them outside so early in the morning.

Actually, he didn't feel like doing much of anything at all.

Being alone in a place like this felt like being a ghost, haunting the empty halls, seeing his own pale, drawn face reflected back at him in the glass of the frames on the wall. Such a large part of him didn't want to be doing this, didn't think he *deserved* to be doing this, but the other part of him knew that if he wasn't castigating himself in this way, he'd be taking it out on himself in a way that was so much worse.

Although he seemed, based on last night, to have found a way to indulge all his regular vices here at the Institute, the only varying factor being that he'd probably be choking himself on the same cock every night, instead of different ones.

Walking to the archive doors was unlike any other experience he'd had at any previous institution, anywhere else in the world. There were no bag checks, no metal detectors to pass through. No one to check his researcher ID card and then scan his passport for no apparent reason. No one to lead him through an interminable number of rules, which he already knew by heart. There was just a note taped to the door, which was slightly ajar.

*I'm sorry*, the note read, spiky handwriting done in perfectly straight lines on a piece of Schechter Institute stationery. An apology. It caught Michael so off-guard that he almost forgot how to read in English. *I shouldn't have pried into your private life. We barely know each other. I'll be more circumspect tonight, if you'll still have me.*

His chest was suddenly too tight again, and it was hard to swallow. Michael hated this easy forgiveness. It grated on him, and made him more upset than he cared to interrogate at the same time. Kindness like this—forgiveness like this—it was something he didn't deserve. The stillness of the archive pressed down on him, the sunlight illuminating dust motes floating through the air causing him to blink furiously. Steadying himself was difficult.

There was a last line on the note, and Michael took in a shuddering breath past the ugly mass of hatred for himself and the way he always fucked everything up and made other people hurt and upset and feeling like they needed to apologize.

*Your files for today are on the desk. Along with something I thought you might find interesting—a peace offering, if you will.*

He'd hurt Jacob enough that Jacob had thought it was necessary to apologize. Michael wished he could go back in time and replay the other night and ensure that he did the right thing, at least making an attempt to comfort Jacob through what was clearly a moment of grief, instead of dumping his painful past onto a perfect stranger.

But that was the problem with time. It always moved forward, no matter how much Michael wanted it to rewind. No matter how much he wanted the chance to do things over.

The only thing he could do was move forward, despite how little he wanted to. Not unless he was willing to do something that couldn't be undone, something that still felt wrong in his brain to even think about, even if there were moments when he went to cross the street and considered what it would be like to just step into traffic.

With a shuddering breath, Michael turned the door handle and made his way into the sanctuary, breathing in the smell of old paper and ink and willing it to settle him. Work had always done that before—been a way to get his mind off the anxiety that had plagued him since he was a child. Something about the order of knowing which documents he had to review in a set period of time, knowing what the person paying for his time wanted him to do, the structure of words and the way that foreign grammar worked never changing, something about that steadiness comforting him. The way that his world narrowed down to a single page at a time, a single line at a time, a single *word* at a time—it all transported him out of his own mind and into the distant past. A place where he didn't need to worry about whether he had done something wrong or hurt another person, whether he had irreparably fucked up his life or set a train wreck into motion. It was just him, and the knowledge of past generations, the mystery of what things had been like hundreds of years ago for people he could never meet and therefore never harm. The joy of making all of that accessible to people in the here and now.

He trailed his fingertips across the spines of books as he walked down the aisles, taking a moment to familiarize himself with their layout. He wouldn't dare to remove any of them from the shelves—he didn't know if he was allowed, or if there were special protocols for handling the library the same way there were for handling the documents he was here to examine. Those were kept in individual boxes along the shelves that ringed the sanctuary, stretching up high enough that there were ladders placed every few feet along the walls.

Michael stood in the center of the largest collection of Ashkenazi Jewish archival material in the United States and breathed.

He stood and let the weight of all the knowledge press in against him, knitting him back together. He had to hold his seams close, had to resist the urge to fray, because this was what he could do for Nate. The last thing. The only thing, now.

Michael opened his eyes and made his way to the desk, where a neat line of gray archival boxes was waiting, along with a small red box off to the side that Michael took to be the so-called peace offering, which he was determined to save for last. And then he cracked his knuckles, sat down, and began.

The hours slipped away from Michael in a pleasant haze, and he didn't even need to dull the edges with drugs or alcohol or sex to do it. He relished the comforting repetition of archival work: open the Velcro on a new box and slide all the flaps open, place the foam cradles in the shape of a book so that he could open and read folios without cracking the bindings too badly, start with the item on the top of the stack. Examine it carefully first, noting whatever he could glean from the context of how it had been made and bound and how it had worn down, things that he would put into his translator's notes, the addenda he always sent to clients as a little extra context along with their document photographs and English text. Then starting to read, his mind working through the translation from Yiddish or Russian or Hebrew into English.

Even though he was fluent in ten languages besides English, Michael was most comfortable in Yiddish, a language his grandparents had still spoken in bits and pieces around the house. He'd passed his Yiddish classes in college with flying colors, and he'd learned modern-day and ancient Hebrew along with Russian and a half dozen other languages alongside them, along with two master's degrees in translation to bolster his skills. His Russian was still razor-sharp, mostly because Nate had been near-fluent and they'd often defaulted to speaking—and arguing—in the language when they were out in public to avoid other people listening in. When they met—Nate a recent transfer from Yale when his advisor had accepted a tenured offer elsewhere, and Michael a contract researcher who accepted the advisor's new influx of grant money to help with the project that Nate was working on—Michael was glad to find someone to practice languages out loud with. It was easy to get rusty with spoken language when all he was doing was reading the words silently to himself.

He'd pretended to be rustier in Russian than he was, mostly because he'd been using it as an excuse to spend time with Nate, who Michael had taken one look at and fallen for. And once they started dating, Michael had never needed to translate anything from Russian again, even though it was his job. Nate did it all for him, reading articles and sources out loud as they lay naked in bed, tracing Cyrillic on Michael's skin as he spoke the words.

It made him ache, thinking about those early days. Michael hadn't been able to conceal his interest for long, but it hadn't mattered, because Nate was interested too. It had been so, so easy to wrap himself up in Nate the way he always did when a relationship was new. Sarah had joked in the early days that Nate had become Michael's entire personality, and that he was at risk of morphing into the rich son of a second-generation diamond dealer who could study for a PhD because he knew he never needed to work a day in his life if he didn't want to. Michael had laughed, because he was a middle-class Jew from Massachusetts. But maybe it had happened that way after all. It was so easy to be consumed by Nate. He was the most charismatic person Michael had ever met, and he was knee deep by the end of their second date. They had walked through the park, hand in hand, while Nate had regaled him with stories about research trips abroad, mishaps and misunderstandings and food that looked like one thing but was definitely another making Michael laugh until he cried. And then Nate had pressed him up against a tree in the darkness, as fireflies blinked across the grass, and kissed him until he couldn't breathe.

After that, Michael would have stopped his own heart from beating if Nate had told him to.

When Nate died, they had been dating for three and a half years. Three and a half years in which they'd built a life together, moving together into an apartment after six months. Nate was captivating, and Michael wanted every minute that he could spend with the other man. He was greedy for his presence and his attention, and when he had both, Michael felt like he was something holy.

Of course, it hadn't been like that forever. Michael's cracks had started to show, and Nate had grown frustrated with the way Michael hadn't been able to mend them fast enough. Nate had been patient when Michael had accidentally courted the wrong kind of attention, and Nate had been kind when Michael concluded that he needed to stop going out so much because he just couldn't figure out how to stop being too overfriendly with every man or woman he met. Nate had just held him close and let him cry and then assured him that it wasn't a problem at all. That he liked having Michael all to himself. That he liked hoarding Michael's attention like a dragon. That he liked being Michael's entire world.

Michael had always tried to be better, but it was never enough. And still he hadn't been able to do the right thing and leave so that Nate could find someone better, someone worthy of him. He'd been selfish, right up until the end.

Nate had loved him until the end, despite all his flaws.

Michael swallowed around the lump in his throat, wondering if he was going to be able to really cry this time. Every time he'd reached the edges of his grief, his body had just shut down into numbness. Like he subconsciously knew that if he let himself sob, instead of allowing just the tears that escaped around the edges, it would start the process of healing, and he couldn't bear that.

He stared down at the pamphlet that he had rested in the foam cradle and his vision blurred, but when he blinked it cleared again. It was just the dust that clung to all archives, crumbles of decaying paper that floated in the air.

Michael went to turn the page, but then took another look and determined that the paper was probably too delicate to touch with his bare hands. He went to reach for the pair of cotton gloves that Jacob had left next to the archival boxes but stopped short.

There was nothing there, and his hand met nothing more than the polished wood of the desk.

"What—" Michael muttered, looking around for the gloves and thinking back to the other day, when the shelf had collapsed and Jacob had caught it. There was definitely some kind of draft in the former sanctuary, and even though he hadn't felt it on his skin, that could totally be because he had never been the most observant. Nate had always said so.

Still, he should mention it to Jacob in a way that wouldn't offend the other man, since he clearly believed that any and all household inconveniences were the work of small demons. Michael didn't know how much of that bullshit he could hear without caving and suggesting

Jacob speak to a psychiatrist. Maybe he could say that he had personally felt a draft from the windows on the side of the sanctuary, and had seen the gloves blow off the side of the table.

He crouched down and stifled a groan at the way it pulled at his side. Something warm trickled down his ribs as he got onto his hands and knees under the table, and he ignored it in favor of crawling around and trying to find the gloves. It took his eyes a few seconds to adjust to the darkness, and when they did, he sat back on his heels quickly enough that the back of his head banged on the underside of the table, causing black to spot across his vision.

The gloves were lying perfectly intertwined, the fingers knitted together like they were on hands that were holding one another. Archival gloves were flimsy things, one-size-fits-all cotton that barely made it through a single session without springing a hole somewhere. But these gloves looked like there were hands inside them, standing up on invisible wrists, the palms and fingers three-dimensional.

But then he exhaled and blinked, and the gloves were lying on the floor in a crumpled heap, just like ordinary cotton gloves that had been blown off a table by a stray gust of wind.

Michael felt vaguely ill as he reached out and snatched them up. He'd been called crazy more times than he could count, but this felt like the first time it could be *true*.

Gloves in hand, he went to crawl back out from under the table, one hand clasped to his ribs, his eyes stinging from the pain. There was a whisper that he couldn't make out, and a feeling like a cat brushing against the side of his thigh, and he scrambled out panting.

Michael was left standing woozily, with a pounding heart, a sweaty pair of gloves in his hand, and blood dripping down his ribs. He pressed his left hand to the incision and drew in a hissing breath as the slide of gauze against ragged flesh stung.

He dropped the gloves onto the desk and realized that his left hand was now tacky with blood. Sighing, he abandoned the hope of finishing the box he had been working on before having to break for lunch, and went upstairs to wash his hands and change his shirt before heading into town to find food for himself, and ingredients for an apology meal to cook for Jacob.

It was the least he could do. And when he tried, he'd always been good at apologizing.

# Chapter 6

The town around the archive was quieter than Michael thought it would be. It was clearly a decently well-off place, with the manicured streets and stately homes, but the town itself was little more than a single street, stretching no more than a mile. Something about it struck Michael as claustrophobic, limited, causing his hands to tighten on the steering wheel.

He drove down the main road slowly, keeping an eye out for pedestrians, wondering if he would be able to stop himself from picking at the incision long enough to get through this trip without causing a town-wide incident.

*Stranger appears dripping blood down his front, everyone rallies together to drive him out of the zip code.* Michael could imagine the headlines now.

He managed to find an empty parking spot that he could get the car into without crashing—it had been a potentially catastrophic length of time since he'd had to do any driving, let alone parking, on his own—and got out, wrapping his jacket closer around his chest. It was far colder here than it had been in the city, and he was already shivering as a cold wind whipped dead leaves against his legs. It had taken him a long time to stop shivering after he had surgery, and even now it triggered something deep within him, the kind of instinct that made his brain want to run from imagined pain. He was glad there wasn't anyone on the street to stare at him as he made his way onto the sidewalk, leaning against the side of his car for a minute to catch his breath and let himself steady.

To distract himself, Michael pulled out his phone and thumbed through the notifications that had come through yesterday and this morning. He'd taken to leaving his phone in his bag for long stretches of time, unwilling to be the recipient of constant concern from everyone who had his phone number. There was the usual litany of check-in texts from his friends, all of which he responded to with the minimum number of words to convince them that they didn't need to call the police for a wellness check.

Sarah had texted, asking how the archive was, which at least didn't make him feel like she was prodding him about his grief. Michael's thumbs hovered over the keyboard, and he debated replying via text before he thought better of it, sighed, and hit dial instead.

"Michael!" Sarah answered on the first ring, which had been so unlike her before the incident and had become her habit after. Like she worried that if she didn't answer him immediately, something dire would happen.

"Sarah," he replied, some of the tension unwinding in his shoulders at her voice. He'd been a shitty friend the last few years, but she'd stuck by him at every turn, far more loyal than he deserved. "How are you?"

"Drowning in midterm grading." She sighed. "The undergrads are better than usual this semester, but I still have a few who seem to make it a challenge of trying to write the most incomprehensible paper possible. One of these is nearly entirely gibberish."

"Email it to me and I'll grade it for you." He smiled despite himself. She had a habit of getting him to do that. Maybe in another life he would have made a good professor, if he could have withstood seven years of additional school. "You know I love that kind of challenge."

Pages rustled on the other end of the phone, and Sarah gave a frustrated grunt. "You have your own work to do. How's the elusive Schechter Institute?"

It was a peace offering. He'd told Sarah—and everyone else—that a client had hired him to go to the Institute in order to translate as much as he could in two weeks. Sarah had given him an odd look, then groused about how the archive had been closed to students and researchers alike for years, and yet apparently the archivist was allowing rich fucks to hire translators to get in before people had the chance to do their actual research.

He hadn't told her the real reason he was there, and he never would, even though she'd probably guessed exactly what was going on and was just too kind to call him out on it. Nate had talked about the Institute enough that she'd have put two and two together. Sarah would never have approved of him continuing Nate's work, because she thought he should be moving on from his grief, and she would see this as staying mired in it rather than an effort at repentance.

Plus, Sarah had been against Michael going anywhere at all, not with—as she put it—his "current mental state." He knew she was worried about him, but a brunch two months after he left the hospital, where she'd confronted him about pursuing inpatient therapy and rehab to get rid of his newly acquired drug habit, had ended up with him storming out because nothing that Sarah said about his avoidance behavior was true.

Of course it wasn't.

A few weeks after their blowup, Sarah had come over with a peace offering of rugelach and an apology, and he'd accepted because she'd sworn she wasn't there to talk about anything more than the latest trashy reality TV. And the peace had held ever since, fragile though it was. Michael hated that he'd fucked up his friendship at the same time as he was mourning his boyfriend. No one could accuse him of not going all out in trying to devastate his relationships.

"It's frustrating, but in that good way." Michael shivered as another breeze blew in, the cold hitting him across the face. He pushed off the car and started to walk down the street, putting in his earbuds so he could tuck the phone and his hands into his pockets. "The archivist is very unusual, and I'm not sure there's rhyme or reason to what he's giving me to look at. You can't request boxes, only read what he gives you."

For a second, only the crunching of what sounded like potato chips echoed in his ears. "That doesn't matter to your… client?" Sarah asked eventually.

A cold tendril of dread snaked through Michael: that she was finally going to force him to admit the truth, and get mad when he wouldn't. He hoped he could sidestep her question by providing her with something else to latch onto. He chose the one thing he knew she wouldn't be able to resist gossiping about. "No, the client doesn't care. But I have something far more interesting for you. The archivist isn't Eleazer Schechter anymore." Hunching his shoulders against another blast of cold wind, he started searching for a store to duck into to escape the weather. He found a conveniently located bookstore and crossed the street to get to it, his body relaxing as he opened the door and warm air greeted him. "It's his grandson."

"Oh?" The crunching on the other end of the line stopped. "Tell me more."

"He's our age, I think." The bookstore had a few other patrons in it, but no one was paying him any mind, so he drifted over to the religion section to see if there were any interesting new titles. When he'd eyed the small shelf, he gave up and made for the romance novels instead. "His name is Jacob, and he took over from his grandfather. Eleazer died, and that's why the archive wasn't answering any emails until now. Jacob said he had a really hard time getting the archive back up and running."

"That tracks. That archive was a notorious mess." Sarah blew out a breath. "I heard from a few older students that it was incredibly difficult to sort through, none of the files were in order or anything—boxes which were supposed to contain one thing containing something else entirely. Jacob must have had to re-sort everything."

Images of a pristine white shirt and carefully done hair, sleeves perfectly cuffed and pants without any hint of a wrinkle flashed before Michael's eyes, chased by a vision of a flushed face and rumpled clothes and looking up at

Jacob from between the other man's thighs. He swallowed hard and blinked, re-focusing instead on the lurid romance covers in front of him. "He seems like the type."

Despite his best efforts, his voice came out just a little bit strangled, and damn her, Sarah knew exactly what the cause was.

"So he's cute," she said with a cackle. "Does he swing your way, or should I be catching the next bus to whatever that town is?"

"*Sarah*," Michael hissed, even though she was on earphones and no one could hear her. "It's not— I don't—"

He coughed and ended up choking on his own spit.

A tired sigh. "So you already fucked him, then."

"Oh my God, Sarah." Michael flushed from his chest to his cheeks. "I—" He was about to lie, but swallowed it down, because he didn't want to do that to his best friend yet again, when he was already lying to her so much. "I— Look, he propositioned me, okay? It wasn't the other way around. It wasn't like you're thinking. I think he's just lonely."

He looked over his shoulder to make sure he was alone, even though he was whispering. He didn't need anyone overhearing him—he knew how gossip could spread in small towns, and Jacob seemed like an intensely private person.

"The way you're lonely?" He could hear the gentle question in it. "It's okay if you are, Michael. You're allowed to engage in healthy relationships, you know. I just want to make sure that's all it is, being interested in someone who's interested in you back, and not you punishing yourself."

"I—" He pinched the bridge of his nose, tension building in his chest. "It just happened, okay? And it probably won't happen again because I'm sure he has no interest."

"He'd be a fool not to have interest," Sarah immediately retorted, and Michael envied the way that she could think he was making bad choices but still be like a mother bear, prepared to rip anyone to pieces who dared to besmirch his honor. "Anyone would be lucky to have you, even if it's just for a night."

"Thanks, Sarah." He realized he was starting to get looks from some of the bookstore clerks circulating around, and he slunk back out the door instead of wasting money buying a book he wasn't going to read. He cast around for a distraction to fill the silence that hung between them, hoping he could come up with something better than his fucked-up sex life. "Hey, you know, Jacob insists that the archive is infested with mazzekin."

"Oooo." Michael could tell that he'd caught Sarah's interest. While she was studying the history of the Old Testament and the archeological evidence that early Biblical settlements had left behind, she'd been raised by Old Country grandparents and still wouldn't drink water left out overnight in case she ingested a demon or some nonsense like that. Unlike him, though, she didn't have the complicated background with her own heritage. She was always interested in this type of thing, and even though it hurt to talk about it with someone who was fascinated by the customs instead of annoyed by them like he was, he indulged it because he loved her. "How does he know? Has he tried to bribe them? My grandma used to leave coins under the rugs for them, I don't know why."

Michael turned right out of the bookstore without the faintest idea of where he was going, leaves crunching under his shoes. "He did say that he left an offering to them when he moved in, but that his grandfather hadn't, and they all just kind of accepted one another."

"You sound like you believe," Sarah said. Michael couldn't tell if her tone was accusatory or amused.

"I don't—" He bit his tongue before he could reflexively deny the existence of supernatural entities in the archive, his mind snagging on gloves worn by spectral hands. "Of course I don't. He's really convinced that they exist, but so far he's just blamed a minor shelf collapse on them that could have been due to old brackets on his bookcase. And you know, it could be the grief that's pushing him toward belief in things he can't see, since his grandfather was old-fashioned and kept to the same superstitions. He was talking about how they're all he has left of his past…"

"Michael," Sarah broke in with wary gentleness, "if you like him, maybe don't suggest that he's hallucinating about demons to mask his heartbreak. People don't take kindly to that. I can almost guarantee you that it's not going to get you any more sex. Or, God forbid, a date."

He blew out a breath from his nose, not sure how to tell her that he wasn't fit to date anyone ever again. Clearly, he had proven himself incapable of being safely in a relationship, and he'd never again be able to trust himself with another person.

The sound of a skull cracking filled his ears, nausea cramping his stomach. He swallowed it down, completely unwilling to break down in public.

"Tell me about the gossip from work," he pled,

hoping that the word *gossip* would distract Sarah. And his lungs expanded a little bit easier when she took the bait, launching into a long and convoluted story about how a student was petitioning to have a teaching assistant kicked out of the program because they got a B+ and were upset about it, and how the honor council got involved, and…

He let her words wash over him until he made it to the end of the main street, where there was a small grocery store. "I need to pick up food, Sarah. Can we talk later?"

"Yeah, sure." She made a sound that he assumed was her blowing a kiss into the phone. "Remember to keep your therapy appointments. Bye!"

She hung up before he could get irritated and snap at her that, yes, he knew that she and his parents were going to come after him if he missed any of his therapy appointments. Instead, he took a few moments to center himself by counting the leaves he could see on the ground in front of him, noting the sounds and smells of the town and the feeling of the cold air on his skin. The exercise helped to dispel some of his anger, and he felt steadier when he opened the door to the grocery store, ringing the bell.

It was a small place that was probably overpriced, but the produce looked fresh and he didn't want to waste time driving anywhere else. He needed to get back to the archive so he could keep going, getting through the boxes he'd been assigned for the day before sundown. He had two weeks at the archive, and he didn't know if there was anyone coming in after him, whether Jacob would kick him out precisely at the end of the two weeks, or whether he'd be allowed to keep going. Either way, he hated falling behind, and he wasn't about to give up his chance to finish Nate's research because he was price hunting for bananas.

He picked up a basket and slid the handle into the crook of his right elbow, resting the side against his undamaged ribs. Unconsciously, his hand drifted to the fresh bandage on his left side, and he started thumbing across the aching skin. Every time he did, the memory of Jacob's thumb in the wound sent a spiral of heat through him that was difficult to ignore.

Maybe Jacob would be amenable to a second round.

Although that would be more about pleasuring himself than punishment, and pleasure was more than Michael deserved. He hadn't been with anyone more than once since Nate because that felt like disloyalty. That felt like rewarding himself for the fact that Nate was no longer here because of him.

If he saw someone once and walked away, he could rest easy knowing that if they died, it wasn't because of him. The danger came from going back. The danger came from letting people get close to him, so that he could fuck them up.

*You're making me do this.*

Nate's voice echoed in Michael's ear as he reached for a tomato, and he winced. He hadn't heard Nate's voice so vividly since he'd been high on painkillers in the hospital and he'd had a hard time telling reality from hallucinations.

That was Nate's constant refrain in the last few months. Michael had made mistake after mistake, and they hadn't been able to get out of the cycle of him screwing up and Nate having to correct him. And he could tell that Nate was getting more and more frustrated with each passing day, but he was floundering and didn't have a way to change things. They were stuck in a cycle: Michael being careless with Nate's heart, and Nate trying to salvage things but not being able to. Constantly being forced to try to teach Michael how to love him better.

He'd spent the last months of Nate's life torturing the man, and he'd never forgive himself for that.

The tomato was cool under his palm, and he blinked back to awareness at a gentle "Do you need help?" from over his right shoulder. It had been a few months since he'd disassociated so thoroughly in public that he'd forgotten where he was, and he flushed with shame.

He turned to see a middle-aged woman wearing an apron with the emblem of the grocery store on it.

"I'm sorry?" He blinked a few times, refocusing his vision.

"Do you need help finding anything?" She smiled at him. "You must be new here. I've not seen you in here before, and since this is the town's only grocery store, I kind of know everyone."

The old him would have smiled and made conversation, because she was clearly one of those small-town people who *did* know everyone, and knew their stories too. But Michael no longer wanted anyone to know his story, not when he knew how it ended. "I'm good," he said, giving her a close-lipped smile. "Thank you, though."

"Are you okay?" Her mouth turned down in concern.

"Yeah." Michael picked up a tomato woodenly and put it in his basket for something to do with his hands. The clerk's eyes tracked his hand as he reached for another.

He'd make pasta with pomodoro sauce, he decided. When he didn't engage in more conversation, she shook her head.

"I'm sorry for bothering you. Let me know if you have any trouble finding what you're looking for." She patted him on the arm, the sudden contact making him jump. She backed away, and immediately he felt bad for scaring her.

He was left mired in humiliated relief as she retreated to the back of the store, and he started grabbing produce as quickly as he could reference the vague grocery list he had drawn up on his phone. He grabbed one of the packaged sandwiches on display for lunch, and then started piling pantry staples into the basket too. There hadn't seemed to be much else to eat in the kitchen, and Michael wasn't about to steal Jacob's food in addition to imposing on his hospitality. He may be a horrible person, but he was determined not to be a horrible guest.

Canned tomatoes, pasta, cereal, flour, sugar, milk, eggs and more weighed him down by the time he lugged the basket to the single checkout lane. The weight on his right side pulled his body down, stretching his stitches into a line of fire that he had to bite down on his tongue against. He concentrated on placing the groceries onto the conveyor belt, and then moving around to help shove everything into reusable cloth bags stamped with the store's name. He didn't say anything to the clerk as she smiled kindly at him and handed him his receipt, giving him a look that he just knew meant she saw *something* was wrong with him, even if she didn't know what.

He dashed out of the store and for the safety of his car, his throat tight. He wanted to hide away from the world and not have more interactions like this. And that made sense, he supposed. Wanting to hide while in pain was an animal instinct that humans couldn't escape. Michael knew. He'd been felled by it.

The car was cold when he got in. He barely felt it on the drive back home.

# Chapter 7

The remaining hours that afternoon passed too quickly, the light fading from the sanctuary just as Michael finished the last of the documents in the boxes.

He'd found more than he'd anticipated for the first day's work. In his experience, and possibly bad luck, there was usually nothing to be found on the first day of translation work. It always started with the most boring documents, the ones he had to slog through, the more interesting ones revealing themselves bit by bit as the days went on, exactly when his focus would be fading. Instead, he'd come across several accounts of strange, unexplained occurrences in a town in the eastern part of Poland, documented in a meticulous hand.

*A case of dybbuk possession: Chasia was seen walking into the forest at night, and then began speaking in Lithuanian despite never having left the village. She could no longer pray without experiencing pain.*

*Eidel accused Yehoshua of sins she could not have known he committed, but upon investigation it was found that he did, indeed, commit these sins-and that the secret-keeper was a righteous man now among the deceased. Eidel had been possessed by his ibbur.*

Michael picked his way through the lines of Yiddish text, taking in each incident, imagining himself there, in the mid-1800s, poor, and barely getting by, the threat of violence constantly hanging over his head, denied access to careers and education that Christians were able to pursue with ease. He'd been to Poland in the first year of his master's degree, while helping a professor do field work over the summer. The villages were modern now, but the woods were still wild, and back then they would have been dark and ominous, cradling fields farmed by smallholders, rolling hills in the distance. Flipping through the pages, he was back there, smelling the wet earth and hearing the birds in the early morning, so different to the sounds of the city waking up back home.

It always transported him, reading through old words.

*The synagogue was crowded on the Day of Atonement, when the exorcism of Chasia was attempted.*

*It snowed heavily the day that Yehoshua was taken to his judgment for theft after Eidel's accusation, and the animals were taken inside.*

It was his favorite thing about being in an archive, the way it helped him pull on the mantle of the past. The way he was able to forget who and where he was and immerse himself in lives that had already been lived.

He'd forgotten how much he craved it, being able to forget that he was himself. In this case, he not only immersed himself in the past—he immersed himself in Nate, in pretending he was Nate, sitting here and reading documents that validated his theory, that fascinated him to no end. Because in order to be successful, in order to carry out Nate's research and finish his dissertation, he had to think the way Nate would have. So, he put his own desires aside and tried to imagine how Nate would have reacted to all of this.

It helped take the edge off the dread he felt reading through the documents, the weight of old traumas, of not knowing his own mind, pressing down on his chest.

The interesting thing about this set of records which Jacob had pulled out for him was that it wasn't just a series of village mishaps blamed on mazzekin. There was also accompanying documentation from someone else—a man who had been traveling through the town and had stopped for several weeks when the snow got too bad for him to continue. He wasn't Jewish, and therefore provided an outsider's view of occurrences that otherwise would have no independent eye on them.

*Any uncovered milk spoils between one moment and the next if left uncovered, no matter how fresh from the cow or goat. The well runs dry until the village prays for release from spirits, reciting incantations, and then the well is restored to working order. I am frightened here, and fascinated in equal measure.*

And… he'd agreed that the occurrences had no obvious causes. Ordinarily, Michael would have chalked it up to someone being swept up in the superstitions of a small, insular community while stuck with them during a period of heavy snow, bored and with nothing else to do but listen to tales at the fireside. But the man had been from the large university at Warsaw, and he'd been traversing the country to do an agricultural survey, so it wasn't as if he was someone unfamiliar with science or patently inclined to a superstitious point of view.

It wasn't much, but it was something. And while it

didn't prove Nate's theory beyond a shadow of a doubt, it also *was* supporting evidence. So, Michael carefully catalogued and photographed each page of the notebooks in which the accounts had been collected and made his own notes in pencil in the notebook he'd brought for the trip.

When the door creaked open after the sun was fully down—the lights had clicked on at some point, so they must have been on some kind of timer—Michael wasn't sure how to feel. He was happy, on the one hand, that he was already finding material that would help support Nate's dissertation. He knew exactly which chapter he'd insert the textual evidence into, and where it was filling holes that Nate hadn't been able to patch with the work he'd done thus far. But a smaller part of him was souring at the idea that there was evidence out there proving Nate correct, which rendered Michael's own beliefs *wrong*. He would ordinarily have looked at these notebooks and dismissed them, but here he was considering them credible evidence.

Michael jumped out of his skin and his thoughts shattered as he felt something brush against his leg, just like before, when he'd been under the table. But when he looked down this time, there was a pitch-black cat winding its way between his legs. He breathed a sigh of relief, some of his earlier anxiety washing away—Jacob hadn't mentioned a cat, and he hadn't seen one here before, but there was clearly one rubbing its chin against his shins. He must have somehow missed her completely when he was searching for the gloves. The sanctuary wasn't well lit, and she was perfectly colored to blend into the shadows, after all.

She turned her eyes up at him, bottle-green and luminous, and then darted back down the central aisle of the sanctuary and back out the door. Michael returned his attention to putting all the documents back into the final box, securing the Velcro straps and standing everything upright. When he was done, the door to the sanctuary opened wide and Jacob strolled in, hands in his pockets and his eyes fixated on Michael.

"I didn't know you had a cat," Michael called, standing up and rounding the desk. He felt pulled to Jacob, the way two magnets would snap together and connect if they were brought close enough.

"Bar-Shiriqa." Jacob glanced over his shoulder, but there was no sign of his pet. "Shiri for short."

"You named your cat after the Jewish demon of the toilet?" Michael had to stifle a laugh. He couldn't tell if Jacob was serious or not.

"Who says she's a cat?" Jacob cocked an eyebrow. "And not the demon of the toilet in the flesh?"

There was no way Michael could keep his laughter in at that, the stitches in his side pulling at the motion of his ribs. Jacob's mouth twitched upward and he chuckled too, the sound rich in the silence.

Michael stopped when he realized that it was the first time he'd laughed like this, free and unbridled, since the night of the incident. And it felt good, and wrong, and it wasn't at all why he was here. He wasn't supposed to be enjoying himself—he was supposed to be atoning for what had happened, in the only way left to him.

"How was your research? Fruitful, I hope." Jacob drew closer, until they were a mere foot apart, the pine-forest and old-book smell of him reminding Michael of that time spent in Poland, among the trees. "I selected those boxes as a starting-off point. I think you will find the material becomes more intriguing with time."

It was hard to concentrate with him so close. Michael blinked a few times and leaned against the nearest bookshelf for support, dizzy once more. "It was… interesting. Nate would have remarked that you don't often get an outsider's point of view on these kinds of community matters."

"Are you closer to believing now?" Jacob took another step forward, their chests nearly touching, Michael pinned against the shelf. "In the world beyond this one?"

The sudden urge to tell Jacob about the cotton gloves flared up, but Michael wasn't about to confess that, for a second, he'd wondered if a mazzekin had jumped out of the archive's documents and into the real world. Instead, he chewed his lip. "No. I already told you, I don't personally put stock in any of that."

"Well." Jacob reached out and tapped a finger against Michael's shoulder. "I'm sure you'll be a believer once your time here is up."

The contact was like an electric shock, snapping against his skin. But he leaned into it, and Jacob's entire hand came to rest on Michael's chest, his fingers curling and his nails digging into the muscle. Jacob held his stare, like he was daring Michael to do something, but he held back.

Jacob gradually brought his thumb and forefinger together, pinching the sensitive skin of Michael's chest between his fingernails. The promise of something as rough and unforgiving as last night rose before him, sending a flush of heat through his body, but he wanted to save that for later.

Licking his lips, he tilted his head back against the bookcase, breaking Jacob's gaze. He was starving, and he didn't want to pass out on top of Jacob. "I got stuff to cook for dinner tonight, if you're interested." It was safer to concentrate on the plans he'd made than to look in front of him, because if he did, his willpower was going to disintegrate and he'd beg Jacob to fuck him roughly right there against the bookcase. "You said you didn't know how to cook, so I thought I could teach you. You know, to thank you for letting me stay here."

Jacob seemed to get the message, because he dropped his hand and stepped back enough to give Michael breathing room. "I'd enjoy that, yes."

His voice was cool and he hunched his shoulders, and Michael immediately regretted his rejection. He'd always hated disappointing people like this, making them feel as though they weren't worthy, or weren't enough. It was one of the feelings that he had the most difficulty with, the innate horror of knowing that the deficiency lay in who he was, and that there was nothing he could do to fix it.

"I—" Michael breathed in and stepped forward, catching Jacob by the shoulder. The other man's skin was burning, hot to the touch. He shuddered with the contact, the delicate bones of his shoulder shivering under Michael's palm. "I want to do it again. I just need to eat something first."

"I'm getting the sense that something is holding you back from fully committing to your desires." Jacob cocked his head, narrowing his eyes at Michael. "Is it that, technically, this is work for you? What if I said I wanted it again? You may have issues reckoning with your desire, but I certainly do not. We're both consenting adults, and if we want to fuck, why can't we?"

*Because I don't deserve it*, Michael's brain supplied. *Because it's supposed to be punishment, not pleasure, not anymore.*

"I don't know," he said lamely instead.

"If you're worried about me telling anyone, I can assure you I will not." Jacob bit his lip. "I have no one to tell. I'm not part of any community, and I have no friends. I'm alone here."

He blinked rapidly, and in the low light, Michael could have sworn his eyes took on a sheen. "It's just me. And I'm not going to apologize for wanting connection, for wanting something more. For wanting something to replace the hollow ache inside of you, pleasure or pain or both. I'm—I'm not saying that it's anything more than sex."

Jacob stepped out of Michael's touch and wrapped his arms around himself, turning around so his back was to Michael. The hitch in his shoulders and the small sniff he gave went straight to Michael's gut, filling him with guilt.

"My boyfriend died seven months ago," he said into the void between them. "I haven't been with the same person twice since then. It feels…" He swallowed, saliva pooling in his mouth. "It feels wrong to enjoy myself when I know he can't."

Jacob paced a few steps toward the nearest bookshelf, then turned around to lean on it. There were tears on his cheeks, the tracks glimmering faintly red in the odd cast of the light. He wiped his face with the back of a hand. "Is that why you're here? You said you were finishing his research, but is it more that you feel the need to subjugate your own intellect to his? As much as I think that you're misguided not to believe in the types of creatures you're here to study, I cannot imagine it's easy to put your beliefs aside. Especially since yours seem rather vehemently held."

Michael's knees were weak; he hadn't expected to have to open up to Jacob like this, but the other man had been vulnerable and honest with him, so he owed him some honesty right back. And it felt easier, somehow, to confess this to another person who had lost someone, instead of a blank-faced therapist on a computer screen. He slid down the bookcase and drew his knees into his chest, and Jacob mirrored him.

"This is really hard to talk about," he said through the persistent, immovable lump in his throat. "But yes. I was— I was responsible for the accident that caused Nate to die." He caught his own use of the passive voice and cleared his throat. "The accident that killed him."

"No one can be responsible for an accident," Jacob said softly, resting his chin on his knees, his pale fingers gripping his forearms. "That's literally the opposite of an accident."

Michael sighed; arguing with him would involve confessing far more than he was ready to share. No one deserved the whole of him, the entirety of his story, not when he'd spent so much time and effort concealing most of himself from everyone around him who mattered, except Nate.

"Well, I *feel* responsible, and that's all that matters." He scratched at his incision, the pain sharpening his mind. "Maimonides had five stages of repentance for a transgression. Naming and owning what you did and the harm you caused, beginning to change yourself, making restitution and accepting the consequences of your harmful actions, apologizing, and making different choices. I can't make restitution and apologize directly, although if I could, I would. I'm here as part of that. I'm here to make restitution to Nate's memory by finishing what he started. What I feel doesn't factor into it."

Jacob huffed. "You're punishing yourself based on the work of a medieval Jewish philosopher?"

"Yes." Michael's face heated. "And no. It's not punishment. It's repairing as much as possible while changing yourself so you don't cause the same kind of harm again."

"Why is it your job to change? And repent?" Jacob fiddled with the seam of his shirt sleeve, staring Michael down.

He hated that Jacob was pushing him, but was determined not to give in to the impulse to snap back at him that this was none of his business, and only he knew what he deserved because only he knew the truth. He took a slow breath in to dissipate some of the acid that was beginning to run through his veins at being prodded. "Because I caused the harm, and because I need to ensure that I don't do the same thing to another person."

"Again," Jacob said dryly, waving a hand in the air. "Accident."

It was a mistake that Michael couldn't explain without telling the whole truth, and because he wasn't ready to do that, he took the easy way out and changed the subject. "Are you hungry?"

He stood, crossing the aisle and offering a hand to Jacob, who took it and allowed Michael to help him up. "More than you know," Jacob said, giving his hand a squeeze before dropping it, at least respectful of the distance that Michael was determined to keep between them. "Lead the way."

Some of the awkwardness dissipated as night set in fully and Michael set about finding pots and pans in the archive's kitchen, centered by the rote motions of beginning a meal. The kitchen had been redone at some point, and while it was far larger than normal, it looked more or less like any other kitchen in a nice house, with marble countertops and wood cabinets painted a deep, rich navy. He narrated as he assembled what he needed, Jacob leaning against the counter with his arms crossed over his narrow chest.

"So pasta is one of the easiest things to make, and you can do a really good version that's quick and cheap and also tastes much better than what you'd get in the average restaurant. My particular favorite is pomodoro."

"Mm." Jacob hummed, seeming completely uninclined to help Michael unearth the rest of the cooking equipment. "I'm sure it's delicious."

"The secret is salt." Michael lugged a huge pot to the sink and started to fill it with water. "Lots and lots of salt."

"Enough to keep away a demon?" Jacob raised an eyebrow. "I'm sure you know the traditional method of warding homes."

Michael did—Eastern European Jews had spent

centuries salting doorways and windowsills to keep out spirits. His own grandmother had done it, and when salt had spilled, she'd thrown it over her shoulders to warn away evil spirits. "I'd say you want to put in as much salt as it would take to ward your average-sized residential window." He gestured to the window over the sink, the one that looked out onto the garden, and fished out the box of kosher salt that he'd put into the cabinet.

Jacob was quiet, so Michael looked over to him, the sound of the water sloshing into the pot the only noise between them.

But Jacob didn't appear to want to talk much, and the good thing about cooking was that it could be done with a minimum of conversation if you needed to. Michael had taught Nate how to cook, and in the beginning, it had always been a prelude to winding up on the kitchen table, doing something completely different than making a meal. There had been a closeness to it, and a sense of fun and whimsy, which had gradually faded away when they moved in together and life became more mundane.

Michael was used to cooking in silence.

Then again, he'd promised Jacob that he was going to teach him how to cook, and that was part of what he intended to do, in addition to providing Jacob with a meal as a thank-you for allowing him to stay there. So, he cleared his throat as he opened the spout of the salt box and poured a huge measure into his hand.

"See?" He thrust his hand out toward Jacob, who actually tripped backward at the motion, only narrowly catching himself on the counter so that he didn't fall over.

Michael hastily dumped the salt into the pot and dashed

forward to put a hand under Jacob's elbow. He remembered Jacob saying that he had problem with his feet, and he felt immediately guilty that he'd caused him to startle and almost fall. It had to be difficult with imperfect balance, trying to navigate the world. "I'm so sorry," he stammered.

"No, no." Jacob took in a shaking breath. "It's alright. I'm fine. I just lost my footing. Go on."

Michael drew his hand away and paused, looking down at Jacob's forearm. It was speckled with tiny red dots, almost like small burns, that he would have sworn hadn't been there before. "Are you alright?" He ran a finger over one of the wounds, and Jacob hissed through his teeth.

"Yes." Jacob pulled away, and Michael let him go. "I'm fine. Just scratched myself earlier." He brusquely unfolded his sleeves, buttoning the cuffs, and Michael decided it wasn't right to pry, even if he was very sure that Jacob was lying—those looked like tiny burns, not scratches. "Teach me how to make pasta."

Michael could recognize a deflection and a request to change the subject when he saw one, and decided to give Jacob a graceful exit. He hefted the pot up and carried it to the stove, even though it was likely too heavy for him to be lifting after his surgery. "Step one—boil the water."

The burner clicked on easily, the flame a vivid blue, and he turned his attention to draining the tomatoes and cutting up the garlic and basil, showing Jacob how to copy each motion.

"I'm not touching that," he insisted after Michael offered him a clove of garlic, his nose wrinkling. "My hands will smell for the next year."

"Fine," Michael retorted, although he couldn't help but smile at Jacob's prissiness. "You can strip the basil."

Jacob stood shoulder to shoulder with him over the cutting board as the water slowly rose to a boil, steam fogging the air and the two of them working in tandem. The silence was quiet and comfortable, not thick and tense the way that so many silences in the last few years had been for Michael, so at least some of the tension in his shoulders was able to dissipate. The part of him that always expected a blow was permanently primed to receive one, and no amount of meditation or visualization or anything else had begun to unwind that impulse. His therapist told him that it was because he was afraid of his own healing and blocking himself from moving on. It might have been a waste of money, but he never said to her what was really on his mind: that he was still tensing up and waiting for the evil he had wrought to catch up with him.

They worked quickly, a small mound of minced garlic joining the pile of basil leaves that Jacob was surgically separating from the stems. When they finished, Michael eyed the boiling water.

"If you put the pasta in now, it will be done roughly when the sauce is finished." He handed the box of spaghetti to Jacob, who looked down at it like he was holding a bomb.

"So I just…" Jacob crinkled his eyebrows. "…put it in?"

The skepticism in his tone was so endearing that Michael couldn't help but laugh. "Yes. You've never even made pasta before?"

"I told you, I'm very good at cooking frozen things."

Jacob pointed an accusatory finger at the boiling water. "This is not a frozen thing. Although I did live in Italy for a time, so I've at least been in the presence of what is presumably very good pasta."

Michael couldn't tell whether Jacob was being serious, but he took the bait, circling around Jacob's back and pressing the smaller man to his chest, reaching around to take the box of pasta from his hands. It was close to exactly what he'd promised himself he wouldn't do, but something about Jacob had a way of reducing his resolve to rubble. "You just... open the box and take out the noodles. See?"

He took the sheaf of spaghetti in hand and tossed the box onto the counter, steering Jacob around until he faced the pot, and then pressing the noodles into his palm. "Go on. Dump it in."

That at least made Jacob laugh as he complied, opening his hand and letting the spaghetti slide in. Michael kept Jacob trapped in the cage of his arms as he stirred the pot, then fished his phone out to set a timer, the numbers ticking down through the shattered glass.

"What's next?" Jacob twisted his head, and then they were close enough to kiss, their lips scant inches apart. It was so hard to keep himself separate, to resist what it was that Jacob was clearly offering—no, asking for—as he leaned back into Michael's chest. The ways in which Michael was so, so weak and defective, the part of him that fell for people faster than falling asleep, was rearing its head. And that was a problem, because giving in would feel good, and so it wasn't right.

This felt too much like a date, like romance. Michael

was okay letting himself fuck another person; there was no way he would be okay letting himself fall in love again.

With Herculean effort, Michael managed to let Jacob go and stepped back, calming the reaction his body was clearly having to the contact, reminding himself that it was alright to be used, but not alright to take. The way that Jacob's face fell ever so slightly hurt.

"And now we start the sauce." He turned away from Jacob, busying himself with dumping oil into a saucepan to heat up, followed by the garlic. When it started to sizzle, he talked Jacob through adding the right amount of chili, just enough for a bit of a bite, then he added in the tomatoes to brown, and then finally the juice that he had crushed out of them. Every time Jacob bumped against him, he bit his lip. When their hands touched, it was difficult to breathe.

How strange, that the two of them were so opposite in their grief. Jacob was reaching out for comfort and contact, and Michael was pushing everything and everyone away. The way they were so opposite shouldn't have been shocking, though—not when Jacob's grief was legitimate, over the loss of a family member, and Michael's grief was mixed so deeply with guilt and shame that it was hard to tell them apart.

They drained the pasta—or, rather, Michael drained it while Jacob looked on—and added in the sauce. Michael swirled in butter, and then cheese. "It's the secret," he said, licking his fingers.

"Besides the copious amount of salt?" Jacob fished two plates out of a cabinet, then pulled forks out of a drawer.

"Yes." Michael rolled his eyes. "Besides the salt. The

butter gives it a creamy finish. It works well with the chili and the freshness of the basil."

They each took a plate to the dining room, where Michael had to get over the fear of accidentally tripping and dumping his plate of tomato sauce onto what was probably a priceless antique carpet. Sitting down facing each other, for a moment there was more silence than Michael could stand.

"You didn't open my present." Jacob saved him from the awkwardness by breaking in. "Does that mean you aren't accepting the peace between us?"

He opened his mouth to apologize, because yes, he *had* totally forgotten to open the red box that Jacob had left for him, caught up in research and all his thoughts. But then Jacob smiled, and Michael got the distinct sense that he was teasing.

"Open it tomorrow," Jacob proffered with a wink. "I think you'll like it. Or at least be curious about it."

"I will," Michael promised. "But for now, eat what we made, will you?"

He remembered how painfully Jacob had eaten the night before, and how thin he was, all ridges and angles. But he couldn't help but want to feed him, to nurture him, and his heart warmed when Jacob lifted a single strand of spaghetti to his mouth and ate it, chewing contemplatively.

"It's good," he concluded after swallowing. "Quite good. Thank you. I haven't had a meal like this in a long time."

He nodded, because Jacob looked so sad then that he didn't know what to say. It was hard for him to know what kind of comfort Jacob was looking for, if any. And he didn't know if, broken as he was, he was even able to provide such a thing—if he could do that without opening himself up to comfort in return, which would be the worst possible thing for him to receive. Better to hold himself away from Jacob and let himself hurt the other man than to open himself up to Jacob and betray Nate's memory.

"You're welcome." He took a bite himself—Jacob was right, it was good. "I'm glad you like it. And now you know how to make it. If, you know, you want something that isn't frozen."

Jacob hummed and didn't say anything else, but kept eating, slowly but steadily. Shiri wandered into the dining room and jumped up onto the table with a *prrp* of curiosity, twining between their plates. Jacob fed her a bit of cheese off the top of his pasta, citing a "cheese tax," and that got Michael to chuckle even as he went to the fridge to retrieve the rest of the container of grated parmesan.

"I appreciate the company," Jacob said after they finished, when Shiri had eaten her fill of cheese and settled on Michael's lap, purring hard. Michael met his eyes, and when Jacob reached a hand across the table, Michael broke and took it in his own, promising himself that it meant nothing, that it *was* nothing. "And the kindness. It's been hard, recently, like I've said. And I appreciate it, especially since it seems to be hard for you too."

Michael swallowed, but the weight of the cat and the solidity of Jacob's hand in his and the fact that he'd had a good meal and he was warm and had let himself be comfortable for the first time all day… it was suspiciously close to feeling something other than numb. It was suspiciously close to feeling content, and safe, and *right*.

He hated that he was too weak to resist it, that he was lured by it, that he was tempted into accepting it. *This* felt like a sin, one he wasn't going to be able to avoid.

He was weak. He had always been weak. For once since Nate's death, he didn't fight it. He sank into it. He let the feeling envelop him, and for the very first time since he'd realized what he'd done, Michael broke down and truly cried.

# Chapter 8

Michael found himself huddled on a couch in the archive's parlor, under a thick woolen blanket with a fire roaring in the grate, the cat back on his lap and Jacob's arm slung around his shoulder. He felt utterly hollow, scooped out like someone had reached into his ribcage and removed his organs one by one. There were still tears escaping down his face, but the sobbing had quieted.

He was too exhausted to be embarrassed that he'd had a breakdown in front of someone who was basically a perfect stranger. Jacob had shepherded him to the couch and held him as he cried, earning a soaked-through shirt for his troubles. His fingers had raked through Michael's hair, and he hadn't said anything, or tried to. It was like he knew this was something that Michael had to purge from himself, the tears that his numbness had buried under a layer of restraint which had finally cracked.

Jacob didn't try to soothe him like Sarah would, and

he didn't mock him for crying like Nate would have done. He just sat, and held Michael, and let him grieve.

Michael stared into the fire, the logs crackling and the smell of woodsmoke comforting. Jacob had gotten up to light it when Michael had started to shiver, probably the effect of exhausting himself emotionally. He'd fished a blanket out of a nearby chest, instructed his cat to sit on Michael's lap (which she miraculously did with only a swish of her tail and a sideways glance), and then stacked logs in the grate and coaxed the flames to life. Shadows lurked at the corners of the room, the light creating a circle of comfort that encompassed the two of them and the couch and left everything else black. There was an eerie scratching noise that permeated the crackling of the flames and the snapping of the logs, and when Michael had looked up, Jacob had just held him tighter. He explained that it was either the mazzekin being disruptive or the branches of the pine trees around the house scratching at the glass of the windows, but that it was too dark to tell. There was no moonlight filtering past the clouds that had gathered over the course of the day, but the way Michael felt right in Jacob's arms made is so that he didn't care if it was truth or a lie.

It was more intimacy than he'd shared with anyone in what felt like years. It was more intimacy than he deserved, but he was selfish and he was going to take it.

"Thank you," he rasped when he felt like he could talk without crying again. "I'm really sorry for this. I know you don't know me, and you're just doing a job, and here I am sobbing all over you and you've been so kind..."

He trailed off when Jacob touched a finger to his lips, shushing him. "Don't apologize. I told you, I've been alone here for a while. I've been here with my grief and there hasn't been anyone to comfort me. I'm glad that when yours came to the surface, I was here to comfort you."

"It's a mitzvah to sit with the grieving," Michael said, sniffing. Memories of every time he'd attended a shiva came back to him, friends of his grandparents dying and them showing up to a child's or grandchild's house with plates of food and words of comfort. He rubbed his palms into his eyes, needing some relief from the hot grittiness. "I just never want that to be me."

"Because you don't think you're deserving." Jacob didn't phrase it as a question, and so Michael didn't feel the need to answer. But when Jacob sighed, he felt it in the motion of the other man's chest. "But what do you take away from others when you don't let them comfort you? If it's a mitzvah, a good deed, to sit with the grieving, then aren't you preventing them from behaving righteously?"

"Figures that I'd be out-argued by a man running an archive," Michael grumbled, because it was easier than really thinking about what Jacob had said, which would lend itself to a whole different kind of self-hatred.

Jacob resumed stroking his hair, and Michael melted into the touch.

"I'm sorry there was no one here for you," he said. "Do you—are you estranged from your family?"

A slight stiffening of Jacob's body was the only hint that the question wasn't entirely welcome. Michael was about to apologize, but then Jacob started to talk. "My family isn't quite like others. We aren't close. Much of that is because of the distance. I haven't seen any of my siblings in what feels like a thousand years."

"But you had Eleazer."

"Yes." Jacob's pulse jumped, and Michael could feel the pounding of his heart through his ribcage. "For a time."

"I think that having something and then losing it honestly makes the grief even worse." His eyelids were heavy, and he had to exert far too much willpower to stop himself falling asleep. "Being happy, and then having it ripped away."

"That's one way to think about it." Jacob's voice was hoarse, and his tone told Michael that he didn't quite agree. "If you don't want anything, if you never let yourself have anything, that means you can't feel the pain of having it taken away. I get that. But it also means you don't get to feel joy. So what's worse?"

Michael couldn't help but sigh. "You say that like someone who has never experienced loss."

"On the contrary," Jacob said, staring into the fire. "I've lost everything and more. I no longer have anything left to lose. And I don't regret holding any of the things I lost in my heart for even a moment. It hurts, sure. But I don't think feeling nothing at all would be better. In fact, I know it wouldn't. Because I don't know what life is if you reduce it to just walking around and eating and drinking and sleeping and looking at things." His voice was hard and brittle. *Full of resentment*, Michael thought. *Laced with pain*.

"If you let that happen to yourself, you're just a soul held prison in a mound of flesh. You're wasting the capacity that you were given, which was to hurt and love and heal and break all over again. That is what mortality is, Michael. This right here, letting out your grief? This is so much better than refusing to delve into your pain so that you can finally actually feel it. Everything you've done, everything you're doing, is avoiding the underbelly of your hurt. Everything designed to keep you safe from your grief and self-recrimination? All of that is just trapping you in that pit. You're never going to get out unless you let it go. It feels safe, but that's because you're buried. You're not safe. You're dead while you're still alive."

There was a vise around Michael's throat. "I don't think that's what I'm doing." He blinked hard before tears could fall, annoyed with himself that what Jacob had said had shouldered its way into his mind. "That's not what I want. I— I did something bad. It's not ordinary grief. It's guilt."

His stomach sank when Jacob gently shifted him off and stood, tucking the blanket back in around Michael's shoulders.

"Sorry—"

Jacob shook his head, frowning. "You apologize far too frequently. I shouldn't have said that—I didn't mean to sound accusatory. I'll be right back. I figured we could use a drink." He raked a hand through his hair and pointed at Shiri. "Stay there, and make sure he doesn't get up."

Michael could have sworn that the cat nodded, but that would have been impossible, and the old fear that he was losing his mind crept in at the edges. After Nate had died, Michael had been convinced for a while that he had been seeing things which weren't there. He was assured by his doctors, when he confessed, that it was merely a symptom of the very high fever he'd had when his shattered ribs had become infected. But still, not being able to trust his own mind had shaken him to the core, and reminded him of times past when he'd suffered from paranoia and delusions, no fever necessary.

"I can trust myself," he muttered to himself out loud. The cat turned her luminous eyes on him and chirped, beginning to knead his lap. "I'm not crazy."

"Who said anything about crazy?" Jacob reappeared so suddenly that Michael jumped, startled.

"Make some noise, would you?" Michael put a hand to his heart, breathing in to slow the frantic beating. "You scared the shit out of me."

"Sorry." Jacob sat back down. "Force of habit. Maybe this will help."

He was holding an uncorked bottle of wine in one hand, and two glasses in the other. He offered one to Michael, who took it, even though he rarely drank. Pills had been his vice of choice over the last few years, but now seemed like as good a time as ever to start with alcohol too. It wasn't as though he was going to get sloppier than he'd already proven to be sober.

Jacob poured for both of them, setting the half-full bottle down on the floor and swirling the red wine in the crystal glass, the firelight playing against the liquid. He took a sip, tilting his head back and closing his eyes. Michael followed suit, the tartness of the wine burning its way down his throat.

They finished off the bottle in silence, one of Jacob's hands resting over Michael's thigh, tucked under the blanket. He snuck looks at Jacob every so often, struck by the sharpness of his cheeks and the hollows under his eyes.

The hours slipped away in a pleasant, warm haze, and finally, Michael drifted into sleep.

Waking up in a bed with the sun hitting his face was disorienting, because the last thing Michael remembered was losing his grip on a wineglass and closing his eyes against Jacob's shoulder. He had no idea how he'd gotten back to bed without realizing it—he hadn't drunk that much—but it wouldn't be the first time recently that he'd lost time or memories to the black hole that his brain had become.

In the morning light, his behavior the night before was almost too embarrassing for him to deal with. The fact that he had sobbed his heart out onto the shirt of a man he'd met forty-eight hours ago was horrifying, and he had no idea how he was going to face Jacob come this evening. The archivist was going to kick him out of the Institute, he was sure, and probably tell everyone else in his professional network that Michael was the single most unprofessional translator he'd ever met. And then Michael would never be able to finish Nate's work, let alone continue on with his own, and he'd be stuck living with his parents and their stifling pity since the accident…

The edges of a panic attack were creeping up, and his vision darkened around the edges as his chest constricted and his breathing shortened. The bedsheets grew sticky against his skin as he started to sweat, and he curled onto his side and hugged the pillow to his chest, desperate to soothe the raw wound that had opened last night.

He panted for a few minutes, shaking, until he remembered his breathing exercises and forced his brain to focus on measuring out his inhales and exhales. It did enough to calm his body so that he was able to stagger out of bed and into the shower, which he turned on to cold, full blast.

Freezing water hit his face and body, shocking his brain back into awareness, and he spared a moment to be grateful that he'd learned this trick. The last time he'd had a panic attack was the night before Nate died, the grief having buried the anxiety deep enough that it hadn't reached the surface—the only good thing about having so much guilt on his conscience that he'd almost ceased to function.

He gasped into the cold spray, tilting his head up so the water ran down his face and over his hair and onto his chest. The panic was thankfully starting to recede, and he tried to distract his mind by going through the motions of shampooing his hair and shaving away his stubble and washing away the sweat that clung to his skin. But the time he had finished, he was shivering from the cold instead of the fear, and his mind was marginally clearer.

Jacob Schechter seemed like a kind person. He'd been the one to say that he was desperate for connection. And while getting sloppy tears all over him the night after they'd fucked was probably against some kind of professional code of ethics, Michael couldn't bring himself to care.

He could do this and leave. Maybe it would be an even more thorough punishment than the series of one-night stands and the bottles of pills, allowing this thing between them to grow for a time. Wasn't that what Jacob had said the night before, that even though having something and losing it was painful, it was worth it?

Michael doubted this was precisely what Jacob had in mind, but maybe it could be the mental equivalent of a thumbnail digging into a wound. He could leave here more broken than before, because that was what he deserved. He could have this, enjoy it, and then relish when it was taken away. That way, instead of getting too comfortable, instead of healing, he would be just as miserable as before.

He decided as he dressed, because he was a bad person, that if Jacob was willing to give, Michael was willing to take.

Careful not to make too much noise, he crept down the stairs and into the kitchen, pulling out the box of cereal and then the milk. He found a bowl and poured himself a glass of water, then leaned against the central island to eat, his stomach churning vaguely with the aftereffects of the wine and the panic.

Shiri appeared in the blink of an eye, winding her tail around his arm as she hopped up onto the counter with an inquisitive chirp. The cat stuck her head into the bowl before he could stop her and came away with a mouthful of Honey Nut Cheerios, crunching happily.

"I don't know much about cats, but I don't think you're supposed to eat those." He tried sticking a finger into her mouth to get the cereal out, worrying that he was going to somehow poison Jacob's cat, but she smacked him with a paw and gave him an electric shock for his troubles, so he decided to leave her well enough alone.

Fed and watered, he had nothing left to do to distract himself besides make his way into the archive. He checked his phone and found that it was seven-thirty in the morning, but it wasn't as though Jacob had told him there was an opening time. He scrolled through his text messages and emails as he made his way to the sanctuary, Shiri winding her way between his legs and doing her best to make him trip. He discarded almost all of them except a few from prospective clients, who were reaching out again because he hadn't responded to their earlier messages, his out-of-office reply that had been up for months informing people that, after a long illness, he was slowly getting back to work but responded much less quickly than before, allowing him to ignore the messages for at least another week.

There were also several amusing GIFs from Sarah which he responded to with a picture of Shiri, and his daily text message from his mom checking in, which he responded to with his usual *good morning, thanks for checking in, I'm fine* so that his parents didn't call the police because they'd assumed that he'd died in his sleep.

He pocketed his phone as he reached the sanctuary doors, which had been taped with another note.

*Thank you for trusting me last night*, this one read. It made Michael's throat constrict. *I'm glad I was able to be there for you as you cracked open your grief.*

Taking it down, he folded it carefully into quarters and tucked it into his back pocket. It was just a kindness from a stranger, but somehow it was the first piece of sympathy that didn't feel like a knife to the ribs.

It was fine, he reminded himself. It would hurt even more when the source of that comfort was taken away.

"Are you supposed to be coming in?" Michael looked askance at Shiri, who was standing patiently at the door to the archive. She swished her tail, and of course didn't respond, and Michael decided that if Jacob didn't want his cat to be in among the books and papers, he probably would have said something, fastidious as he was about all the other rules.

"Come on in, then." He opened the door and let her sprint ahead, her tail pointed straight up as she darted into a corner, probably to hunt down some bug or other. It made sense, he supposed, to have a cat in an archive to help with pest control.

There were four more boxes laid out on the table for Michael, along with the small red box that had been placed there yesterday. Michael's present from Jacob. He skirted the desk and sat down in the chair, pulling the red box toward himself.

His breath caught as he lifted the lid to find a perfectly intact incantation bowl, a shallow clay dish with spirals of Hebrew writing from the edges to the center, where a crude demon had been sketched, little more than a triangle with a cartoonish head, horns, and clawed feet. They had been used throughout history by Jewish communities looking to trap demons, and were often buried in graveyards or at the corners of homes after magic spells and even pictures of demons were inscribed on the crude clay. Michael had never been this close to a real one, not when most of the intact specimens that had been found were locked in museum cases or private collections.

A little dirt still clung to the edges of this one, remnants of having been buried to anchor the protection. Face down, the bowl would have "trapped" the demon, rendering it harmless to whoever had made the bowl and written the spell.

Chapter three of Nate's dissertation was dedicated to incantation bowls and their uses in times of catastrophe, when events happened that were too big to be blamed on minor household spirits—pogroms, plagues, natural disasters. And here he was, holding a real one in his hands, closer to the history he'd spent years translating than he'd ever been.

Despite his better judgment, Michael lifted the bowl up out of the foam cradle it was resting in, turning it around, brushing his thumb over the pits in the bottom. If he closed his eyes, he could imagine himself desperate and scared, shaping crude clay into a bowl and then praying to God as he inscribed it with incantations. The terror he would have felt, painting the likeness of the demon he thought was chasing him into the center of the bowl, trapping it. Digging up the earth, placing the bowl face down, and then burying it deep.

Would it have felt like a betrayal if it didn't work? If the pain and the horrors kept coming? Or would he have held out hope that the ritual had worked and that, even if things were bad now, there could have been a much larger disaster if he hadn't trapped the demon stalking him?

A chill crept down Michael's neck. *This* was why he did what he did, for all those people who hadn't had a voice, who left something written behind, something which he could now bring to the world through the minor miracle of turning one language into another. And this was also why Nate did what he did, because this was a link to Nate's past which he hadn't wanted to be forgotten. Nate had done this for all the people who had no choice but to believe in a higher power because there was no one in their daily lives who cared to protect them. Because there were people who were trying to hurt them. Because clay bowls and salt and superstition were all they had, and that had to be enough.

He nestled the bowl back into the box it came in, running a finger around the rim one more time, the clay warm from being held. When he lifted the lid to put it back on, he blinked. His hand was covered in blood, his fingertips tacky. A quick glance down confirmed that for the first time in weeks, he'd been good this morning and hadn't picked at his incision, so the blood wasn't coming from there. He lifted his hand to the light—he must have cut himself on a sharp part of the bowl without realizing it, and then bled all over—but he blinked because, in the light, there was nothing there.

No blood. Just unblemished skin.

It had to have been the light, coming in from the stained-glass windows. They were mostly in tones of blue and gold, he confirmed with a glance over his shoulder, but light worked in funny ways. Even though he could have sworn the stickiness on his fingers had been hot and slick and very much there.

Michael shook his head, chided himself for worrying so much about losing his grip on reality, and went to work.

---

This trip was like researching with a ghost. Michael could practically feel Nate sitting next to him, adjusting his glasses as he muttered to himself while jotting down notes in his favorite leather-bound notebooks, his hand smearing the pencil since pens were never allowed in archives. They had always traveled together, since Nate hated them to be apart, and for Michael being able to save money on hotel rooms and rental cars had been invaluable. He'd chosen clients based on where Nate was going next, which almost always worked out because there was always someone who needed to hire a translator or a contract researcher to go to an archive for them when they couldn't do it themselves. And it had been nice not to be alone during the long hours of sitting and paging through dusty books, even though they weren't allowed to speak to one another in more than a whisper, and Nate often got so immersed in his work that he refused to leave to eat or use the bathroom or even go outside to take a breath that wasn't full of dust.

Michael missed the company so much that it made every bone in his body ache.

Today's materials were long lists of attacks that townspeople had attributed to various kinds of demons, from mazzekin to the demoness Lilith. On their own, the tales of men seduced by demons they swore were their wives, crops failing spontaneously between one day and the next, and more would have been good fodder for either his or Nate's dissertations. They were more of the same kinds of tales that were told throughout the region, and would have been unremarkable. Nate would have considered them mundane.

If not for the police reports.

It was rare for the community to have involved outsiders in these occurrences—the rabbi would be the one to deal with any purported demonic activity, offering ways to banish the offending presence. But these reports had been filed by wealthy, secularizing Jews; those who had been gradually moving away from religious practice, and those most likely to be able to escape antisemitism, to the extent that that was even possible.

And the police couldn't explain any of the happenings either.

> Plates were pushed off the table of the complainant with no one near. No drafts were found from the doors or windows. This I saw with my own eyes.
>
> Gila drank from the river, and directly after began to speak in tongues. She was well respected in the community. The doctors could find no cause for this insanity. She was cured after the rabbi came to pray over her, a last resort.
>
> Thefts were reported at night, food and drink stolen from the homes along one street. We set up watch for the entire night. No intruders came and went, but in the morning more food and drink was gone. The imprints of a rooster's feet were seen in flour scattered across the kitchen counters.

All of the complainants were judged perfectly sane, and none of the incidents had been found to have any explainable cause. Michael combed through hundreds of pages of carefully written reports, mouthing along with the Russian words as he translated in his head.

It was remarkable, and he wasn't sure if he should be elated because this helped his research for Nate, or more confused than ever because he was looking at more evidence in this one box than he had ever found, and none of it proved his own beliefs about the subject right.

He gave up on wondering what the archive's materials meant for him personally and instead sank into his usual fugue state of reading and translating and pretending like he was in a different time and place. Every so often he'd feel a brush against his calves that he assumed was Shiri, although every time he ducked his head under the table, he saw no sign of her. With the shadows that the light from the windows cast, though, he wasn't surprised that seeing a black cat was difficult.

When his phone alarm sounded for lunch—he always set one, since he knew that he ran the risk of getting so caught up in his work that he would forget to eat until he fainted—he startled hard, blinking dry eyes. He had been reading for hours, and his hand was cramped from taking copious notes. The tripod for his camera was still folded, because he'd gotten so absorbed in the texts that he hadn't wanted to stop and take pictures. He'd have to go back through all the documents before he boxed them back up so he could photograph them.

Standing up, Michael rolled his shoulders and moved his neck around, trying to ignore the ways in which his muscles were already so tight that he'd likely be immobile by the end of the day. His body was so much less resilient after the surgery, and along with the fatigue and pain and lack of stamina, he was constantly stiff and sore. His doctors had looked pityingly at him when he mentioned it from the hospital bed and asked when it would go away after surgery, and they'd gently told him that it was likely psychosomatic, and that trauma to the ribs wasn't going to cause muscle tension in his neck.

He'd stopped asking after that and proceeded to just deal with the tension as best he could, with CBD-infused lotion and stretching when he could manage it and an amount of Advil that was probably slowly killing his liver, but which at least kept him mobile. His therapist kept telling him to meditate more, and he probably should, but it was easier to keep going and try to forget than it was to clear the crowded, anxious thoughts out of his head.

When he looked down from stretching, though, he froze. It couldn't have been more than thirty seconds since he'd stood after putting the papers he'd been looking at back in the neat stack they'd come in, and while he hadn't fastened the lid of the archival box yet, he certainly hadn't left the papers fanned out on the desk, completely out of order and upside down.

*It's fine*, he told himself as he looked at the mess, which he couldn't have caused—could he? He would never treat documents this way. They were fragile and had to be handled in a particular way to avoid damage. Michael had been trained to handle documents like this without harming them, and this wasn't that. The longer he looked at the mess, the more his hands started to shake, and he reflexively prodded at his incision just to ground himself with the pain.

He hadn't done this. Except if he hadn't, who had? He was the only one in the archive, and even if the cat had managed to somehow jump onto the table and scramble everything up in thirty seconds, and then vanish again, he was sure he would have heard her making a mess.

Jacob's warning about the mazzekin that lived in the archive came back to him, but there was a clear difference between being enthralled by tales from the past and believing there were literal demons haunting an archive. This wasn't supernatural—this was his mind failing. He was hungry, and tired, and washed-out from everything that had happened last night. He needed to rest, and clearly if he was hallucinating like this then something was going haywire in his brain.

The old, familiar fear kicked in, hammering inside his chest and turning his limbs cold and weightless. The ways he'd managed to insult or slight Nate without remembering it, the times when he'd flirted with another person without being cognizant of his actions, the instances of them arguing over something Michael had done which he couldn't for the life of him remember now. He'd never had the best memory, and he'd never been the most attentive lover, and sometimes he was too in his own head to realize what was going on in the real world. He'd relied on Nate to point out these failings when they occurred, but now that Nate was gone, he was on his own.

It hadn't been this bad since he'd gotten out of the hospital, though. He hadn't felt a distrust of his own mind like this since he'd been forced to recount the events of that afternoon over and over and over, so many times that it felt like he must have been lying because there was no way these events had happened in that order at those times. There was no way he was telling the truth because he was a liar and a cheat and the only good thing in his life was gone, because he'd killed him.

Michael found himself hunching over the table, his hands gripping the sides, the spiral of anxiety fighting to take control as much as he was fighting to push it back.

He busied himself by carefully collecting each of the documents, making sure they were right-side up, and then stacking and stowing them in the archival box, which he made sure to Velcro shut this time. He placed it with the others, and just for the sake of his mental health, took a picture with his phone of everything neatly organized, just so he could remind himself while he ate lunch that he wasn't that crazy, not yet.

There was no sign of Shiri as he left the sanctuary, checking over his shoulder every few steps to make sure the boxes were all still where he'd left them. The doors were closed—he thought he'd left them open, so the cat could come in and out, but a draft had probably blown them shut—and he tugged on the handle. It was stuck, the handle slow to turn, and he had to yank on the door to open it, the wood creaking in protest.

"Fuck," he muttered as the door slammed into his shoulder with the force of the motion. He leaned his forehead against the edge, taking in a breath as deep as he could manage and letting it scour his insides. This was far more frayed than he'd felt in a long time, but perhaps it was just the mental strain of returning to work when he'd spent about half of the last few months alternating between taking the easiest, shortest jobs he could possibly find and lying practically comatose on the couch, watching every show on Animal Planet because none of them involved people dying. "Fuck."

Collecting himself was easier knowing that there was no one around to see him scrub his hands over his face, shake his body like a dog, and give a muffled, wordless scream of frustration to try to clear his head. It didn't work, but it at least propelled him forward and out of the sanctuary. Shiri reappeared between his feet and he nearly face-planted to avoid stepping on her; thankfully he was able to maintain enough balance that he at least didn't crash into anything valuable hung on the walls.

A frighteningly audible growl from his stomach made Shiri meow in response. "Sorry," he snapped at the cat, because he was at the end of his rope. "Didn't mean to disturb."

She just stared at him, hunkered down, then sprung up onto his shoulder, digging her claws in before winding around his neck like a scarf, her legs hanging down either shoulder and her tail tickling his nose.

Michael sighed, resigning himself to being a cat tree to an animal far heavier than one small cat had any right to be. She purred loudly in his ear as he retraced his earlier steps to the kitchen, pulling together the ingredients for a sandwich and grabbing a bag of chips from the cabinet, along with one of the bottles of Diet Coke he'd stowed in the fridge.

"Don't you *dare*." He nudged Shiri's paw away as she made a grab for his peanut butter, and the mundane action of trying to prevent a pet from stealing food at least made him feel a bit more grounded in the real world.

In the kitchen, the light was brighter and clearer than it was in the sanctuary, and the garden visible through the kitchen window was inviting despite it being late fall. Jacob had laid out specific rules for the use of the archive and told him not to go up to the fourth floor of the building, but he hadn't said a word about not going outside. Maybe the weather would clear his head.

He set the food down on the counter and decided that it wasn't worth trying to remove the cat just yet. The stairs creaked as he walked up them, and he hoped that wherever it was that Jacob was sleeping, he wasn't disturbing his rest, not after what he'd done for him last night. Jacob looked so tired and hollow that he rivaled Michael for looking unwell, and he wondered if part of the reason why Jacob seemed to stay shut in the Institute was because he was exhausted, as Michael was, of people telling him that he looked like death warmed over.

Michael was glad that he'd packed a few sweaters in addition to his jacket, and he murmured an apology to Shiri as he picked her up and placed her on the bed so he could tug on a warm, cable-knit sweater that his grandma had made for him in cream-colored yarn. The weather app on his phone told him that it was just over forty-five degrees, and rather than risk having to come back inside, Michael opted to pull on his jacket too, shoving a pair of gloves into one of the pockets.

"Come on, then," he called to the cat, who gamely hopped off the bed and trotted after him as he traced his path back down the stairs to pick up his food from the kitchen. He didn't know if she was allowed outside, but when he made it to the front door and she stretched her body up to pull the handle down and crack it open, he figured that a cat who knew how to open doors probably didn't need his permission for a supervised walk outside anyway.

The breeze was crisp and cool, and after hours spent reading it felt unspeakably good to get fresh air. Michael followed the gravel path that wound around the side of the old synagogue and found the cast-iron gate that had been set into the brick wall. Shiri ignored him opening it while balancing his food all in one hand, and instead vaulted over the wall and into the garden in one smooth motion. "Show-off," he accused as he made it into the garden without dumping his sandwich on the ground.

She padded over to a bench and sat down, curling her tail around her small body as a gust of wind made dead leaves skitter over the ground. He sat down next to her, and after getting over the shock of the stone's coldness seeping through his jeans, he ate in methodical bites while leaning against the side of the synagogue and staring into the forest that ringed the grounds beyond the edge of the property.

"I wonder what it was like here when there was a congregation that used the building," he said to the cat next to him, which he should have taken as a sign of his degrading metal acuity and instead chose to interpret as being respectful of all God's creatures and their ability to listen to him prattle on. "Maybe the archive has pictures of what it was like in its original state."

Shiri meowed and stretched out one paw to touch his thigh.

"Thank you for not telling me I'm crazy," he said. "For talking to a cat."

She turned narrowed eyes on him, as if to say *of course you should talk to me*, and that was when he decided to pull out his phone and engage in actual human contact.

Sarah answered on the first ring, and she didn't seem to mind that he was talking through mouthfuls of salt and vinegar chips.

"I only have a few minutes. I'm heading to class." She was hard to hear through the loud whine of a siren, and Michael could imagine her jaywalking across Broadway because she was running late to teach, as always. "But you know I'm always happy to talk to you, doll. What's up?"

"The translation work is going well, I'm unspeakably exhausted, and I think I might be losing my mind."

He didn't need to hold back with Sarah, at least not what he was feeling inside, and yet saying it all like that, in one rush of self-consciousness, still made him flush with embarrassment.

"Well, we'll start with the last complaint. Michael, you're not losing your mind. Have you still been talking to your therapist every week? Are you sure you don't want to reconsider talking to the psychiatrist too?

He opened his mouth to refute her, as had become his habit. "I don't need—"

"Because you're traumatized, and if I hear you blame yourself one more time for the accident I'm going to—"

"Sarah," he warned her, curling his shoulders inward and squeezing his eyes shut. Maybe he should have chosen the conversation with the cat. "I don't need drugs."

He very carefully didn't think about how he'd conveniently omitted the fact that, yes, he had five different psychiatrists on speed-dial, and yes, he had a rotating cycle of drugs he took at what was likely far too high a dose because he wanted to opt out of the pain he felt for what he'd done.

"Fine." This was an old argument, one they'd rehashed many times since he'd gotten home from the hospital, and Sarah knew well enough to let it go. "So talk to me about your work, then. What is this quote-unquote mysterious client with unfathomable access to the best domestic archive having you look at?"

It had been kind of her to continue letting his lie slide, and for that he put up with her very clear sarcasm. It felt good to talk like this, to pretend like this was an ordinary trip. To pretend he'd done nothing wrong.

He stuffed the last bite of the sandwich in his mouth and stood up, chips in one hand and phone pressed between his shoulder and his ear, and started to pace.

"The documents here are unlike anything I've ever seen before." He stuffed another chip into his mouth and headed toward the back of the garden, which stretched quite a bit farther back than he'd originally thought. Shiri hopped off the bench and kept pace with him as he crunched across the gravel path toward a fountain that had chipped and fallen into disrepair, ivy climbing around the empty bowl. He told Sarah about everything he'd seen over the last few days. "It's remarkable that these documents exist, let alone together."

"Eleazer Schechter was a legend for a reason." Sarah's voice crackled as he got farther into the garden, hedges forming pathways that branched out from the fountain. He glanced down and saw that he only had a few bars of service. "It seems like if there's any place that was going to have this type of material, it would be the Schechter Institute. But yeah, Michael, I know you're not the biggest fan of this stuff. How are *you* doing?"

He massaged his chest, trying to banish the tightness her question caused.

"This trip is like taking a firefighter and telling him

that his new job is to become a professional arsonist," Sarah continued. "I want to make sure that this, on top of everything you're already dealing with, isn't impeding your recovery."

Michael crumpled the empty chip bag in his fist. "I'm fine. I owe it to the… client. I need to finish what I'm supposed to do."

"If you weren't in this particular archive, I'd tell you to leave," Sarah said gently. "You're going to end up in an early grave, with the way you punish yourself like this."

It was too much every time she spoke like this, and while he would always forgive her, every single time, it never made it easier to hear.

"I *killed a man*," Michael hissed into the phone. "We're not talking about someone with a bad habit they're trying to break, Sarah! I'm not supposed to be feeling better about myself because there's *nothing to feel better about*. I'm a fucking horrible person who did a fucking heinous thing and I will never, ever be cleansed of that sin because unless you can tell me that *you shall not kill* is no longer a commandment, it's over for me."

He was breathing too fast and his incision was burning as much as it had when he'd first woken up in the hospital. As Nate had died, Michael had passed out on the sidewalk from blood loss and pain, or so he'd been told. And the first sensation he'd felt when he'd blinked back into awareness had been a firebrand across his chest, so agonizing that he couldn't even get enough air into his lungs to not panic. He'd cried involuntarily as the nurses had loaded him up with enough painkillers to fell a horse, struggling to place additional IVs because he'd been shaking so badly.

"I do not know how many times I'm going to have to tell you this," Sarah said in her infuriatingly calm voice, "but it's not your fault. I know that's hard to believe because you're far too good a person, but I hope that one day you see it."

A long pause followed, and Michael could have sworn that she was sniffing on the other end of the line. "I've got to go," she said thickly. "Class."

Sarah hung up without another word, but it didn't ease the churning in his stomach or the guilt sitting heavy on his conscience. He turned off his phone because he didn't want to deal with either getting a guilt-ridden apology from Sarah in an hour or not getting one at all, and tucked his hands into his jacket pockets as he walked to the far edge of the garden and tried not to cry.

He was gradually becoming horrified with the self-indulgence he'd shown last night in sobbing all over Jacob, something that wasn't appropriate and also wasn't deserved. He'd felt better, after, and that was something he couldn't forgive himself for.

*That's not why you're here*, he reminded himself as he swallowed down the emotion threatening to choke him. Being numb had been a way for his psyche to avoid the pangs of gut-churning sadness that were wracking him now, and something told him that on the other side of letting it all out was healing, and no, he wasn't going to let that happen.

Michael picked at the incision, slipping a hand under his sweater to thumb at the ridge in his skin.

The corner of the garden was bordered by a wrought-iron fence, and as Michael leaned against it, he realized why—it was a small graveyard. Most of the headstones were decidedly old-looking, with moss growing over the stone and obscuring the words. They were written in Hebrew, and it was clear from the number of graves—no more than ten in total—that this wasn't a general cemetery. It was probably a place to bury prominent members of the congregation, or perhaps rabbis. Michael would have opened the small gate and gone to look at the headstones, to try to determine what he could from the old inscriptions, but the freshly churned rectangle of earth in the center of it all gave him pause.

Jacob must have buried Eleazer here, too.

The grave was small, and Michael wondered if Eleazer was as fine-boned and delicate as Jacob. He wondered if Jacob had dug the grave himself, or whether he'd had people from the local burial society come and help him. There would have had to be a rabbi, at least, but Michael wasn't sure where the nearest congregation was.

It hurt, deep in his chest, to think about Jacob standing here all alone as he buried his grandfather, and then going back into the Institute alone, surrounded by his grandfather's things, sitting there through the night with no one else to talk to. And for the first time, he wondered how he hadn't seen it before. Jacob was clinging to the idea of mazzekin in the Institute, and he insisted that his grandfather had believed in them. It was just like his grandparents and their grandparents before him, a reliance on something difficult to explain to get through life's traumas.

Michael sighed. He looked down when he felt a nudge against his leg, and he didn't protest when the cat jumped up and clung onto his shoulders again. He wasn't wearing a watch so he couldn't tell how much time had elapsed since he'd left the house, but he was beginning to shiver slightly and the crescents of his nails were faintly blue, so he decided it was probably far past time for him to be going back inside to resume work.

"Come on," he said to the cat, even though she had no choice in the matter. "Let's go back inside."

He left the grave behind, but for the rest of the afternoon his thoughts were stuck on the image his mind had formed: of Jacob Schechter standing in front of the freshly churned earth, feeling completely alone in the world now that his only close family was dead.

It took hours more to finish reading through all the documents, translating and taking notes, then going through them again to photograph them. The creaking of the door was his only warning that Jacob had joined him, absorbed as he was in the final stack of papers.

"Did you find today's collection satisfactory?" Jacob sauntered up to the desk where Michael worked, a black button-down shirt tucked into charcoal slacks. Michael wondered for a moment whether Jacob ever dressed casually, whether when he woke up his hair was rumpled and he blinked slowly as he gained his bearings, or whether he was always this put together. "It's quite an unusual set, and I thought you'd be intrigued by it. Or, rather, I'd hoped you would be."

Michael swallowed the urge to run a hand through Jacob's hair to mess it up, and instead looked down at the final document he'd been cataloguing, running a finger down the lines of text. "It's a remarkable collection, that's for sure."

"Assembling it wasn't easy." Jacob circled around the desk and nudged Michael aside with his hip, perching on the edge of the chair. Everywhere they touched felt like it had been set on fire. "Eleazer was an assiduous collector, and a lot of these documents had to be obtained from private collections."

It was hard to ignore the way Jacob's thigh was pressed against his own, and Michael had to talk his body down from the fever pitch it was reaching just from the other man's proximity. "It's why the Schechter Institute is famous. I'm sure you know, but among the comparative religion and Judaic studies crowd, this archive is like the holy grail. When Nate got the email that he'd been allowed in, it spread through the program like wildfire. It was an incredible coup."

Jacob reached out a delicate, pale finger and traced the same line of text that Michael had. "Tell me about him. Nathaniel."

Michael's heart stuttered in his chest. The thought of sharing Nate with Jacob did weird things to his breathing. "He was... he was brilliant. Complicated. Charismatic and dedicated to his work. He had already managed to gain quite the following for his research by the time he..."

"Died," Jacob finished for him when Michael trailed off into silence. "I know."

Michael was glad they were sitting in the same chair so he didn't have to look Jacob in the eye. The weight of the night before, that quiet intimacy, hung over the two of them like a shroud, and he didn't know where they were supposed to go from here. Was he supposed to open up to Jacob, now, and show him the ugliness festering inside? Would Jacob expect it, or were they supposed to pretend like last night hadn't ever happened?

"You don't have to talk about it," Jacob said, relieving him of the burden of wondering what came next. "But if you want to, I'm here. Keeping it all inside must be hard. I get the sense that you don't have many people in your life that you share your heart with."

That stopped Michael in his tracks, pausing with a folio cradled in his hands. "No, I don't. Not anymore. It's—it's been hard for me to relate to people ever since the accident."

He was careful to couch what he said in generalities, because he didn't want Jacob to know the truth. That his family and friends were mad at him for taking Nate's death on his own shoulders, not understanding why he was so crippled by guilt when it had been an accident that had caused Nate's death. He'd not told anyone—not the police, not his friends, not social workers or his therapist or his family—what he'd really remembered from the moments before he'd stumbled out of the alley and into the street, then fallen unconscious. It was easier to pretend that he didn't remember. Michael's unwillingness to come clean, to confess, to keep living the lie, had driven what felt like a permanent wedge between him and every other person in his life who he might have gone to for support.

Thankfully, Jacob didn't press the issue.

"Grief rarely makes sense." Jacob took the folio out of Michael's hands and added it to the top of the stack rested in the open archival box. "But it seems that you had a... complicated time of things."

In that moment, the two of them sitting shoulder to shoulder, Michael almost wanted to confess to Jacob what he had done. He almost wanted to say *look at me, this is all of me, I killed the man I loved and everyone told me that it wasn't my fault, and then I was forced to grieve in secret and hate myself in secret and I feel like there's an invisible wall between me and the rest of the world because I sinned in a way that can never be forgiven, but everyone else still thinks I'm a good man.*

He almost wanted to. Instead, because he was a liar and a coward and a traitor, he turned his head and kissed Jacob Schechter.

Jacob's lips parted and burning hands wove their way around the back of Michael's neck and into his hair. Jacob turned his body and moved his thigh over Michael's legs so they were pressed chest to chest, Jacob sitting on his lap. He deepened the kiss, one hand drifting down Michael's chest until it was resting on his scar, the heel of Jacob's palm pressing into the incision like he was trying to hold Michael's lung inside his body. Like Jacob was the only thing keeping him sewn together.

They drew apart, panting, and Michael felt just how much Jacob wanted this, and how much he himself wanted it in turn. It had been years since he'd felt desire like this, like fire in his veins. He was shivering, tiny tremors wracking his body as Jacob anchored a hand to the back of his neck and pulled him forward, bringing their mouths to touch again. And then he nipped Michael's lower lip with his teeth, and he was lost.

This was a bad idea. This didn't hurt. It felt good, too

good, and would it feel bad enough when this was ripped away to make up for the pleasure? The familiar litany played in his head, and then he looked into Jacob's eyes, luminous in the dark, and it just… stopped.

His brain shut down, and his doubts went quiet. He was trapped, hypnotized, and when Jacob leaned forward again and ran his thumbnail over Michael's scar, everything went blank. Michael wasn't even sure if he could remember his own name as Jacob took him to pieces with a soft mouth and clever hands and more tenderness and passion than he'd felt from anyone in a long, long time, all the desire for pain and grief and someone to hate him as much as he hated himself gone quiet.

"Michael?" The question was soft.

"Yeah?" he rasped.

"How long will it take you to forgive yourself?" Jacob sat back on Michael's thighs. "Do you think you ever will?"

"No," he replied hoarsely. "I don't think so."

Jacob sighed, tilting his forehead to meet Michael's. "Do you think, if you can't forgive yourself, that you can at least let yourself forget?"

"Yeah." The answer came too fast, too sure, but right now he was beyond self-hatred and he was weak.

Jacob's half-smile broke him. "Then come to bed."

When Jacob stood, Michael followed, and even though he'd promised himself it would never happen again, he got the distinct sense that he was falling, and there was nothing he could do to stop it.

# Chapter 9

The next morning, Michael was torn between floating and self-castigation.

They hadn't made it to bed, just to the living room couch, Michael draped over the back with his hands fisted into the pillows. He'd almost protested when Jacob had spent what felt like forever on foreplay, but Jacob had just placed his other hand on the back of Michael's neck and held him down while he teased, then eased inside.

But even without force, without pain, without the distinct feeling of being used, it had been even better than their rushed first encounter, even if neither of them had managed to get their clothes all the way off, Jacob still wearing his shoes with his pants half-hanging off his hips, his shirt unbuttoned to reveal surprisingly defined abs and a snowy expanse of skin over his shoulder blades that Michael had discovered got marked with astonishing ease.

He was failing at repentance, at repair, and he didn't

care. He was going to hurt Jacob the way he hurt Nate, and he didn't care. He couldn't care, because when he was lost in Jacob's gaze nothing else mattered. The world fell away. What he had done fell away.

It was like being under a spell, and he found he didn't mind.

Until he thought for more than a second about the delicious ache in his core that twinged with every movement as he shifted in bed, and realized that, by letting another person in like that, he had betrayed Nate and everything their relationship had been.

They'd eaten dinner together, crispy slices of frozen pizza that Jacob had nearly burnt and a decent salad that Michael had thrown together. He'd urged Jacob to eat more and he had, some of the color coming back into his face. There had been another bottle of wine, and another night on the couch with a blanket and the cat and a roaring fire, Jacob telling folktales from ancient Babylon like he'd invented them himself. Michael had almost asked him to come to bed and just sleep—it was one of the things he missed most about Nate, being able to curl up with another person and drift off—but then he remembered that Jacob was practically nocturnal and had left him to go work in the archive while he took himself to bed.

It was a perfect evening, and last night he'd told himself he didn't mind.

It was so much more difficult, in the light of day, to rationalize that contentment. Michael tried to remind himself that he was here at the Institute as penance, and that the ease with which he forgot Nate, dead and buried for less than a year because of him, was a mark of just how broken he was. As he lay awake, blinking in the light struggling in through the window, self-hatred slid back over him, and while it felt right, for the first time in a long time he also hated that it was necessary.

When he stood up to begin his second full day at the Institute, the view out the window looked bleaker than ever. The tree must have lost much more of its foliage in the wind of the day before.

He showered and dressed and hated the way that it washed away the smell of Jacob, the heady scent of crushed rose petals and damp forest that he'd spent the whole last night breathing in.

Falling too hard and too fast was his curse, and his growing attraction to Jacob Schechter was no different. But the circumstances, Michael reminded himself, had changed. He was no longer fit to be that person, the perfect partner who knew just how to keep a person happy. He'd proven that he was broken in this fundamental way; Jacob was far more than he deserved.

He should probably finish as quickly as possible and then leave, so that Jacob would have the chance to forget all about him, and so he wouldn't have the chance to hurt him by accident. Or worse, on purpose.

The sickening swirl of his thoughts followed him downstairs, and he contemplated a bowl of cereal for breakfast before the nausea in his stomach compelled him to go back for his jacket and his car keys and head outside.

Maybe a drive into town would clear his head. Ordinarily he'd talk things like this through with Sarah, but when he'd turned on his phone again in the morning, there hadn't been a single message from her. It was possible that he'd finally ruined that too, by being so rude to her, but the thought of losing his best friend was too much to contemplate on top of all of it, so Michael turned on a stupid podcast and looked up places in town serving breakfast, putting the car into reverse and backing down the driveway.

Driving, and the change of scenery, cleared his head. Alone in the archive with Jacob, it was far easier to pretend than it was in the light of day, with cold wind whipping at his face through the open window. The Institute felt suspended in time, the two of them in their own little bubble for the last fifty-something hours, and the isolation was messing with Michael's head. He had to remember that there was a reason he had come here, and it was more important than anything else. He had to remember who he was, and what he did and did not deserve. He did not, for example, deserve sleeping with the same person twice.

The little town was just as quiet this morning as it had been the other day, and Michael began to wonder whether there was anyone who actually lived here at all. It could be because of the weather—he could barely see the sun behind the gray clouds hanging low in the sky, and the air smelled of the promise of bitter cold and oncoming rain. Maybe everyone else had the good sense to stay home and out of the path of a potential storm, but it did mean that when he walked into the small café, there wasn't any line. It took him a minute to decide, standing in front of the teenage girl who was working the register, but he settled on ordering a chai latte and a bowl of slow-cooked oatmeal, and there wasn't anyone to block him from taking the small table set into the bay window.

It was cozy and cheery here despite the bleakness of the weather outside, the kind of place that Michael would ordinarily have loved to stumble upon. This was a café where he could spend hours sitting and writing, ordering drink after drink so that he wasn't taking up space without giving anything back. Fairy lights in the window framed the autumn-hued trees that lined the sidewalk, and vanilla-pumpkin-scented candles clustered on the window ledges. The view was as relaxing as the smell of muffins drifting from the back. Even the music was ideal, a piano soundtrack on just loud enough to keep him focused without being something that would distract him.

Images of coming here with Jacob in the morning on a weekend, his arm around the other man's narrow waist, Jacob's head tipped onto his shoulder and the two of them laughing together about some inside joke, flashed across Michael's mind. He wanted it so badly that it felt like being punched in the stomach, but that wasn't either of their lives. It was a fantasy, and nothing more.

At least he was gratified that the thought of never having Jacob to call his own *hurt*.

"Here you go, dear." An older woman with a name tag identifying her as Lena placed a bowl of oatmeal in front of him with a *thunk*, the berries on top arranged in the shape of a smile. He couldn't help but smile back at the absurdity of it, and the woman bustled away, only to come back with his latte and silverware.

"You're new in town." She put her hands into her apron pocket and looked at him with the kind of assessing gaze that immediately told him she was sizing him up for a grandchild. "Are you here visiting family?"

"No." Michael wasn't going to be impolite and ignore her, so he dipped a spoon into the oatmeal and took a small bite before responding. "My name is Michael. I'm here doing research."

"Oh?" The woman's eyes shot up. "And what is it that you do?"

"I'm finishing up a PhD dissertation." He took another bite of the oatmeal, which was unexpectedly good. "It's about folk beliefs of the Jews of 1800s Eastern Europe."

"Ah! So you must be Jewish yourself. And a scholar!" Lena pulled up a chair, her eyes twinkling, and every Jewish grandmother that Michael had ever met flashed before his eyes as he fought back a groan. Still, it would be impolite to tell a grandmother that she couldn't try to make him a match because he was a murderer and didn't deserve happiness, so he took a sip of his latte and shut his mouth. "But where are you researching? My synagogue is two towns over, and there isn't a closer one. It's not like the community is so big here anymore, not with so many people retiring and moving to the city."

Michael's brow furrowed. He'd thought the Institute was close enough to town that most people who lived here would have known about it—especially most Jews—but maybe it was the difference between something being academically famous and actually famous. Plenty of people in his field, himself included, would geek out over so-called famous document caches or scholars that no one else on the planet had ever heard of, and this could be the case. Even if it was sad that people from his own community didn't know they lived practically next door to a treasure trove of knowledge.

"I'm at the Schechter Institute for two weeks." The oatmeal was warming him from the inside out, and he shrugged off his coat. "Doing research for—the dissertation." He stumbled over it, but he didn't need to share everything with this perfect stranger.

"The… Schechter Institute?" The woman pressed a hand to her mouth. "Oh dear, you haven't come here just for that, have you? I'm afraid to tell you, young man, that you're going to have to turn back."

Michael set his spoon down, turning to give her his full attention. "Why is that?"

"Because poor Eleazer Schechter died a few months ago, may his memory be a blessing." The hand that Lena had over her mouth drifted down to her heart.

"Oh." Michael shook his head. "Yes, I know he passed away. But his grandson has finally gotten the archive back up and running in his grandfather's memory, and I'm the first researcher who's been able to get into it since Jacob took over."

The chai latte was strong when he took a sip of it, but not as strong as Lena's confusion. "Jacob? Is that— You said it's his grandson, dear?"

"Yes." Michael took another sip too quickly, scorching his tongue. "Jacob Schechter."

"But Eleazer didn't have any grandchildren, at least not that I knew about." Lena's lips were pursed, and she had a hand on the edge of the table. Her knobby knuckles were dusted in flour. "At least, none that he ever mentioned to me. He came in here at least once a week before he died."

Something shifted uncomfortably in Michael's stomach at the confusion evidently written on her face. It could be distressing to realize that someone you thought you knew was actually someone completely different. That you didn't know all the creases and corners of their lives, that they had only ever allowed you to see the surface of who they were. Especially when they were gone, and you couldn't ask them why they hadn't trusted you to see all of them. Why you weren't given that privilege.

"I think it may have been a complicated familial relationship," he replied, thinking back on Jacob's claim that he had no family now that his grandfather was dead. It made a kind of sense, if something terrible had happened between the family members, that Eleazer wouldn't have mentioned anything to people in town, and why Jacob would assert that he had no remaining family even if that could hardly be true, absent some kind of horrific mass casualty. "He must not have shared with the rest of the community."

Lena sighed. "What a tragedy. You never really know people."

"No," Michael replied, thinking about how this kind old woman was sitting across from a killer, chatting to him about his life. "You really don't."

"Well, if you'd like to come to services at the synagogue I go to, you're welcome," she said, rattling off directions to her synagogue. "I have three granddaughters and a grandson, all of them doctors. And Jeanie has a grandchild, they're in law school, and Sharon has a granddaughter who just founded something in *tech*."

She winked as she stood, and Michael did his best to muster what would pass for a genuine smile. But all he could think about as he finished his oatmeal and his drink was Jacob sitting, all alone, writing an obituary. Eleazer, who Jacob said had been very ill, doing his best to appear normal for his friends up until the very end. The loneliness and the lies and the ways that people kept their true selves hidden so they didn't hurt others. So they didn't have to hurt themselves.

He spent the drive back to the archive wishing he could have been there for Jacob, and realizing that despite his best efforts, despite trying not to be weak, he was in deeper than he'd thought.

Jacob had left him a stack of diaries for his second day in the archive, which yielded yet more terrifying anecdotes. Michael got so wrapped up in reading that when his alarm dinged to remind him of the fact that he needed to eat lunch, he would have ignored it if not for the appearance of Shiri, who slunk into the archive like she was on a personal mission to make him take a break.

"I'm coming, I'm coming," he grumbled, following her out of the sanctuary—after carefully boxing up all the materials to avoid a repeat of the day before—and grabbing food to stick into the pocket of the hoodie he was wearing. The temperature in the archive had seemed to drop ten degrees since that morning, but maybe it was just that he didn't have Jacob's obscene warmth at his side and felt cold by comparison.

The front door wasn't stuck like it had been the day before—come to think of it, it hadn't been stuck when he left that morning, either—and Michael followed the same path out to the back garden as before. It was still cloudy and cool, the air still smelling like it was threatening rain and the trees creaking as the wind blew their nearly naked branches against one another. He wondered how the trees in town had managed to cling to their leaves, but everything here was basically desolate.

Instead of sitting down on the bench—he'd done enough sitting already for one day, and he had hours more left to go—he opted to walk the perimeter of the garden. It wasn't a perfect rectangle, and he wondered if the congregation had gradually bought up land as it expanded or grew wealthier. The graveyard, at one extreme, made Michael nauseous as soon as he got near it, something about knowing that he was just feet and a layer of dirt away from Eleazer's body causing acid to rise up his throat. He made his way past the old fountain and the cemetery, heading for the back left corner of the walled-in backyard, where it looked like trees were growing wild inside the property.

Michael took tiny bites of an apple as he followed the path, Shiri trotting ahead of him with her tail up like a flag, almost like she was trying to lead him somewhere. He wasn't hungry, but he knew that if he didn't eat, he'd regret it. Still, the apple tasted like ash in his mouth.

The far corner of the garden hosted a greenhouse, which Michael peeked into and found held a profusion of roses, still growing despite the season. They'd gone a bit wild, the bushes puffing out past their neat rows, and he wondered if Eleazer was the one who grew them, and if Jacob hadn't bothered to prune them after his grandfather's death. He'd gardened as a kid, working with his mother in front of their house, and he wondered if he should offer to help Jacob put the roses to rights. Or whether that would be a far too painful reminder of the grandfather he had lost.

An insistent meow pulled Michael out of his contemplation. "Okay, okay." He glared at the cat, who had hopped up onto the edge of the brick wall and looked like she was waiting for him to follow. So he did, the apple core dangling from his fingers as they reached the back of the garden.

And then Shiri hopped over the fence into the forest beyond.

"Hey!" Michael shouted after her, instantly panicking that he was going to be responsible for losing Jacob's pet cat. "Come back!"

There was a small gate set into the wall, much like the one that led into the garden. Michael pried it open and it squealed on rusty hinges, the noise grating in his ears and setting his teeth on edge. As soon as he slipped out onto a dirt path that led into the forest, his heart jumped as he saw a flash of black tail leading off into the woods.

He dashed after her, wondering if he could lure her back with the peanut butter sandwich wrapped in a napkin in his pocket, and also wondering how he was going to explain to Jacob if he couldn't get her back. He didn't want to know what would happen with that level of fuck-up, although he'd deserve it.

But thankfully, his tension drained away as he pushed past another few trees and came into a clearing. Shiri sat in the middle of a circle of cleared dirt, surrounded by shards of broken pottery scattered across a bed of dead leaves. His heart thumped as he approached her slowly, not wanting her to dart away again, and he breathed a sigh of relief when she hopped up into his arms without complaint.

Which left him to stare down at what he was standing in the middle of.

The pottery wasn't just a collection of broken plates that had ended up in the woods, as strange as that would have been. Instead, it was a scattered mass of clay shards with Hebrew writing on them. A chill crept down Michael's spine as he realized what he was looking at.

These were the remnants of incantation bowls, just like the one that Jacob had left for him during his first day working in the archive. Some were nearly pulverized, while others were still in shards large enough to display long sections of writing, the ink black on the mud-colored clay. He put a hand up to steady Shiri on his shoulder and bent down to pick up one of the larger pieces, but when he did, a pervasive sense of unease ricocheted through him, causing him to jerk his hand back as Shiri hissed, likely upset with the way she was being jostled.

"What is this stuff doing here?" Michael muttered, half to himself and half to the cat. He stayed crouched down, wishing he had more experience analyzing material objects and that he could tell whether he was looking at antique incantation bowls or new creations. Some of the ink seemed darker and more vivid than on other shards, and the handwriting all differed. But it didn't make sense—why would there be a huge collection of what had to be dozens of rare, valuable objects smashed to pieces in the woods behind the Institute?

Eleazer must have done this, because it didn't make sense otherwise. The Institute was isolated and Michael hadn't seen any neighbors around for miles—and even if there were, how many neighbors were into the recreational collection and destruction of Jewish folk magical objects? This had to be connected to the old archivist somehow, because otherwise it didn't make sense. Jacob displayed far too much care for the objects he protected to ever deliberately harm this many irreplicable items—Michael scanned the clearing and saw what must have been the remnants of twenty shattered bowls.

He bit his lip as he wondered if he should tell Jacob about this. It could have been a symptom of dementia or a side effect of Eleazer's illness somehow, in which case the finding might be distressing to Jacob on a number of levels—not just as evidence of his grandfather's illness, but helplessness and possibly even anger that so many rare objects had been irreparably destroyed.

The dead, gray grass crunched under Michael's heels as he straightened up, the ache in his side protesting with Shiri's additional weight. She flicked her tail back and forth and purred, as though pleased to have led him on the wild goose chase that had nearly given him a heart attack. "Did you want me to find this?" He scratched absently behind her ears. "Did you want me to tell Jacob?"

She purred louder, directly into his left ear, the sensation rumbling through his neck and chest.

"Cats," he groaned to himself as he turned to leave the clearing, his shoes slipping on the tamped-down earth. He was almost at the tree line, picking his way through the shards so that he didn't crush one or spear his own foot through his shoe, when he looked down and stopped dead in his tracks.

One of the biggest shards was lying in his path. It was the center of a bowl, the part where a depiction of the demon that the maker was trying to trap would be drawn. There was a tail visible, and what looked like the tops of wings, but the rest of it was smeared in what looked, disconcertingly, like glimmering, wet blood.

Fresh blood.

He bent down and picked up the shard, wanting to touch it to reassure himself that no, it wasn't blood, it was mud or it was part of a leaf or anything that would mean he wasn't crazy. But the moment he did, his hand clamped down on it like it was spasming, and he immediately felt like he was going to be ill. He shook his hand until his fingers unclenched and he dropped the pottery, falling onto his hands and knees.

Michael couldn't help it, turning and retching into the bushes as Shiri yowled and then jumped up on him to dig her claws into his shoulder. Goosebumps had risen on his skin, and he flushed hot and cold. By the time he straightened up, he was slick with sweat and shaking like a leaf. He was having some kind of panic attack, he was sure of it, and all he could think about with any kind of clarity was that if Jacob was there, he could probably snap Michael out of it with a hand in his hair and an arm around his shoulders.

But he was alone. And so there was no one to help him as he stumbled back to the gate, his hands searching out tree trunk after tree trunk for steadiness, Shiri jumping off his shoulder and leading the way back like a furry black beacon. As soon as he got back through the gate, he sank down against the brick wall and let himself shake apart, his head in his hands and his breath coming in gasps. Cold rain was beginning to fall, plastering his hair to his head and his sweatshirt to his shoulders, and Shiri was meowing from under the cover of a large leaf acting like an umbrella.

Standing up took Herculean effort, but Michael managed it. He pulled off his hoodie and wrapped the cat in it, ignoring that there was food in the pocket that was undoubtedly getting crushed. Shivering and shaking and wet, he made his way to the Institute's front door and gasped with relief when the warmth of the foyer hit him. Shiri jumped from his arms and promptly vanished between one blink and the next, and Michael found himself dripping water on the oriental carpet and shivering like he'd been immersed in ice.

There was no way that he was going to be able to do more work today, he knew it. And despite the crippling sense of disappointment that crushed him at the thought, he took off his muddy shoes and headed up the stairs, shutting the door of his small room just in time for another wave of sobs to break free. Somehow, he managed to shuck off the rest of his clothes, get himself into the shower while gasping for breath, and clean himself off so that he was at least dry and warm when he crawled into bed with just a pair of gym shorts on.

The pill bottle was on the nightstand, and he broke and reached for it, fishing out a pill and hoping that it was going to be the right thing to calm him down. He didn't want to feel whatever this was anymore, and he didn't want to be awake or sentient or thinking. So, he swallowed the pill dry and hugged the spare pillow to his chest and closed his eyes and just focused as best he could on the sound of rain hitting the windowpane, a steady and insistent drumming.

The medication, whatever it was, did the trick, and he found himself gradually pulled into a steady, warm state; his brain empty and his thoughts clear, and his body relaxed enough that he stopped shivering, everything fuzzy around the edges and the sour panic gone from his core.

The rain lulled him to sleep, and he let himself go.

He woke to a weight on the bed and hands in his hair, combing the strands back from his forehead.

"Are you alright?" Jacob's voice was low, like he was afraid of spooking Michael, and it took him a minute to realize that he had slept through the entire afternoon and it was dark outside, the storm still raging with the addition of an occasional peal of thunder. "You've been here all day?"

"No." Michael sat up and bit his lip against the wave of dizziness that accompanied it. Whatever he'd taken, it still had something of a hold on him. "I went out to the garden to have lunch and I—" He paused, unsure whether he was doing the right thing. "I found some shattered incantation bowls in the woods."

Jacob's hand stilled in his hair. "Ah. You found the remnants of Eleazer's pet project, then."

"You knew about it?" Blinking helped Michael's eyes to focus, his dried-out contact lenses gradually floating into place. Jacob was sitting on the bed, his legs dangling off the side and his body angled toward Michael. He was wearing an emerald button-down shirt with dark jeans this time, and that little bit of casualness went straight to Michael's belly. "I wasn't sure if… I didn't know what I was looking at. There were a lot of bowls, and they were all smashed."

"He made them himself." Jacob reached a hand up and kept stroking Michael's hair. He couldn't help but lean into the touch. "He had an obsession with incantation bowls in particular, and he liked to try to make them. When he didn't like the result, he took them out of the property's boundaries and disposed of them. Shattering them would break any spell that he put on them."

"Oh." Some of the tension fled out of Michael's shoulders at the fact that Jacob clearly knew this had been going on—and at the confirmation that he hadn't just found a treasure trove of utterly destroyed priceless ancient artifacts. "I didn't know if they were real or not."

Jacob laughed, but there was no humor in it, only a dry bite. "They were real to him."

His hand dropped to Michael's shoulder, and then to his chest, fingertips trailing over his pecs and down the edges of his abs, making Michael shiver but for a totally different reason than panic or pain.

"I— There was…" Michael didn't know if it was smart or very, very stupid to mention that he had been seeing things that didn't exist. He ended up swallowing his tongue and pausing. "Never mind. I'm sorry. You know, I left the boxes out downstairs. I didn't finish the diaries you left for me, and I'm sorry to have messed up the schedule. I know it's probably too late to finish for the day."

"Stop apologizing." Jacob withdrew his hand from where it was resting on the blanket over Michael's hip bone and stood. "It's evening, but I'm not particularly hungry. If you'd like, we can go down to the archive together and work side by side for a few hours before dinner."

Michael wondered if he was going to embarrass himself by falling over upon standing, but he managed it just fine, and didn't even flush too hard at the obvious way that Jacob's eyes raked down his bare chest.

"Maybe later?" Jacob shifted, licking his lips, his hands tucked into the back pockets of his jeans. "If you're amenable."

They were standing so close that Jacob's body heat warmed Michael, and it took barely a thought to lean forward and cup the smaller man's cheek in his hand, his thumb caressing one sharp cheekbone and his lips coming to meet Jacob's.

It was different than any kiss he'd shared with Nate, heating his blood and steadying him, the physical contact solid and grounding instead of leaving him wondering whether he was doing things wrong, being pleasing enough, or living up to expectations. Sex with Nate had been a performance, graded and analyzed after the fact, a lesson that he'd never quite learned how to master to fully please his partner. But with Jacob—with Jacob, it was easy. Effortless. Perhaps too much so.

With a start, he realized that he'd never once wondered if Jacob was satisfied. He could simply tell, looking at the pleasure on his face like he was a cat with a bowl full of cream, listening to the whimpers that slipped from his mouth as Michael backed him into the wall, pressing his slim shoulders to the plaster. Something about Jacob was simple, the transactional nature of things making it clear that they were offering each other comfort, and that it was being received and appreciated.

Michael wished everything could be this easy. That he couldn't hate himself when he was making someone else this happy, when he was reducing someone else to a boneless, quivering heap.

He knelt, holding Jacob's hips to the wall, and went to unlace Jacob's leather shoe. But he got a knee in the chest for his troubles, and a hand in his hair, and Michael pushed away all thoughts of undressing the man before him and just set about making him feel as good as possible in the shortest amount of time he could.

When he was finished and Jacob was rumpled and gasping, his shaking hands redoing the button on his jeans, Michael left him leaning against the wall and shrugged on a shirt and sweatshirt, remembering how cold the archive had been that morning and figuring it was probably draftier than he'd realized, and that the wind from the storm was likely fighting against the heating system.

"You're not interested in me returning the favor?" Jacob called from the wall, raking one hand through his hair to return it to some semblance of normalcy, the dark strands briefly illuminated by a flash of lightning.

"No." He was still fuzzy from the pill he'd taken—Xanax, probably, given that he wasn't still asleep—and the middle-of-the-day nap, and his limbs were still boneless from all the panic that had washed through them. "Not right now. I just wanted to make you feel good."

"Later, then." Jacob padded over to him as Michael

looked down at his feet and decided to forego socks, because he'd never had the chance to look through old documents without shoes on and something about that tickled him. Jacob leaned into him from behind, tucking his hands into the pocket of Michael's sweatshirt and hooking his chin over Michael's shoulder. He could feel Jacob's body shift, tilting forward, and looked around to find him standing on his toes.

"What?" Jacob raised an eyebrow. "You're much taller than I am. I can't help it."

"If you'd let me take your shoes off, you could stand on the tops of my feet and gain an inch or so," Michael said with a laugh. "Plus, you could change into something more comfortable. Do you ever wear sweatpants?"

"No," came the prim reply, and Michael couldn't help but laugh at the affronted expression on Jacob's face. "I keep my shoes on because I told you, I have problems with my feet. They're ugly."

Michael rotated around in Jacob's arms and tapped him on the nose, feeling more playful and at ease than he had in years. "They can't be that ugly. I bet they're cute, just like the rest of you."

Jacob wrinkled his nose. "And they hurt. Shoes help."

"So does that mean if we ever end up in bed together, you're going to have your shoes on?" Michael couldn't help but tease him, even if he understood hating a part of your body and what it reminded you of. "Because that's certainly something I've never done before."

"Two pairs of socks," Jacob muttered under his breath, shutting his eyes like he was long-suffering instead of someone who had been putting up with Michael for just a few days. "I wear two pairs of socks to sleep. My feet get rather cold, too."

"Maybe one day." Michael stepped back and untangled himself from Jacob. "For now, do you want to go do research?"

Jacob nodded and followed him out the door, and Michael marveled at how much more centered he felt than he had that afternoon, panicking and half-broken in a muddy garden. Like Jacob was some kind of balm for his fractured mind. Like Jacob was putting him back together after he'd been shattered apart.

Good. It would hurt all the more when he left and shattered into pieces again.

The door to the archive room was open, just the way he'd left it. And Michael was relieved to see everything still in its proper place, the archive boxes in a neat stack and nothing on the floor or spread over the desk like the previous few days. Michael's shoulders relaxed at the sight, and he followed Jacob to one of the bookcases, where he carefully removed a heavy book with a plain green leather-bound cover. "I'm researching ways in which people believed that protective or binding spells could be broken." Jacob tapped the book's cover. "I was inspired by Eleazer's work, and I've gradually been reading through everything he had here, starting with the secondary sources."

It was an interesting concept, and Michael couldn't say he'd heard of anyone doing that kind of research before. Maybe that also explained the existence of actual broken bowls in the garden—Eleazer could have been attempting to recreate some kind of ritual. Or he just didn't care about things he'd made himself that weren't ancient ritual objects; or maybe he was just taking his frustration out on the bowls he made when he felt they hadn't done what he'd wanted them to do. "How much does he have on it in his collection?"

Jacob waved a hand. "These four shelves."

"Oh my God." Michael blinked. "These shelves are huge. That's hundreds of books. And you want to read them all?"

"I don't have anything else to do, do I?" Jacob passed him and headed up the central aisle, the cat appearing from among the shelves and sprinting ahead of him. "Now that the archive has been taken care of, my time is mostly my own."

"Do you think about opening things up to more researchers?" Michael reached the desk a few steps behind Jacob and pulled out the chair he'd been sitting in earlier. Jacob pulled one forward from where it had been tucked into an alcove in the wall. "If you have the time, and the inclination."

"Too many people." Jacob shrugged. "I may not have enjoyed being alone recently, but I'm selective with my company. And I don't want to have to put on a brave face for researchers coming in a constant stream. I need time to gather myself in between. And dealing with multiple people here at once would be wearying."

"Ah." Michael opened the box and pulled out a diary, which came with a puff of dust that made him sneeze. "Is that why you don't go to your grandfather's synagogue? Because it sounded like he was close to the congregation. I was talking to Lena at the café this morning."

Jacob stilled, his hand on the cover of his book. "You've been going into town?"

"Yeah." Michael fought the urge to roll his eyes. "Where did you think I got the groceries?"

Jacob let out a breath and raked a hand through his hair, the strands in the front falling over his eyes as they were dislodged. "I don't know. Anyway, the townspeople can be nosy, and they're all a bunch of gossips. Eleazer always said so. I've avoided going many places because I don't want to have to talk about him to everyone who knew him."

Michael's heart gave a twinge. He knew how that felt. "If you wanted to go out, you know, I'd go with you. I could keep any busybodies away."

"I appreciate the offer, but no." Jacob's voice was clipped. "At least, not right now. I don't really think I can leave the Institute."

"Well, if you change your mind." Michael ran a hand down Jacob's arm in apology, and Jacob sighed and upturned his palm so they could tangle their fingers together, resting in the middle of their books.

Michael understood the hope that one day things would be different, coupled with the reality that right now, they weren't. So instead of pushing, he did what he wished everyone would do for him and just squeezed Jacob's hand back before turning to reading the next diary.

They worked in companionable silence for a while, both of them reading and taking notes. Jacob was left-handed, so Michael was able to spy on what he was writing out. It was, bizarrely, all in French, but Michael wasn't about to question the notetaking habits of another scholar. Everyone had their own superstitions when it came to research, like only using the same type of pen to write notes or wearing the same pair of socks on every archival trip.

Shiri made him jump when she landed on the table from the top of the nearest bookcase, and it took him a few breaths to settle himself down. Jacob laid one hand on his forearm and used another to shoo the cat away from Michael's documents and onto a free corner of the desk, where she curled up in a huff. They kept reading to the sound of the storm, and everything was going just fine until, suddenly, one of the lightbulbs in the fixture overhead burst in a shatter of glass.

Michael seized up, watching the shards fall. They weren't directly over their heads, but he felt a few slivers brush his cheeks as they cascaded to the ground. Jacob made a disgruntled noise next to him and scooped the cat up, presumably to stop her from walking over the shattered glass, when the next bulb in the row shattered too.

"Is it the storm?" The room was darker now, and Michael watched as a third bulb burst. "Is it causing some kind of electrical surge?"

"No," Jacob sighed. "It's not the electric." He put Shiri down and looked at her. "Do you want to stop them?"

Michael's eyes nearly bugged out of his head as the cat sat on her haunches, wrapped her tail around her feet, and shook her head.

"Useless," Jacob muttered under his breath. Then he turned his head to the ceiling where another light burst, the glass tinkling against the ground. "Stop it, please," he called out in a stern, undeniably annoyed tone that made Michael's hair stand on end for reasons he didn't care to interrogate. "I'd really rather you not break every one of my bulbs, thank you."

And incredibly, the shattering stopped, the rest of the light fixtures swinging from their hangings.

"Mazzekin," Jacob groaned. "I thought we had come to an accord. They're probably just mad at you."

"Mad at *me*?" Michael half stood, forgetting for a moment that Jacob was talking about household demons.

"If you haven't been responsive to their requests for attention, they've probably gotten annoyed." Jacob looked at Michael, his eyes narrowing. "Have you been ignoring them?"

Michael thought back to the gloves holding each other up, scattered papers that he'd sworn he'd put back, sticking doors and hands that looked like they were coated in blood. "Uh. Maybe? Why do you think it's mazzekin that busted the lights? I mean, it's happened before to me in my apartment, and there's a storm outside that I'm sure is causing power surges."

"I know because I can see them, the little brats." Jacob slumped back in his chair. "I know you don't believe, but the little gremlins are still hanging on the light fixtures. That's why they're swinging." He sighed, before turning his attention upward. "I know you're upset with him, but you're going to hurt yourself if you don't stop."

The swinging ceased.

"You can *see* demons?" Michael turned to Jacob, still caught between disbelief and wondering if he had finally gone completely insane. "What do you mean?"

"The mazzekin. I can see them." Jacob pointed to one of the intact light fixtures. "There are three of them sitting on that thing right now."

"Are you—" Michael almost said *joking*, but he found

that no, he didn't really believe that Jacob was kidding. At least, Jacob didn't *think* he was kidding. "How can you see them?"

Jacob shrugged. "If you put the powdered afterbirth of a black cat in your eyes, you can see demons."

Michael's mouth dropped open as he looked to Shiri on the table—who had quickly gone back to snoring lightly while curled into a tight circle—and then to Jacob. "You—"

The other man lasted roughly ten seconds before bursting into laughter loud enough to startle the cat awake and make Michael jump. "Oh, you should have seen the look on your face." His shoulders shook and he wiped tears away from his reddening eyes. "No, no, I didn't do anything that disgusting. I've always been able to see demons. Something of a family trait."

Caught between relief that Jacob hadn't just confessed to one of the more disgusting folk traditions Michael knew of and skepticism, he couldn't help but laugh back. "Oh really?"

"Would it kill you to believe?" Jacob asked softly, his laughter fading into silence. "Haven't you experienced stranger things in your life than this? Than believing what your ancestors knew to be true for hundreds of years before science replaced faith and tried to explain away everything with equations and formulas?"

Before coming to the Schechter Institute, before everything he'd seen, before reading these materials and talking to Jacob, Michael would have launched into a vehement defense of his own supreme rationality. That those folk stories were exactly that, a way for poor people with no formal schooling to explain the world around them in a manner they could comprehend. A way to have the hard things in life displaced onto a force that could be within their control when they said the right prayer or performed the right ritual or wrote the right name of God onto an amulet that they wore every day. A relic of the old world, an intolerant world, a world that should rightfully give way to this new one, which was so much better and kinder and more forgiving, even if there was still a long way to go.

But that was before, and this was after. And while Jacob had made him feel steadier than he had in months, Michael wondered if it was coming at the cost of going insane in other ways.

"I don't know," he admitted. "I don't know. Believing goes against everything I know and everything I believe. But..." He paused, looking for the right words. "...I don't trust my own mind. I've... seen things, while I've been here, which can't be explained other than by you being right or by me losing my mind."

"You have trouble trusting your own version of events." Jacob propped a foot on the edge of his chair, folding his arms around his shin and resting his chin on his knee. "It's easier for you to think that you're crazy than that what you saw with your own eyes was real and true. Why do you think that is?"

Michael scoffed. "I already pay my therapist to dissect my brain once a week, thank you. I don't need more psychoanalysis."

"I think it's because someone told you that you were wrong enough times that you started to believe them." Jacob wouldn't stop staring at him, and Michael was pinned. "I think it's because you rely on others to tell you what's right and wrong because if other people tell you what to do, you won't ever make a mistake. Except that's not true, is it?"

"I—" He swallowed, his hands shaking, and broke Jacob's gaze. "I don't want to talk about it, okay? I really don't."

"Fine." Jacob turned back to the book he'd been leafing through, and Michael was flooded with relief that he wasn't going to be questioned further.

They read together, side by side, until Michael made it to the last page of the final diary. There hadn't been anything worth photographing, and so he made his last notes in his notebook, biting his tongue as he wondered if he was doing the translation right, puzzling over a particularly tricky turn of phrase.

"It's the other way around," Jacob said, breaking the last few hours of silence. "You inverted the words."

"Oh." Michael erased the offending translation as he looked at Jacob, who was still leafing through his own book. "You speak Russian?"

"And Yiddish, and Hebrew, and Arabic, and Aramaic." Jacob licked his lips. "A few others, too."

Michael whistled. Jacob taking notes in another language suddenly made sense. "That's a lot of languages. You should have been a translator."

"I've an affinity for languages," Jacob countered. "Are you finished?"

He slid a bookmark into place and snapped his book shut, standing to offer Michael a hand up. Together they carried the archival boxes to the far wall, where Jacob instructed him on where to reshelve them in the correct order.

"Dinner?" he asked.

"Dinner," Jacob confirmed.

Michael walked Jacob through the creation of halfway decent burgers to go with his frozen French fries, and asked Jacob to explain his research while they worked.

"It's been a personal interest of mine since I was young." Jacob poked at his burger experimentally, like he had never seen one before, and then deigned to take a bite. "Eleazer inspired my more recent direction, though. I want to understand how and why some spells were made to be reversed, while others were permanent."

"It depends on the strength of the demon you're trying to contain," Michael said through a mouthful of French fry and ketchup, remembering a long-ago lecture that Nate had given him on the subject. "A minor demon might be released after entrapment with a promise of good behavior. But say you catch Lilith in your incantation bowl and manage to bind her—why are you letting the queen of all demons go?"

Jacob snorted. "Queen of all demons. Talk about an inflated ego."

"Tell that to all the families who thought Lilith was responsible for stillbirths and miscarriages," Michael countered, playing devil's advocate. "Imagine your wife is pregnant and you believe your incantation bowl has trapped Lilith or one of her demonesses. Why would you then want to free her? What is the purpose of undoing that spell? It makes sense that some would have release mechanisms, for lack of a better word, while others wouldn't."

"Every demon loves a bargain." Jacob poked a fry into his mouth, and Michael was gratified to see that half his burger was already gone. Maybe by the time he left, he'd have managed to put some meat on Jacob's bones. "You could catch one and then ask it for a favor, bargain with it for a piece of knowledge or advice. You wouldn't chain another person you were trying to do business with, would you?"

"I mean, if I thought they were coming to kill me or harm my family, I probably wouldn't be looking to them for bargains."

"I've tried to make them, you know." Jacob pivoted in his chair, his knee brushing Michael's. "Incantation bowls. Like Eleazer did. I wanted to see if I could trap any of the mazzekin—just temporarily, out of intellectual curiosity. I haven't been able to get any of them to work, though."

That gave Michael pause—had Jacob tried to continue what his grandfather had been doing? He thought back to the shard of pottery he'd picked up, slick with fresh blood. If that had been Jacob's, why would he have lied and said they were all Eleazer's?

There was no reason for him to have lied. Michael was just being ridiculous and imagining things.

"I'm not sure what I'm doing wrong," Jacob continued. "Maybe tomorrow night you'd like to help me?"

Michael wasn't sure that he'd be able to make a demon trap any more effectively than Jacob, but what was the harm of playing along? Jacob obviously had a sincerely held belief in the existence of demon-kind, and in a way, it reminded Michael of Nate. The two of them would have gotten along well, sparring with each other over which kind of demon did what and which incantation was best for repelling what subtype. If Jacob had been introduced to Nate, Michael never would have stood a chance with either of them. They instantly would have been caught in each other's orbit, two brilliant, handsome scholars who believed in the same theories and would build off one another's intellect, instead of constantly butting heads over their work and everything else.

Michael breathed in and out, and reminded himself that Jacob was here and Nate was not, and that the other man had invited him to do something and it would be rude to decline.

He found he didn't want to decline.

"Sure," he said. "I'd love to."

Jacob's answering smile was even brighter than the flash of lightning that broke through the sky.

# Chapter 10

Michael had scheduled his mandatory weekly therapist appointment for 8 a.m., so he wouldn't miss much of the time for his third full day in the archive, and when his alarm went off the next morning, he instantly regretted it. He rolled over, head spinning with the aftereffects of the two bottles of wine he and Jacob had downed while watching a stupid romcom on Michael's laptop, since Jacob had admitted there wasn't a TV anywhere in the building and the only computer was Eleazer's old desktop, kept in a back room.

"Technology doesn't like me," Jacob had groused. "Every cellphone I've ever had has died within a month. Landlines were better."

Michael had teased him, and then Jacob had shut him up with a kiss, which they'd surfaced from just in time to see the two lead characters finally get together. And then when Michael couldn't stop yawning, he'd gone to bed while Jacob, insomniac that he was, headed back to the archive to keep working.

And now he was dealing with the remnants of a hangover while brushing his teeth and dreading having his head examined. When he logged onto the online therapy portal, his therapist's serene face immediately irked him. No one should be smiling that widely at this hour of the morning.

Not that he wasn't usually a morning person. It just put a damper on things, having to wake up from continual nightmares and then retell them to someone else.

"How are you doing this morning?" His therapist's name was Miranda, and he hated her. "I see you're in a new place."

"It's that trip to the archive."

She hummed and wrote something on the pad propped in front of her at an angle so her camera wouldn't capture what was on it. "The one you're doing to finish Nathaniel's dissertation."

"Yeah," he said, hating this already. "That one." It was weird to be talking about this to the one person besides Jacob who he'd revealed most of the truth to, simply because she wasn't able to tell anyone else unless she wanted to lose her license.

"And how are you feeling now that you're there? We discussed that you thought this trip would be healing for you."

Or at least that was how he had phrased it to her. And it wasn't entirely a lie—if he could feel better about at least having finished Nate's work, then he supposed that would be healing for him, in a way.

"It's going fine." He bit the inside of his cheek.

"Do you not feel like talking today?" Miranda asked after a long minute's worth of silence, one which Michael hated that he was paying for. "Because I'm getting the sense that today, speaking is difficult for you."

He shifted in the chair, looking out the window. The lawn was strewn with branches from the storm the night before, and the sound of shattering lightbulbs echoed in his ears. If he was paying for this, he might as well use it as a way to confess some of the thoughts that had been haunting him. "I'm just processing a lot. I think that being here is much different than I expected."

"How so?"

"It makes me miss him." Michael tried to speak it like a statement, but it came out as a question instead. "I— It reminds me of him, being here. Working on his research. It's kind of making me believe that he was right and I was wrong."

"How so?"

Michael ground his teeth together at the repeated question, but that was always how these sessions went. Him going in reluctant and angry, and coming out sad and scraped thin. "The evidence that the archivist compiled here is extraordinary. It tells exactly the story that Nate said it would. If he had come here, he would have had a field day. With what I'm finding, his dissertation would be groundbreaking."

"And have you gotten permission to publish it?"

Michael went still. Because no, he hadn't. He was here on the premise that he needed to finish Nate's research for him, and that once he did and he'd completed the half-finished manuscript, he'd be able to publish it in Nate's name. But of course, he'd have to seek permission from Nate's family, and he had no idea if they would even give it.

"No." He pinched the bridge of his nose. "I haven't."

"So are you really doing this for him? Or are you doing this as a way to punish yourself?"

She'd asked him that question before, and he'd always insisted that he was doing this to honor Nate. To repent. But now, when he thought about looking at Jacob and answering that same question, the words stuck in his throat.

Jacob would see the lie in it. He'd know that Michael was here as a self-inflicted punishment because that was what this was, wasn't it? He was so selfish that he couldn't even do this good thing for someone else. He was so selfish that even his attempt at repentance was self-centered.

"I think I'm doing this to punish myself." The minute he said it, the lie stripped away, it felt better. He felt lighter. Like the lie that he had anything left to give to Nate had held him down.

"Why do you deserve punishment?" Miranda was staring at him through the screen, her pen gone still. "This is the first time I think you've admitted that's how you feel. What's driving that thought?"

"Because, Miranda," he said with a voice full of acid, "I killed my boyfriend and I deserve to be in jail for it. But because I'm not, I have to punish myself. I can't just go… walking around and living my life, can I? Not when I'm such a horrible person that I can't even look myself in the eye. I can't spend a minute alone with my thoughts, or I'll go crazier than I already am."

"Michael," his therapist sighed, "do you really still believe that? This is still how you feel?"

"I'm really tired of people telling me that what I feel is invalid," he spat.

"It's our job to challenge the lies you're telling yourself, Michael." She went back to scribbling something on her pad, and Michael wanted to set the paper on fire. "That's the work we're supposed to be doing together here. I've treated horrible people, and you're so far from being one of them. Your problem is that you want to make everyone around you happy, but it always comes at the cost of your own happiness. You equate being a good person with making it so that other people get exactly what they want out of you, like you're some kind of servant. Like you're responsible for their happiness. But you aren't. That's not the role of a romantic partner, or a friend, or even a family member. People are responsible for their own emotions. And their own actions."

"I was responsible for this," Michael whispered.

"Really?"

He stayed silent, the question rattling around in his brain. Ten sessions in and Miranda kept posing questions that he couldn't answer with a lie, not without knowing it, and all he could do was curl into himself, hunching down, his arms crossed across his chest and his thumb smoothing over the incision in his side.

They stayed quiet for the last twenty minutes of the session, Miranda letting him ignore her. When it was time to end, she gently reminded him that she'd see him at the same time next week and logged off. When Michael looked up, it was to a blank screen informing him that the host had left.

The last thing he wanted to do was go downstairs and work, but if he didn't do *something*, he'd pass an entire day sitting here, frozen, staring at nothing and becoming more unstable by the minute. So, he forced himself to get up and pull on jeans and a sweater, thinking of Jacob and his offer to make incantation bowls together that night. He anchored his mind to that promise and used it to get him through going downstairs and making breakfast, eating mechanically to fuel himself so he didn't pass out on top of the documents he'd be reviewing, even though he couldn't taste a thing through the metallic tang of his post-therapy session guilt.

The documents that Jacob had laid out for him were reports from non-Jews plagued by Jewish demons, labeled as such when rabbis had successfully banished them after being consulted by desperate victims. The words skimmed by Michael in a haze.

dead livestock

drawn to the graveyard

cannot understand why

woken up at night choked by a

He didn't know why he was so rattled, why that morning's session had broken something within him that had held him steady since the accident. If he couldn't cling to his own guilt, then what was supposed to hold him up?

Instead, he focused on the documents, photographing

each one even though they were hardly all worthy of being catalogued. It was something to do, something to focus on that wasn't his brain floundering about whether or not his worldview had to be rearranged.

Jacob's words from the night before kept coming back to him. *I think it's because someone told you that you were wrong enough times that you started to believe them.* No one had ever told him that before. No one had ever connected what had happened before the accident to what came after, all of them focusing on the one event itself.

But there had been so much more than that, hadn't there?

He was so focused on the mess inside his head that he didn't realize a chilly breeze had started up and was rustling the pages in front of him, spreading them across the table and causing some of the onion-skin sheets that were as thin as tissue paper to blow clear across the room. The temperature dropped twenty degrees, his breath misting out in front of him and his body starting to shiver. Cold air scraped against the back of his neck and he turned, wondering whether there was a window that Jacob had left open the night before which he somehow hadn't noticed until just now.

When he looked up, his stomach plummeted.

Where the massive stained-glass window had been set, there was now just a circular hole in the side of the building, open to the elements. There was no shattered glass, no jagged edges, nothing to indicate that the window had somehow broken and cracked. It was just like the window, with its field of midnight blue and twinkling gold stars, had never existed.

Michael blinked, and stared, and didn't know exactly what to do.

If he trusted his own senses, he would have gone to get Jacob from wherever his bedroom was, waking the other man up because surely this qualified as an emergency that was worth losing a few hours of sleep over.

But this was impossible. What he thought had happened—that what must have been hundreds of pounds of leaded glass had simply *vanished* into nothingness—was impossible.

Unless…

Shattering bulbs and swinging chandeliers haunted his mind. The way the destruction had stopped when Jacob had asked out loud. It could have been coincidence, an electrical surge that stopped at exactly the same time as Jacob had claimed to be talking to household demons which he could see and hear and communicate with. Jacob could be crazy, and Michael could be right: all these happenings in the archive were due to easily explainable natural causes.

Or Michael could be the crazy one for not believing. Because what kind of natural cause led to an entire stained-glass window vanishing?

It took him a few heartbeats to decide that it wouldn't hurt to trust his own eyes and the voice in his gut that said it was worth a shot.

"Can you…" Michael said into the empty sanctuary before his voice gave out. He cleared his throat and tried again. "Can you put the glass back?"

Nothing happened, and then Michael remembered how careful Jacob had been to be polite the night before.

"Please? I'd, uh, appreciate it. I'm cold, and the wind might hurt the papers."

There was a shudder through the air in the blank space previously occupied by the window, like the heat waves that rose over the road in the middle of summer. And piece by piece, glass started reappearing, a sped-up version of what must have happened when the window was put together. Panes of blue glass bricking up the frame one by one, the stars added in last to plug the remaining holes. And then everything was as quiet and still as it had been before.

Michael turned back to the table and saw that every page was as it had been left, nothing missing, no documents lying in the middle of the archive's central aisle. Nothing to indicate that wind had been blowing in through a massive hole in the wall just seconds ago. The room was back to its usual toasty temperature, and if there had just been frigid near-winter air blowing in through the space where the window had been, wouldn't it have taken a while to warm back up?

Nausea twisted through his stomach as he raked his hands through his hair, clutching at the roots. What the actual fuck was happening? He'd waffled on the veracity of what Jacob was saying, but there had always been something in his mind holding him back from truly believing the other man's claims that the archive was haunted with the same kinds of creatures that Michael was here to study, the same kinds of demons that his own work was decidedly against the existence of. Now he had two options.

One: everything he knew and believed was wrong,

and the world he lived in was full of the kinds of creatures that haunted the folktales he'd heard all his life.

Or two: he was completely, irrefutably crazy, with the kind of hallucinations that should probably have him checking into a hospital with a good psychiatric ward.

He paced up and down the aisles, his ability to work completely shattered. Shiri appeared after a few minutes, as though drawn to the waves of mental distress, and he gratefully scooped her into his arms, just for something real to anchor himself to. He counted the tiny, fluttering beats of her heart under his hand, and each of her breaths, and stroking her glossy black fur at least provided some kind of distraction.

Eventually, he slumped against a shelf, exhausted from the anxiety and the pacing and the mental turmoil. Shiri clung onto his chest like a warm blanket, kneading her paws into his sweater and spearing him with her claws, tiny pinpricks of pain that kept him grounded.

Maybe this was some kind of psychological break resulting from his earlier therapy session. That had to be it. A temporary kind of insanity. Maybe he just needed to take a nap and watch something stupid on Netflix and rest his mind. He'd had stress-induced hallucinations before, when he'd studied for nineteen hours a day for his final exams in college and barely slept and didn't eat, and ended up so disoriented he didn't know where he was.

It happened. He was fine. He was going to be fine. Maybe it was time to stop therapy for a while, or maybe it was time to cut his losses and leave the archive and just go home and try to move on.

But the thought of leaving Jacob here, alone, slid into

him like a blade. So no, that wasn't going to be what he did. At least, not yet.

Instead, after checking one more time that the window was still there and hadn't vanished again, he took Shiri into the kitchen. It was somehow already lunchtime, his phone reminded him, and he needed to eat. He grabbed the bowl of leftover salad from two nights before and a bottle of water, and marched himself outside, the bracing cold scouring his skin. Shiri trotted after him, yowling, presumably annoyed that she had lost her perch.

He ignored the graveyard and the gate that led to the forest with the remains of the incantation bowls, instead making his way to the greenhouse and thanking God when the door opened without protest. Shiri shot inside ahead of him, flying under a rose bush, and the rush of heat made his muscles unwind.

There was a bench against one window, and he settled onto it, the wooden slats groaning under his weight. It smelled like roses and wet earth, the same scent as Jacob's skin, and Michael wondered if he spent time in here overnight, if that was what he was smelling every time he leaned in close.

He'd forgotten to bring a fork, and since he didn't feel like going back inside, he opted to eat with his fingers, licking dressing off them with every bite. The hush in the greenhouse and the way that everything was the way it was supposed to be—no missing glass, no scattered papers, no strange wind that had no source—settled Michael. It was just like so many blog posts said—spending time in nature was a great stress reliever.

When he'd eaten as much as he could stomach, he made

a circuit around the small greenhouse, running a finger against the silky petals of the roses. There were white ones, yellow ones, red ones with centers that looked like blood. Whoever started it had clearly loved to grow things, because the greenhouse was jam-packed with flowers.

He paused in front of a deep-burgundy rose bush in full bloom, the branches gone wild with thorns as long as his fingernails arching up toward the sky. He cupped one of the flowers in a hand, letting its weight rest there, breathing in the scent, feeling the small ripples on the edges of the frilled petals. He brushed his thumb over the flower's center and jerked away as the back of his hand was scratched open by the bush's thorns, the pain stinging as he hissed. He looked down at his hand and saw that he'd ripped the petal he'd been touching off the rose when he'd jerked backward in pain.

He couldn't touch anything beautiful without hurting it, apparently.

Michael couldn't help it.

He turned on his heel and went back to the house without looking back.

Trying to focus that afternoon was useless. Michael resorted to photographing all the pages he flipped, figuring that he would go through them later and that it was more important to just collect the information than to force his scattered brain to figure out what it said. The shaking in his hands had returned, just like in the aftermath of the accident when he couldn't control the movement of his limbs at all, and he kept having to readjust the camera angle after constantly knocking it off course with his trembling.

Belatedly, he realized that not only had he left the remains of his lunch in the greenhouse, but he'd also locked Shiri inside. He hauled himself back to the greenhouse, whose door had slammed shut. He earned another scratch on the hand from a cat very reluctant to leave her spot curled around the base off a rose bush.

"I can't leave you out here," he snapped, the guilt struggling to escape from his body coming out in an agitated rush. She'd hissed at him but had slunk out of the greenhouse and let him chase her back to the house.

So now he didn't even have the cat for company as he tried to keep working, everything that had happened, all of his guilt, *all* of it weighing him down like he was turning, slowly, to lead. He was vacillating between confessing what he'd seen to Jacob, and hiding the fact that he was clearly going crazy—or that, yes, demons did exist. But Jacob seemed like the kind of person who wouldn't judge—and fuck, he believed that demons were real, clearly—so he wasn't likely to accuse Michael of having utterly lost his mind.

And maybe that was what Michael was truly afraid of: someone looking at him and telling him that, yes, he could trust his own senses and his own mind. No, he wasn't crazy. Yes, this was real.

Because then Jacob would be right, and everything else he'd chalked up to his own mental instability would potentially be true. And every superstition that he'd ever heard—all of that might have real weight to it, too.

He was grinding his teeth in frustration when Jacob walked through the door to the sanctuary, calling out, "Are you alright?"

Making a snap decision between one breath and the next, Michael shot up out of his chair, made a beeline for Jacob, and practically collapsed into the other man's waiting arms.

He was crying, and he didn't care. Because this was terrifying, almost as terrifying as waking up disoriented and in pain in a hospital. "I think I'm going insane. Or the world is broken. I don't know, Jacob. I don't *know*."

Jacob held him tight, strong despite the difference in their sizes, and made soothing noises while stroking a hand through Michael's hair. "Shh," he whispered in Michael's ear. "You're alright. I've got you. What happened?"

Michael pulled away, wiping at his cheeks with the cuffs of his sweater, shivering like he was standing outside in the middle of the snow. "The window disappeared and I wasn't sure if I had lost my mind entirely, and then it came back when I asked it to, and I don't know what the fuck is wrong with me."

"Ah." Jacob ran his hands down Michael's shoulders, gripping his upper arms just above the elbows, steadying him. His green eyes were huge in the dim light of the archive, his proximity the only thing that was preventing Michael from shaking completely apart. "The window disappeared?"

"I— Maybe— I thought so, but I don't know how the hell that could have happened because clearly it's back now." Michael turned his head to confirm that, yes, the stained-glass windows were all still intact. "I'm crazy.

I'm sorry, I'll leave. I don't need to finish the rest of this research."

Jacob's hands gripped him tighter, his nails digging into the backs of Michael's arms enough to hurt. "You're not going anywhere. And you aren't crazy. Why can you not believe what's in front of your own eyes, Michael?"

"Because it's *not real*," he gasped through the panic closing in on him. "It's not real! Windows don't vanish and reappear, gloves don't hold themselves up and lightbulbs don't shatter because demons are playing with them: it's not real. It *can't be real*."

"Anything can be real if you believe it to be," Jacob said. "Look at me, Michael."

Michael did, responding instinctively to the authority in Jacob's voice. "You aren't crazy. I told you when you got here that the archive was infested with mazzekin. I know you didn't believe me, but I was telling the truth. This place is stuffed to the brim with creatures that most humans have never encountered. Do you trust me?"

"Yes," Michael mumbled, his cheeks heating as he found it was true, even though they'd known each other for mere days. "I do."

"Then you have to believe me when I say that even though it doesn't accord with your previous beliefs about the world, everything you've experienced here is very, very real."

Michael swallowed back bile. "It's easier for me to believe that I'm crazy. Maybe I am."

"No, you're not. Come on." Jacob extended a hand, and Michael took it, Jacob's grasp grounding him. "Let's go make an incantation bowl together."

The second floor contained a room that Michael hadn't been in before, the walls lined with shelves and boxes. A table draped in plastic sat in the center, with several large buckets scattered around. Pulled up to the side of that was a stool smeared with clay, and a jar of ink and several brushes lay on the work surface.

"Welcome to my project," Jacob said, finally dropping Michael's hand and spreading his arms wide. "If you're looking for the right place to recreate an incantation bowl from hundreds of years ago, you're in it."

A few of the shelves had been cleared, the boxes tucked into a corner and plastic laid down on the wire mesh. There were, indeed, several incantation bowls in various states of dryness sitting out. Michael crossed over to look at them, the swirls of lettering done in Jacob's careful hand. None of them had pictures in the center, all of them finishing in neat spirals with symbols that Michael recognized as variations of the seal of Solomon, an ancient arrangement of shapes that mystics had believed held immense power.

"Want to make one?" Jacob called out from behind him, distracting him from studying the bowls. "It's fun. It might settle you, too."

"Sure." Michael let Jacob steer him to the stool and sit him down, shrugging off his sweater and tossing it aside so that he didn't get clay on the wool. Jacob pried the lid from one of the buckets, revealing plain brown clay wrapped in plastic. He took a plastic knife from the work surface and sliced into it, pulling off a slab and slapping it down on the table in front of Michael with a grin.

"So, the first step is making that into a bowl."

Michael's lips quirked up. "I got that. But I've never done pottery before, so this is going to be a shitty-ass bowl."

"I'll help." Jacob rounded the table to press himself to Michael's back, wrapping his arms around Michael to grab the clay. "You start like this," he said into Michael's ear.

Michael watched as Jacob's fingers dug into the clay, the veins standing out on the backs of his hands. Jacob gave him a nudge and he joined in, their hands tangling in the clay as they worked to smooth the lump into a bowl.

"I don't think this is very good," Michael said when he smoothed an edge too far and poked a hole through the rim. "Whatever demon we're going to trap is going to have an easy time getting out."

Jacob rolled his eyes. "That's not the point." He batted Michael's hand away and folded the clay over on itself, ruining their work. "You're smiling. And your heart is beating normally again. I can feel it. Are you feeling better?"

The realization that, yes, Jacob was right washed over Michael. "Yeah. I feel better."

"Do you trust yourself yet?"

"Maybe in another twenty bowls." Michael smoothed a thumb over a divot in the clay, wiping it clean. "It's hard for me to believe this stuff is real. I'm not saying it's not, it's just a very different reality than the one I've lived in for thirty years. A very different story than the one I've trusted."

Jacob hummed. "I had the benefit of growing up differently. So yes, I can see why it's taking you longer than it took me to accept this is a special place."

"I—I'm trying." Michael gave up trying to make the clay into a bowl and just leaned back into Jacob, who took his weight. He reached up to scratch at an itch on his face, but only succeeded in smearing his cheek with clay. "I'm filthy, too."

Jacob stepped away, nearly tipping Michael backward before he rebalanced himself. "Bath?"

Michael couldn't deny that as soon as he pictured Jacob wet and naked, all self-doubt flew out the window. "If we can take one together."

"I wasn't suggesting you clean up alone."

Scrambling off the stool, Michael had no trouble leaving the mess of clay—which certainly didn't resemble a bowl in the least—on the workbench. Jacob didn't mention needing to clean up, so Michael didn't press it, because Jacob had turned around and was looking over his shoulder like he couldn't believe Michael was so slow.

"Are you coming?" One of his eyebrows arched.

"I plan to." Michael bit down on a smirk. "This time, at least."

Jacob laughed as he left the room behind, crossing the hall to Michael's bedroom. Michael was surprised, because he'd assumed that he was finally going to get to see where Jacob slept, but the tub in his room was big enough that the two of them would undoubtedly fit.

They crowded into the bathroom, where Jacob turned on the tap, steaming water filling the tub while the two of them began to strip. Michael was glad that he'd at least tried to get back into shape after his surgery as Jacob's eyes raked down his nude form appreciatively once he'd thrown his T-shirt, jeans, boxer briefs, and socks back out into the bedroom, leaving him dressed in nothing but the gauze taped to his side. Jacob stopped undressing long enough to peel the gauze off, laying a hand flat over the ragged incision like his touch alone could seal it shut.

"Are you taking the rest of that off?" Michael plucked at Jacob's slacks. "Or are you planning on bathing with clothes on?"

"Don't make fun of me," Jacob grumbled, "but I'm keeping my socks on."

He worked his pants off his hips as Michael laughed, and then he was nude too, the long, lean lines of him stark and beautiful in the bathroom light. He could have been a painting, all dips and hollows and snowy skin, and Michael took a minute to appreciate the sight before glancing down to Jacob's feet.

"You don't have anything to be ashamed of," he said gently, his lips quirking up as he took in the socks patterned with black cats. Jacob's feet were indeed bent at an odd angle, the sides sticking out on the edges like he had severe bunions, or some other kind of deformity. "But if you want to keep your feet hidden, I'm not going to force you to take your socks off. They're pretty cute, anyway."

"I have a very extensive collection. And people don't get to see my feet unless we've known each other for a few decades," Jacob huffed. "So you're quite a bit short."

Michael laughed. "In other words, no one has ever seen your feet."

"Shut up," Jacob shot back, but there wasn't any heat in it, just playfulness that Michael wished he could make stick. He'd kill to have this version of Jacob be the one that the other man got to be all the time, not having to suffer being crushed by grief for his family.

The tub was done filling and so Michael turned it off, stepping into the water to test the temperature before easing himself down to sitting. He offered a hand to Jacob, who clambered in after him, settling down on his lap with a leg on either side of Michael's thighs. Jacob grabbed the soap that Michael had left on the edge of the tub and lathered his hands and arms, the clay slipping off and washing away. He did the same to Michael, scrubbing each of his fingers until the evidence of their arts and crafts project was gone.

Once they were both mostly clean again, Michael scrubbing shampoo through both of their hair and then cupping water in his hands and pouring it over Jacob's head until he was sputtering like a drowned cat, his hair dripping water into his eyes, he let his hands wander. Jacob was more than obliging, the heat and weight of him pressing down against Michael's chest solid and steady enough that for the first time in days, Michael's mind was quiet.

Until he broke free from the kiss they were sharing to look down, thinking to appreciate the sight of Jacob's body stretched out before him, and instead saw that the water had turned a thick, crimson red.

"Holy fuck," Michael gasped, jerking enough with surprise that Jacob made a pained noise and flinched, holding him down by the shoulders. "The water—"

Jacob looked down. "Oh."

The liquid in the bath was so much warmer now, thick and viscous and heavy like it was going to suck him under. It was creeping up his chest as he slipped downward, the pressure of Jacob on his lap weighing him down. Jacob's hands slid down to Michael's abs, his nails digging into the indents between each pair of muscles, and when they came back up, he was painted to the wrists in red.

The air smelled so much of iron that Michael could taste it on his tongue.

"Is it…" Michael's heart was hammering again, his stomach twisting with something other than arousal now. "Is this blood? Are you bleeding?"

But it couldn't be, because this wasn't blood in the water. Michael lifted his hand to watch whatever they were bathing in drip off his fingers, staring in horror. If this was Jacob's blood, the other man was dead. There was an ocean of it. Bodies' worth of it. He slid farther down into the water and jostled Jacob on his lap, and for a moment he was worried that his head was going to slip under and he would drown here, in a tub barely big enough to fit his whole body.

"I'm not." Jacob didn't seem nearly as perturbed as Michael was, grinding back against his hand impatiently. "Why'd you stop?"

"We… it's…" Michael didn't know what to say, but then Jacob grabbed his cheeks, forcing Michael to look right into his eyes, the green more vibrant than ever against the backdrop of red all around them.

"Does it matter?" Jacob rasped, his gaze insistent. "Water or blood, it doesn't matter, just surrender to the moment. You're here, and it's real, whatever you think this is. You know the mazzekin play tricks, you've seen them yourself. This is just another one of them. They're trying to get to you. I need you to trust yourself. I need you to breathe."

Jacob leaned forward, planting a hand on Michael's chest, right over his heart, leaving a trail of hot, sticky liquid across his skin.

"It's real," Michael repeated, because if it wasn't real his mind was gone, and suddenly, he was fighting against the prospect of losing himself. "It's real."

Maybe if he said it enough, the truth of it would sink into his bones. He was sitting in a tub full of blood, the iron tang of it thick in the air, the liquid resisting movement far more than water ever would have. Jacob was a solid weight on his lap.

It was blood, not water, and everything was fine.

Michael reached down, dipped a hand into the blood, and brought it to his face to examine it. Jacob captured his wrist and drew Michael's index finger into his mouth, his tongue drawing down its length. His nails dragged down Michael's skin, leaving burning trails, and he couldn't help but groan when Jacob shifted and brought them together at last, one smooth motion with no warning.

Jacob gasped as he took Michael in, and Michael had to remind himself to breathe as the warmth of the blood they were submerged in and the heat of Jacob tight around him drew him down into a spiral of pleasure. Jacob's mouth met his and he tasted blood, and when Jacob twined his hands through Michael's hair, he could feel it smearing all across his face, his neck, his chest. Their skin slid together, slick, and the blood rose around them, filling the tub and spilling over the sides, flooding the room, but Michael didn't care.

He tipped his head back as Jacob moved, and for the first time since arriving at the Institute, Michael believed.

# Chapter 11

Waking up alone the next morning was a disappointing way to start his fourth day in the archive.

By the time they'd both come, Jacob panting against Michael's shoulder, the water had turned back to just that. There was no hint or sign of anything different, no moisture on the floor where the blood had run over the sides of the tub, and Michael had felt the doubts creep back in about whether he was totally insane. But once again, Jacob had kissed his eyelids and told him that it didn't matter, that he needed to trust his senses, and Michael had let that carry him through.

They'd eaten dinner dressed in pajamas, Jacob sneaking off wrapped in a towel and wearing sodden socks to change in his room, insisting that Michael not follow. He came downstairs dressed in a worn old T-shirt and flannel pajama pants, cocooned in a fluffy white bathrobe and wearing fuzzy socks.

Michael had laughed at the way he'd made himself look like a snowball, and Jacob had given him the stink-eye before cuddling up against him as Michael made them paninis.

And then they'd gone back upstairs and fallen into Michael's bed, curled around each other under the covers. Shiri had come to join them, perching on the pillows above their heads like a furry hat. For the first time since the accident, Michael had drifted off to sleep peacefully, feeling blissfully safe and warm and whole. Not berating himself, not wondering if he was going crazy. Jacob in his arms and the cat above his head kept him solid, and anchored, and he wondered if there was some way, any way, for him to do this for the rest of his life without fucking it all up.

But by morning, all he found himself curled around was Shiri, the cat snoring directly into his face with one paw jammed into his ear. He sighed, staring at the ceiling and fighting back disappointment that he hadn't woken up next to Jacob. When his elbow met something crunchy as he rolled over onto his back, his heart picked up a beat.

It was a note. *Couldn't sleep and didn't want to wake you. See you this evening.*

There was a sloppy heart that made his stomach flip, and a scrawl that Michael assumed was Jacob's name. Placated, he went about his morning routine, alert to any signs of unusual activity but finding nothing out of the ordinary. Maybe spending the last evening with Jacob had soothed him enough that he'd reset his brain.

The boxes laid out on the desk in the archive contained lecture notes from a class on demon summoning given at a Hungarian university in the mid-1800s.

Spirits are everywhere: They haunt dark places, homes, even the crumbs left on the dinner table. One who seeks to know that the demons exist should place fine ashes around his bed, and in the morning the demons' footprints appear like chickens' footprints, in the ash. One who seeks to see them should take the afterbirth of a firstborn female black cat, born to a firstborn female black cat, burn it in the fire, grind it and place it in his eyes, and he will see them. He must then place the ashes in an iron tube sealed with an iron seal lest the demons steal it from him, and then seal the opening so he will not be harmed. Rav Beivai bar Abaye performed this procedure, saw the demons, and was harmed. The Sages prayed for mercy on his behalf and he was healed.

There were detailed drawings and sketches of summoning circles, the plans laid out in an academic way that Michael had never seen before. Usually, materials like this were couched in mysticism, not science, and he didn't quite know what to make of them. It was somewhat far afield of Nate's dissertation, and Michael wondered if Jacob had been distracted last night as he'd pulled material for today's session. This seemed like it would fit in more with Jacob's own project on how to break spells holding demons in place, like maybe he'd mixed up their two projects.

His face flushed remembering the night before, and he didn't want to flatter himself, but maybe it really had been that good.

With every page he turned, Michael half-expected something to happen, another sign of supernatural… something. And he found that he almost craved it, another test of whether he could do as Jacob had ordered and trust his own eyes. Whether he could rely on his own mind. Whether he could surrender the way he had last night.

Whether he could do it all without Jacob pressed against him.

The hours dragged on and working got harder. Michael couldn't focus, his thoughts drifting back to Jacob with a magnetic pull. He avoided the garden and ended up eating lunch in the dining room, tracing the evil eyes on the carpet with the tip of his toe as he chewed his way through a granola bar, the most he could stomach.

Last night had convinced him of a lot, and now every single argument he'd had with Nate was playing on repeat behind his eyes. He was torn between still wanting to believe, deep down, that he was insane and all of this was just one big hallucination, and admitting that something beyond the realm of human explanation was happening at the Institute, proving Nate's theory effectively right.

If *he'd* come here, he would have been ecstatic. Michael had taken that chance from him, and given everything, there was no way the world was going to know that Nate was correct. Michael could steal his research and publish it as his own, but enough people in the field knew what Nate had been working on that he would be found out in an instant, and what kind of piece of shit plagiarized from his dead boyfriend?

So much of what went wrong between them had been arguments over academic hypotheses, neither of them truly able to give in and consider the other's side as anything other than a personal affront. Michael had taken to completely avoiding the topic after a year of constant combat, tired of being berated and told that he was an idiot, too dedicated to rationality to see what was in front of their faces, a traitor to ancestors who had documented the existence of the supernatural carefully enough that to doubt them was an act of betrayal. It was one of the things that had caused the first layer of frost to form between them, compounded by Michael's knack for making Nate upset and drawing attention from others in all the wrong ways. But that was the first, original sin.

And it turned out it had been Michael's, too.

His incision was itchier than ever today, and he scratched at it so aggressively that it started to bleed again. Ignoring it meant that Jacob would come downstairs that evening and find Michael in a ruined shirt and stinking of blood, but given what had happened last night, Michael chose to assume that Jacob wouldn't care about a bloodstained shirt. Michael's mind kept flashing back to the sensation of the blood rising around him, to the feeling and the smell of it, and somehow, yes, he still believed.

Jacob had gotten him to believe.

The pull and burn of the incision stole his breath with every step he took back into the archive. Looking at the desk with its neat stack of archival boxes made him vaguely ill—what was he even doing here, anymore? What was even the point? If he couldn't publish Nate's research, and he couldn't bring Nate back, was this really going to do anything at all besides give him more time here with Jacob, hiding from the rest of the world?

Michael flinched to realize that that didn't seem so bad. And his stomach churned as he realized that it had been too long since he'd felt the pain of grief for Nate.

He ended up wandering the aisles full of books, trailing a finger across the spines. He pulled down a few Yiddish novels and curled up in a corner on some black fur-coated cushions that had been stacked by a heating vent, presumably as a place for Shiri to sleep. His eyelids drooped as he paged through the books, reading familiar jokes and folktales and processing none of it, because his mind was clear but it was also a mess of contradictions.

What did it mean for him to believe? What of himself would he lose in the process?

He could tell Jacob he was leaving tonight and be gone by the next morning. He didn't have to stay. He didn't have to believe.

But he was broken, and he wanted to.

He wanted to *stay*. He didn't want to leave and hurt. He wanted to always be here.

The same way he'd looked at every previous girlfriend or boyfriend and known that he'd fall deep in love with them—if not right then, then soon—he knew that he wasn't going to be able to escape Jacob. Maybe it was his innate desire to people-please, the instinct in him that *wanted* to care for others, that demanded he fawn over them, that saw something in Jacob and *knew*.

It was scarier than the realization that his entire worldview had shifted, because it meant he hadn't actually repented. He wasn't actually fixed, or even close. He was the same person who had loved a man and then killed him, and instead of staying away from people like he'd sworn he would, he'd managed to become entangled.

Hurting Jacob was an inevitability. It was as clear as day to Michael that he was going to do it. He wasn't yet sure if he would hurt him physically, the image of slender wrists and a slim waist so fragile compared to his own frame, still clinging to the remnants of yoga-honed muscles. Maybe instead he would be the source of all of Jacob's anger and frustration, tearing up his life from the inside out like he'd done with Nate.

Maybe it would be both. Maybe he'd torture him and then hurt him, and Michael wasn't going to be able to help himself. He wasn't going to be able to stop himself because that was what he did.

Blinking, he looked down at the open book and realized with a flush of embarrassment that there were water droplets on the page. He brushed the backs of his hands across his cheeks, and they came away wet.

With an unsteady lurch, he got to his feet and snapped the book shut, dusting clumps of fur off his pants. If he was brave, he would stop lying to himself and tell Jacob what he'd done, and he would leave it up to the other man to decide if he stayed or if he went. He'd abide by the decision.

Michael wondered if he'd have the courage to tell the true story, the unflinching story, the one that didn't make him seem like some kind of innocent victim. He decided he'd do it after dinner, because there was no sense in torturing himself any longer, or letting Jacob be exposed to someone who was effectively living a lie.

He hadn't told anyone the full story. The real story, not the lies formed of bits and pieces in response to questions from his parents or the police or the social workers in the hospital, not the guarded truths he'd told his therapist. Jacob would be the first, and he was sure that it was going to be a rejection that *hurt*. What he'd do after… Michael didn't know. He couldn't see returning to a solitary life of traveling around the world, translating documents for other people's interests. Being alone, having no one next to him, just him and his pain and his grief.

It just seemed so… hollow, compared to the hush of the archive and the brush of Jacob's hand against his, the quiet mystique of this place and all the places like it, the thrill of discovering knowledge and envisioning himself connected to that person hundreds of years ago who had put pen to paper to tell what they had seen, to record their secret fears. He'd had an idea of the way his life would go: jaunts around the world to places of sacred knowledge, debates with Nate over a kitchen table that ended in intellectual curiosity and not screaming. Shelves in their home full of their books and the journals their respective works were featured in, matching tweed jackets hanging in a closet, Shabbat dinners with friends and families that Michael was sure they could have knitted together if he had more time, more courage, more love for Nate inside him to outweigh the attention-seeking parts of him that did so much to make Nate feel worthless.

He thought about the box he'd found when finally cleaning out Nate's drawers, the simple white-gold band perfectly fitted to the fourth finger on Michael's left hand, and the way that had shredded him to pieces.

There had been a whole life in front of him, a steady path that he just had to walk and not fuck up, and somehow, he had stepped off the trail anyway and ruined everything. And no matter how much he wanted to get back onto that trail, he couldn't. It wasn't there anymore, and even if it was, walking it alone was meaningless.

Every time he looked into Jacob's eyes, he saw a new path forming. It was the same each time he fell hard for a new person, even before he knew whether they felt the same way. He should probably do Jacob the courtesy of deciding whether he was even interested in Michael before he let his imagination run wild. And Jacob deserved not only to know who Michael really was, but also to have Michael make sure this wasn't just another symptom of him trying to evade responsibility for what he'd done by falling into someone else's arms.

Jacob deserved to be wanted for who he was, not just as an escape. But as Michael paced the aisles of the archive, thinking about Jacob's laugh and his smile and the way his eyes dimmed when he was sad, the way that he hadn't flinched away from Michael when he'd grieved but held him close instead, the way he'd named his cat after the Jewish toilet demon and was reluctantly learning how to make something for himself to eat that didn't come out of the freezer, he couldn't see wanting Jacob for any reason other than that he was brilliant and kind and good.

He eventually paced enough that his feet hurt, and the tangle of nerves in his stomach still hadn't abated. The idea of Jacob looking at him with disgust after he knew—really *knew*—already hurt, the anticipation of pain somehow just as bad as the pain itself. But this was something that Michael couldn't be a coward about. Jacob had given him the gift of beginning to trust his own mind again, hadn't he? So, Michael owed him something in return, and that something was the chance to say no.

The only thing left for him to do was go back to the desk and the archive boxes, the student's notes still spread out on the surface of the table. He shuffled through them, and then decided to put them back in the box. After securing its straps, he turned to the second box on the table and drew it closer to himself to open it.

As soon as the lid flopped open, Michael lurched backward so quickly that he toppled his chair, hitting the ground with a hand flung out to try to stop himself from cracking his skull open. Because there were no papers inside the box, at least not that he could see. Instead, the hollow cavity teemed with locusts, the chittering of their legs and the rustling of their wings deafening in the silence of the sanctuary. As he looked up, a few of them must have realized that they were now free, because they started to fly out and toward the ceiling, so many more of them than could possibly have fit into a single archival box, as if that was the most unbelievable part of the situation. He remained paralyzed on the floor, his wrist throbbing, as a black blur flew through the air. Shiri jumped onto the table—thank God he'd put all the documents back into the box first—and started swatting at the locusts, bringing down several before biting into one with a crunch that made Michael nauseous.

"Oh dear."

The dry humor was evident in Jacob's voice. Michael struggled upward, swatting his hands around his head as the bugs dove for him. He didn't care how undignified it looked—he grabbed his phone from the table and dashed out of the path of the bugs, who had formed a cloud around the desk, flying in an increasingly tight circle with Shiri batting happily at the edges. As soon as he reached Jacob, standing in the doorway with his arms crossed and his eyebrows raised in amusement, he grabbed him and towed him backward, shutting the door behind them with a definitive *click*.

He hoped locusts couldn't sneak under doors and through cracks the way that cockroaches could.

"I *hate* bugs," he panted, leaning against the wall. "They scare the shit out of me."

"I cannot say that I'm an enormous fan." Jacob stared at the shut door, a half-smile playing across his face. "Locusts are an incredible pest, and quite hard to get rid of. But still, in this instance, a very effective cat toy."

"I didn't know they existed in the United States." It felt like there were bugs crawling all over him, and Michael ran his hands through his hair to make sure the sensation was totally phantom and not because he was actually covered in the creatures. "How did they get inside that box?"

"Phenomenal question." Jacob looked down at Michael's chest. "It seems like it wasn't the only plague visited upon the archive today, though."

He gestured meaningfully to Michael's stomach, which was coated in a large, tacky bloodstain. He hadn't bled this much in a while, and he was surprised he hadn't felt it. "Fuck." He plucked at the fabric and hissed as it pulled away from the incision. It had dried enough for the shirt to stick to his skin, and he hadn't even noticed.

"I'll go clean myself up," he said. "I need a shower anyway, after that."

He didn't say another word as he mounted the stairs and fled. Looking at Jacob reminded him of the promise he'd made to himself to tell the other man the truth, and the inevitability of his rejection weighed on him. It was, as always, far easier to escape than it was to stand firm.

He was going to do it, but he just needed a little time first. He reached his room and closed the door, scanning quickly for anything that wasn't supposed to be there and breathing a sigh of relief when he didn't find another plague of locusts or frogs or whatever was coming next.

As he stripped off his clothes and got into the tub, turning on the shower head, he realized that he hadn't, even for a minute, wondered if he had been hallucinating the cloud of bugs that had flown out of the archival box.

Trusting his own mind felt strange, like a skill he'd had that he'd lost and was only now coming back to. It had been years—before the accident, before Nate—since he'd been so sure that what he perceived was real, and true, even if it was difficult to explain.

Now, he just had to hope that when Jacob saw the real him, it wasn't going to be the end of whatever this was.

# Chapter 12

Jacob was unusually quiet when Michael made his way back down for dinner, freshly dressed and with a new bandage wrapped tightly around his ribs, hopefully enough to discourage him from picking at it. The other man was sitting on one of the stools pulled up to the kitchen island, hunched over the marble on his forearms. Michael didn't know how to begin this conversation, not really, so he just sat down heavily on the stool next to Jacob so he at least wouldn't have to look him in the eye.

He sucked in a breath. "I wasn't honest with you when I came here."

Jacob's hands spread flat on the counter. "About what?"

"About why it was me who showed up."

Jacob didn't say anything. Michael didn't know if it was an invitation to keep going, or whether it was a sign that Jacob wasn't ready to hear what he had to say.

He licked his lips, seized by the same gnawing anxiety

as every time he faced something uncertain, every time he faced the precipice of gaining something good. It was the feeling of life as a series of corners that you couldn't see around, but knowing bone-deep that there was something terrifying around each one of them. And even if one corner was turned and there was a surprise, or something good, Michael knew that his brain would always tell him *it's a trick, it's designed to make the horrible thing around the next corner feel even worse, because you held this good thing inside you and let yourself feel it*. And so that good thing would itself turn into fear, because once you had something, all that was left was to worry it would be taken away.

He should have worried more about everything he had being taken away. Maybe if he had done that, it wouldn't have been so shocking when it happened. Maybe he would have been better prepared to turn that corner.

"What's holding you back," Jacob asked, "from telling me?"

This time, the answer came faster, a confession that he couldn't stop himself making. "Once I tell you, I don't know if you'll want me here. And I—"

"You want to stay," Jacob finished when he couldn't, when the words wouldn't fall from his lips.

"I do." He got up and walked around the kitchen island, staring out the window, his hands grabbing the ceramic edge of the kitchen sink. "Jacob, I do. But—"

He didn't know if he could do this.

Michael turned to see Jacob staring at him with glittering eyes.

"Trust me, there's nothing you could tell me that's worse than something I've already done myself," Jacob said. "You think you're evil, but you don't even know the meaning of the word."

"I didn't come here for sarcasm," Michael snapped, anxiety bleeding into frustration, because it sounded for a minute like Jacob was making light of this, and that was the last thing he wanted.

"No, you came here to finish your dead boyfriend's dissertation because you thought doing so would absolve you of something that you didn't even do."

And that was it, the spark that kindled Michael's anger and let it flare to the surface. "You don't even know what happened." He whirled back to where Jacob was sitting, his angular chin resting on steepled fingers. "You know nothing about me. You've known me for less than a week. It's nothing you could ever understand because you weren't there."

"You think I had to be there to understand what you did?" Jacob cocked his head, his eyes narrowing. "I'm a researcher at heart, Michael. I know what the internet is. 'Twenty-eight-year-old doctoral candidate dies after assault by stranger in back alley, twenty-seven-year-old translator severely injured, manhunt for suspect ongoing.' That was the headline, wasn't it? Of the story the *Times* wrote?"

He knew.

He *knew*.

All this time, he'd been thinking that he'd been hiding who he was, what he was, from Jacob. And instead, Jacob had known. He didn't know for how long, but as he stared at the man who had comforted him through his grief, who had held him close, he realized that Jacob didn't seem shocked or surprised. He seemed calm. Fine.

Like he was ready to use it as a weapon against Michael. He could already feel the blade pressed against his neck.

Michael swallowed hard, the lump in his throat growing by two sizes. "What are you saying? You cyber stalked me and now you want to hold over my head what a terrible person I am?"

"No," Jacob said, staring Michael down with a challenge in his eyes. "I'm saying that I can read a newspaper article and look at your guilt and listen to everything you've said over the last few days and put two and two together. I can understand what it is that you haven't said, not to the police, not to anyone else. Do you know you flinch every time someone comes up behind you? Do you know that when something drops, your face goes white? It wasn't a stranger who assaulted you both, was it? It's clear."

"What's clear?" Michael managed to choke out the question after a heartbeat of silence.

"That he abused you," Jacob replied, his voice soft this time. "That he deserved it."

Michael stared at Jacob, his green eyes calculating, and he didn't know if it was too much or not enough or exactly what he'd needed to hear for so, so long.

But the one thing he was sure of was that he couldn't be in the room with Jacob one second longer. He made it past the threshold of the kitchen before he let the tears fall in earnest, staggering up the stairs like he was a wounded thing, making it to his bedroom and stripping off his clothes and shutting the door and curling up in the bed like blankets could protect them.

*He abused you. He deserved it.*

Two statements. Separate, yet tied together.

So many people, in the aftermath of Nate's death, had said things like *it wasn't your fault*, or *it was an accident, don't blame yourself, it was random violence.*

Jacob didn't say that. Jacob knew what Michael had done. But he took away the blame by turning murder into retribution.

He hurt you, so you hurt him. Your anger and your actions were righteous. He deserved it. He deserved to die for the way he harmed you.

It was too much. Michael hugged one pillow to his chest and buried his face in the other. He had been prepared for anger, but he hadn't been braced for absolution. He knew how to face anger. He'd been angry at himself for so, so long.

He didn't know how to take this forgiveness.

Pulling the blankets tight around him, he willed himself into the pleasant space between waking and sleeping where he didn't have to think, barely had to breathe, and could avoid feeling much of anything at all. This fugue state was soothing in its blankness, its effortlessness. It was calming.

It worked, until there was a knock at the door an hour later.

Michael's eyes were hot and swollen with tears when he cracked them open.

"Are you still alive in there?" Jacob called from the other side of the door. "Because if you aren't, I have quite a bit of dinner to eat myself."

For a minute, Michael stared at the ceiling, picking at his incision, until basic decency compelled him to croak out, "I'm coming."

"It's going to get cold," Jacob sniped as Michael eased himself out of bed. "Are you going to take forever? Hurry up."

Michael rolled his eyes at the way Jacob was clearly hangry—it figured that someone who barely ate would be prone to hunger-induced rage—but when he'd redressed himself and opened the door, Jacob didn't seem that annoyed. Instead, he ran one hand down Michael's chest, slipping his fingers into the waistband of his jeans, and tugged him forward, a smile playing around his lips.

He'd never been so grateful for someone else's mock annoyance, something to get him out of his head and into the present. He'd never been so grateful that another person had changed the topic, that another person had decided to drop the subject and wasn't digging their fingers into the wound.

"I hope you like pasta," Jacob said as he towed Michael down the stairs. "Because I made a variation on your recipe. It's probably not as good as yours, but I think you need to eat."

"You're a quick study." Michael's throat was dry. "You didn't need me to teach you. You could have just watched the Food Network."

"You enjoyed it," Jacob said haughtily, and Michael nearly laughed. He let Jacob slide his fingers out from his waistband and into Michael's hand, their fingers tangled together as they arrived in the foyer.

The door to the archive room was open. "Are there, uh, more bugs?" Michael blinked, his eyes still tacky.

"Shiri took care of them." Jacob pointed to the window seat in the parlor, where a very rotund-looking cat was resting in the flickering light of the fire, splayed out on her back and dead asleep. "Nothing to worry about anymore."

Michael wished that his worries could be dealt with as easily as locusts, crushed and disposed of and not to be feared again.

"Come on." Jacob's voice was gentle. Michael realized he had frozen. "Let's go eat."

True to his word, there was a steaming bowl of pasta on the dining room table. Jacob pushed Michael into a chair and started dishing some out onto the plates. "I hope it's edible."

Michael couldn't help the slightly hysterical laugh that bubbled up in his chest. "You told me you know I murdered my boyfriend and then I have a breakdown, and you make me *pasta*?"

"Oh, Michael." Jacob ran a hand through his hair. "I know you blame yourself, but I've known you for just a little while and I can already tell you that your version of events, whatever you've been telling yourself, is just not true. I don't mean what actually happened. That seems black and white. But the reasoning behind it."

Michael swallowed, staring down at the plate that Jacob had placed in front of him. He grabbed the fork.

"You said he abused me." He stared into the pasta like it was going to save him from all of this. "Why?"

A dry, humorless laugh. "As people say, I've been around the block a few times, even though it doesn't look it. I know the signs. If it wasn't him, someone was hurting you. Someone was telling you that what you believed wasn't true. And it was going on long enough for it to become ingrained in you, bone deep."

Michael finally looked up and met Jacob's eyes and wondered if the same thing had happened to him.

"He was going to propose to me." Michael didn't know why that was where he started. "I found the ring after he died."

"Proposing marriage is hardly a marker of a good person." Jacob cocked his head. "Or a litmus test of a healthy relationship."

Michael didn't know what to say to that. He stalled by twirling some pasta on his fork, but fell short of eating. He didn't know if he could, with the nausea twisting his stomach.

"I want you to tell me what happened before the accident, in your own words." Jacob separated a single strand of pasta from the rest on his plate, popping it into his mouth. "You know how you didn't believe in the mazzekin, and it took you a while to accept it? Because you didn't trust yourself? I think that what's going on is much the same."

"Gaslighting," Michael mumbled, massaging his temples. There was a vicious headache forming there, probably from all the crying and the panic. "It's what they call it."

*They* were innumerable articles on the internet that he'd found in some of his darker hours, the ones when he'd been angry at Nate instead of himself. He'd fought against it, because Nate didn't deserve to be painted like that, not when Michael was the one at fault. Not when they'd argued, and Michael was the one who survived.

"And that's what he did to you." Jacob's expression turned stony. "That's why you came here to me and you couldn't accept what you were seeing."

"I—" This was harder than Michael had thought it would be, being honest. He couldn't lie, not to Jacob, and while this wasn't going the way he'd thought it would, it was somehow worse. "When Nate and I met, I was drawn to him instantly. He was charismatic, and everyone loved him. I had always been shyer, with just a few good friends here and there, sticking close to the people I dated. Because you see, I..." His cheeks flushed hot. "I've always gotten really attached really quickly to the people I've fallen for. I'm demisexual, and that's just how it goes for me personally, how it always has."

Jacob didn't press Michael for more, but he reached across the table and put his hand on top of Michael's. Like he understood what Michael was saying.

"We argued, like any other couple. About work. About the people I hung out with, and how much time I spent with them. About me making the wrong choices and attracting the wrong kind of attention."

"He didn't even have to isolate you from people who would disagree with how he was treating you." Jacob's voice was hard. "You did it yourself. It's why, for the most part, you haven't spoken to anyone else while you've been here."

Michael gaped, wondering if he was being spied on. "How did you—"

Jacob shrugged. "Most people in the modern day are attached to their phones. They're always texting, or tweeting, or doing whatever else. Humans crave connection. But you've barely done any of that, even though you're desperately lonely. It doesn't take a genius to guess that you don't have many people you want to talk to."

With any other person, shame would have weighed Michael down, because that statement would have been delivered with derision, or scorn, or pity. But Jacob just laid it out like he was reciting facts, no judgment behind the words. "He wasn't okay with the idea of Sarah. She was my best friend, and we went out to dinner when Nate and I first started dating..." His mouth was dry, and he paused to take a sip of water he nearly choked on. "He came and sat at a separate table, watching us. Maybe he was hoping that I'd cave and introduce them. But then we finished dinner, and when she got up she hugged me and kissed me on the cheek, just like she'd done every day for years. And Nate saw. And when she left, he started yelling at me. We were on the sidewalk, and I was upset with him for being upset with me, and he..."

It stuck in Michael's throat.

"He what?" Jacob prompted after a minute of dead silence.

"He slapped me across the face so hard that he split my lip open against my teeth." Michael tried to recite it like it was a police report, clinical and dry, not loaded with the terror he had felt in that moment. Not fear of Nate. Terror that he'd done something so bad that Nate would leave him, the utterly consuming fear that he'd fucked up so badly that Nate had had no choice but to hurt him to make him see it.

Jacob's hand curled around Michael's, his nails as sharp as talons against the skin. "You felt like you deserved it instead of walking away from someone who'd physically hurt you."

"Yes." Michael didn't have to ask how he knew.

"How many times?"

Michael shrugged. "I lost count. I did a lot of things wrong."

"Until whatever argument happened that night, when you finally protected yourself from the abuse."

"It didn't feel like it." Michael swallowed. "It didn't feel like abuse. It didn't feel like protecting myself."

Jacob bit his lip, closing his eyes. "It was. I promise."

"I don't know what to think about what happened."

"I've… been with a lot of people, in a lot of different ways." Jacob kept his eyes closed. "I've been in a few partnerships where, when the other person looked at me askance, I flinched because I was afraid. And I'm usually not like that. I can usually protect myself, but there have always been people who have managed to get under my skin and past my defenses. It hurts differently every time."

Things clicked: the delicacy with which Jacob had handled him, and the perceptiveness with which he'd assessed the situation. He knew, and he understood.

"When was it, for you?" He wasn't sure if he was allowed to ask, but he did anyway.

"The last time was a while ago." Jacob's eyes finally blinked open, and there was pain there. "But it still feels raw. I still worry about it, every time I… meet people."

Michael recoiled. "I would never. I hope you know that."

"Not you." Jacob shook his head. "You don't have it in you. I never worried for a second. It's not in your nature to want to control others, not in that way."

Aside from a few performative bites taken out of the pasta, neither of them had really touched their food.

"I just want to be clear," Michael said to banish the last lingering vestiges of doubt. "You know that I pushed my boyfriend into the edge of a building and caused a massive brain hemorrhage that ended up killing him on the way to the hospital. Before that happened, he had pulled me off the street and into an alleyway and beaten me up because I told him that I was going to go to Lithuania for three months on a job. And when I fell down, he kicked me until he broke seven of my ribs and one of them punctured my lung. But I didn't run away when he let me get up. I attacked him back. And he was the one who died. And then I lied to everyone, from the police to my family, and said that a stranger did it so I didn't have to confess that I was a murderer."

"I know." Jacob stroked a hand up his forearm. "I know."

"I don't want to leave here," Michael admitted, his voice cracking. "I don't want to leave you. I swore it wouldn't happen again, that I would keep myself apart from other people so I wouldn't hurt them, but then I met you and I—"

Jacob shut him up by putting a finger to his lips. "Trust me. Even now, there is no way you could hurt me that I couldn't recover from."

"This is wrong," Michael mumbled against the finger. "I was supposed to be better than this."

"What happened to trusting what was before your eyes?" Jacob dropped his hand and knocked up Michael's chin with the knuckle of his index finger. "This doesn't have to be anything more than what you want it to be. And for right now, you can want to just stay. No one else is coming. It's just the two of us, for as long as you want it to be. Can you give up the pretense of doing your abuser's work for him, though?"

Michael nodded, his throat thick. "Yeah."

"Good." Jacob smiled, and it was like the sun. "Now, eat. And when you're done, I'll show you more of what I've been doing."

He made it through most of his pasta, but still ended dinner lighter than he'd felt in weeks. Months. Maybe even since before he'd met Nate.

His abuser. It kept ricocheting around his head.

How long he could stay here, holed up like this, was something he didn't want to think about. But at least for now, he'd found a place that was safe, a person who salved the wound that his heart had become.

"Thank you for telling me your story," Jacob said, once they'd eaten enough of their meal that there was barely anything left. "I know it wasn't easy to do so, and I appreciate you being honest with me. It's rare to find someone who trusts me enough that they're willing to do that."

"I don't know why that is. You seem trustworthy to me." Michael couldn't imagine anyone meeting Jacob and not falling for him. "Even if you do wear socks in the tub."

Jacob rolled his eyes. "You're never going to get over that, are you?"

"Nope," Michael replied, popping the end of the word and grinning. "I'm not. How long will it take you to get sick of me because of it?"

"Two hundred years, give or take." Jacob shrugged. "I'm resilient."

Michael got up and started stacking empty plates, allowing Shiri to steal the last piece of grated parmesan that had fallen onto the table. "Good, because I'm not going to be ready to give you up for at least that long."

It felt so normal and domestic to be bickering over dinner that Michael could have cried. This was what he'd been missing for so long, the part of being with someone that he craved. It was intoxicating all on its own.

They headed back up to the third floor room where Jacob had been working on his incantation bowls, stopping to make a detour in Michael's room so he could change into a T-shirt he'd brought with him in the vague hope of working out, and so that he could force Jacob into a T-shirt too, on the premise that it was ridiculous to make pottery in a button-down. It also gave Michael the opportunity to laugh at the way his clothing swamped Jacob, even as it lit a flare of possession inside his chest, seeing Jacob's shoulder slip out of the collar of the V-neck.

"It hadn't been working for me, so I want you to try." Jacob cut a new hunk of clay and plopped it on the plastic-coated table.

"That's because you're not doing it right." Michael took the clay and began digging his thumbs into the center of the lump, trying to form it into a respectable bowl this time. "None of your incantations are specific."

Jacob cocked his head. "You really think that's the difference between it working and not? What if the mazzekin I was trying to trap doesn't have a name, or distinguishable features? What if I don't know who or what I'm trying to trap?"

Michael didn't know everything that had been written on incantation bowls, but he did know that they typically contained three things: an entreaty to God to trap the demon, a specific demon they were trying to trap, and a depiction of the demon itself. "I think you would make it work by just calling it the mazzekin that was harming your cattle, or ruining your cooking, or whatever. You don't need to know its name, and the drawings were all very crude. They just feature something demonic looking with its feet bound. That's part of how they're trapped, besides the metaphor of the upside-down bowl. Most bound demons in Jewish folklore are said to have worn golden chains around their feet to keep them contained."

"The powerful ones, at least." Jacob exhaled. "That I know."

"Yes, the sheyd." This hadn't ever been Nate's main area of expertise—he was far more interested in the mundane than in the stories of powerful demons that had the ability to disguise themselves as humans, and who had been fought, and sometimes bound, by talented Jewish mystics—so Michael didn't know too much about them. "There are definitely incantation bowls trapping them, like with Lilith and her demonesses. They were more threatening because they could look like humans. God gave them that power, along with the ability to eat, drink, have sex, and even reproduce."

Michael prodded the clay into an even more bowl-like shape, careful to keep the edges from getting too thin again. "Sorry to lecture you. I know you probably know all this already, but I can't help myself. I've been told I go into lecturing mode too often."

"It's interesting to hear it from you, though." Jacob pulled another, smaller lump of clay and rolled it into a thin snake, then took Michael's rudimentary bowl from him and flipped it over, pressing the additional clay onto the rim. "I'm never upset to get a different take on the stories."

He righted the bowl and handed it back to Michael. "So would you let this dry first, or would you paint the incantation on it now?"

Michael stuck his tongue between his lips. "Maybe I'd dry it in the oven?" He had only the vaguest knowledge of pottery, but he knew that it had to go into the kiln to harden. "But I'm not really sure how to do that or what temperature to do it at."

"You look it up." Jacob scooped the bowl up in his hands, holding it in front of him like it was a crown he was presenting to a king. "I'll carry this downstairs."

"I'll kill you if you drop it." The words slipped out naturally, a jibe that he'd made countless times over the years, but unlike the last seven months, this time it didn't make him feel bad to say it. "I worked hard on that thing."

"I know." Jacob kissed him on the forehead as he made for the door. "It's beautiful."

Michael got up to follow Jacob, pulling out his phone to google how to fire clay in a home oven without blowing anything up or setting it on fire. "Don't blow smoke up my ass. It's hideous."

Jacob just turned and smiled at him, his hands coated in clay that Michael wanted to wash off the same way they had the other night. The thought made desire seep through him, but at least he still had enough willpower left to focus on the task at hand first.

"I think we should bake it for ten minutes at five hundred degrees." He paged through a few more results as they made their way into the kitchen, but that seemed like the most common answer. "And if it gets ruined, I'm going to have to make a new one, I guess."

"You got it." Jacob transferred the bowl to Michael's hands, since he was far less covered in clay, and rinsed himself off in the sink before setting the oven.

"How do you want to test this?" Michael turned the bowl around in his hands, wondering what it would have felt like to be doing this in a cottage in the middle of rural Eastern Europe, not for academic curiosity but instead for safety and security and hope. "I mean, I personally don't know how we'd tell if it was successful."

"We're going to see if we can get the mazzekin to be reined in." Jacob fiddled with the collar of his borrowed T-shirt. "I thought we could set up in the sanctuary and use you as bait, and then we'd see if you could use the bowl to trap them. I assume that I'd be able to see some result of them being bound."

Michael had nearly forgotten that Jacob had claimed he could actually see the demons in the archive. He cocked his head at Jacob, because if he was in for a penny, he was in for a pound, and he was determined to believe. "What do they look like?"

"The mazzekin?" Jacob scrunched up his nose and narrowed his eyes. "Um, they're small. They're kind of… cat shaped? But they're not furry. I would say it looks more like scales than anything else, but they don't feel like snakes. And they have much bigger teeth than cats do, and longer tails. Perfect for causing trouble. I've seen them walk on all fours but also on just their hind legs, and they come in plenty of different colors but most of them have pitch-black eyes, no irises like cats have. And then there are the wings. Like bats. Their ability to fly makes them particularly annoying and hard to catch."

Michael didn't know what to say other than, "Sounds cute?"

"Kind of." Jacob took the bowl back from Michael and popped it into the oven, which had beeped to indicate it was at temperature. "I'd be more inclined to say they were adorable if they weren't troublemakers. These ones are fine for the most part, if you give them the attention they crave and the right offerings at the right times. Others are much ornerier."

Michael peered into the oven, clicking on the light to see whether the bowl was still in one piece, or whether it had been immediately shattered. "What other kinds of demons can you see?"

"All sorts." Jacob shrugged. "They're everywhere."

"And everyone in your family can? What about Eleazer?"

"Him too." Jacob leaned back against the counter, his forearms on the marble and his wrists draped over the sides, the crescents of his nails dark with clay. "I think that was, in part, why he was so interested in what he studied. He could see whether or not his experiments were working. I suspect there are so many mazzekin here because he trapped dozens, if not hundreds, before he died. He'd moved on to more… practical experiments, moving things out of the realm of the purely academic, in his last two years. I found some of the incantation bowls trapping them, but me shattering them in the kitchen sink didn't break the spell."

"Or they just liked it here." Because where else would they go? "They have lots of stuff to mess with, you can see them and you believe they're there, so you give them a lot of attention—it's the perfect setup, isn't it? It's practically a small demon playground here."

Jacob shook his head and sighed. "Unfortunately."

The timer that Michael had set on his phone dinged after ten minutes, and he opened the oven door to find the bowl lighter and decently dried-out looking. He grabbed a kitchen towel off the oven handle and used it to pull the bowl out and set it on the counter. Jacob immediately prodded it with a finger.

"That's hot!" Michael grabbed his hand and pulled it away. "Don't touch that, you'll burn yourself."

"I'm very burn resistant, I assure you." Jacob shook him off but tucked his hands into his pockets. "It looks done."

Michael wrapped the bowl in the towel, totally not understanding how Jacob touched it with his bare skin as the heat seeped into his palms. He cradled it to his chest as they made their way into the archive room, Jacob brandishing a Sharpie.

"I think it's supposed to be done in ink." Michael let Jacob open the door and flick on the lights—the ones that weren't shattered, anyway. "Like with a quill, or a paintbrush, or something."

"This *is* ink," Jacob grumbled. "We cooked it in a gas oven, Michael. Do you think they had those in ancient Israel? I can assure you, they did not."

It was a fair point. Michael sat down on the floor in the

center of the aisle and put the bowl down on the carpet, cradled in the kitchen towel. "Give me the Sharpie, then."

Jacob sat down across from him so they were knee to knee, the bowl between them. He handed over the marker and Michael bit his tongue, thinking of the right words to use. Ultimately, he went with a classic version, asking God and every angel whose name he could remember how to spell in Hebrew to bind, seal, counter seal, hobble, and silence the mazzekin in the archive room for as long as the bowl stayed intact. The bowl was probably too small, and he had to cram the words in to fit it all, spiraling from the edges to the center. For good measure, he wrote out one of the shorter names of God from the mystic tradition, and then handed the bowl over to Jacob. "You've got to sketch it. I can't draw."

With his tongue between his teeth, Jacob accepted the marker and started to draw, rendering a surprisingly lifelike version of what he had described in the kitchen. Michael watched him until there was a loud *thunk* from behind him that made his head whip around.

"Right on time," Jacob said, sketching the tail. "Just keep ignoring them. Or project the fact that you don't believe what you're seeing in their general direction."

The sound had come from a book falling off the top shelf of the nearest bookcase, landing on the ground with its pages splayed open. Michael watched as another book teetered closer to the edge of the shelf, like a cat was testing its owner and trying to grab their attention by gradually pushing something breakable off a table.

Michael did his best to think loudly in the general direction of the shelf that no, this had nothing to do with the supernatural, and it was probably from very weird air currents in the building, or maybe Shiri had somehow snuck onto the shelf behind the books and was now pushing them out one by one to make a mess.

Jacob shook with laughter as four books flew out at once, violently this time, crashing against the opposite shelf before smacking down to earth. "Nice work."

He tossed the bowl into Michael's lap, and Michael took it in hand. "So ordinarily you'd want to bury this, but because we can't do that in here—unless you want to tear up your floorboards—we're just going to have to go for the symbolic."

"Sure." Jacob nodded. "Try it."

Michael took the bowl and closed his eyes, pretending he was doing this the right way, thousands of years ago, a bowl commissioned from a mystic and blessed by a rabbi, a last-ditch effort to save a child or a marriage or protect a home.

It wouldn't work if he didn't believe, he knew that in his bones. But luckily, that wasn't a problem anymore.

The constant noise of books thumping to the ground ceased the second that Michael sent up a quick prayer to God and overturned the bowl onto the carpet with a hollow sound.

He opened his eyes to see a book teetering on the edge of the shelf, too far gone to be suspended there by anything other than a hand holding it. Or a tail.

"It worked," Jacob breathed. "You did it."

"They're frozen?"

"That one is." Jacob pointed to something Michael couldn't see. "And that one too. I only see the two, but they're not moving for once. It actually worked."

"See?" Michael couldn't keep the smugness out of his tone. "I told you that you needed to make it specific."

He reached down and plucked the bowl up off the carpet, turning it right-side up. The book remained suspended in air, so he stood up and offered a hand to Jacob, pulling him up to stand beside him. "Break it."

"Me?" Jacob raised an eyebrow. "You made it work."

"You're wearing shoes," Michael countered.

Jacob's eyes crinkled in a smile as his heel came down on the bowl, the sound of snapping clay followed almost immediately by yet another thump as the suspended book hit the ground.

"And they're gone." Jacob pointed to the ceiling. "Escaped up into the rafters. Probably wary of getting caught again. Maybe I'll have to bribe them less now they know there's someone around to punish them."

"I wouldn't." Michael bent down to scoop the sections of pottery into the towel, wrapping them up for safety's sake. "I don't think it's right, trapping them like that."

"You don't?" The question was quiet and soft, and Jacob searched Michael's face like he was looking for honesty and didn't think he'd gotten it.

"They're annoying, and they're causing property damage, but so do cats and we don't chain them up. I think that unless they're actively hurting people, they should be allowed to roam free. But it doesn't hurt that they know we can punish them. Like you said, maybe they'll behave better." Michael ran a hand down Jacob's shoulder. "I'm not in the habit of trapping things that aren't supposed to be chained, not unless they have to be."

"Oh," Jacob breathed. And then, without saying why,

Jacob stood up on his tiptoes and flung his arms around Michael, burying his face in Michael's shoulder. From the wet coldness against his skin, it felt like he was crying, and Michael didn't understand why, but grief could surface in strange ways. So, he held Jacob as tightly as he could for so long that it felt like he had never been anywhere else but here.

# Chapter 13

Michael had gone to bed far later than usual, after promising Jacob that he would keep looking into his research project in the morning, now that all pretense of working on Nate's research had been disposed of. He'd also, against his better judgment, said he'd help Jacob work his way through the secondary source books that he was committed to reading for his research. He wanted to eke out as much time as he could with Jacob each day, and he wondered if it would be possible to reset his body's clock so that he went to sleep and woke up at the same time as him.

He wondered when he was going to get the chance to see Jacob's room and spend the night with him. But it had been just under a week, and Michael hadn't been told to leave, so maybe his basically moving into Jacob's room was too much, too fast. He wasn't going to push, not on that.

So, on his fifth day in the archive, six days after arriving at the Institute, he made his way down to the kitchen to get breakfast, finding a stash of frozen waffles in the freezer that he made for himself with a generous amount of butter on top, flicking through his phone while he did so. He responded to his parents' texts and still hadn't gotten anything from Sarah. He finally responded to his clients that he'd have to postpone working on their projects for personal reasons and could refer them to another translator if it were urgent, and left it at that.

He didn't really intend on going back. Who knew where the path would lead from here, but it wasn't back to his old life. It was somewhere forward, somewhere he couldn't yet see, but even with that uncertainty he felt steadier than he had in years. Something about telling Jacob his story the night before felt like scouring a wound clean. It had hurt, and it was still raw, but there was none of the urgent pain and heat of infection. Contrary to everything that Michael wanted to admit, talking about it had actually helped.

It felt like cleansing the past—at least in this small way—allowed him to contemplate the future. His lease was up in two months, and he'd had vague plans of trying to find another place to live, one that wasn't so full of memories. Maybe he would make a short trip back to the city to pack up his stuff and sell his furniture, then use the money he wasn't spending on rent to buy a car instead of renting one. He needed to talk to Jacob about how serious he was with his offer to stay *here*, but even if that was a bridge too far, he could find somewhere nearby to settle down. Maybe he could work in the café or the bookstore and tutor on the side for one of those online companies that taught kids the SATs. It wasn't going to be nearly as hard to make ends meet here, not like it was in the city.

Thinking about that led him to thoughts of the joint bank account that he hadn't been able to bring himself to touch since Nate's death, the one that his family must not have known about because it hadn't been reclaimed or emptied or shut down or whatever happened to accounts after someone died. The one with nearly two million dollars in it from Nate's trust, money he had transferred over a month before he died because he'd been talking about buying them a bigger apartment, insisting that it was embarrassing they were still living in a one-bedroom because they could do so much better, no matter how attached Michael was to the small space.

He hadn't been sure what to do with it and had tried extraordinarily hard not to think about it, but now he wondered if he wasn't owed it. Damages for pain and suffering, in a way, which he could use to start a new life after everything Nate had taken from him. Years, and security, and self-confidence, and his physical well-being. His career and his friends and his very sense of self.

Michael knew he may not find a way to get all of that back, but that didn't mean he wasn't going to try. At least now he could name what he had lost. What had been done to him.

*He abused me. He deserved it.*

Jacob had left his notes for Michael in a disused storage room, full of dust-covered boxes and an old, sagging armchair in the corner. It was positioned by a window, with a lumpy footstool in front of it, and when Michael brought Jacob's notebooks over to start reading through them, he found it surprisingly comfortable. The window let in more than enough light to read by, and with the silence and the dust motes that were swirling in the sunbeams, Michael almost felt like he was back in the library on his college campus.

The Institute had so quickly become a safe place.

Jacob's notes had been made in nearly a dozen languages, some of the notebooks old and battered, bound in scratched-up leather like the ones Michael liked to use, others newer and more pristine, the ink still a rich black. He tried to determine if there was rhyme or reason to what language was used when, but gave up when he found no discernible pattern, instead focusing first on the notes in English.

Jacob was clearly a masterful researcher and an even better scientist. He was the kind of man who would have been a famous mystic had he lived five hundred years ago, someone who became known by a single name or an acronym and whose wisdom was handed down through the generations. There were biblical verses matched with sections from the Gemara, modern day principles of physics and chemistry intertwined with old folktales. It was a life's work, all on the subject of how incantations far stronger than the one they'd formed last night could be broken.

As he flipped through the pages, Michael wondered why Jacob was so focused on incantation bowls, and why he'd failed to realize that the ineffectiveness of the ones he'd formed had to do with missing the essential parts. It was a bizarre oversight from a man who seemed brilliant, but then again, Michael was intimately familiar with how grief and not being in the right mindset for research could fuck with the ability to do good work.

An incantation bowl was one way to bind a demon of the sort Jacob was interested in, but as Michael had said, these were enchantments that weren't meant to be undone. Jacob seemed to be searching for his own solution, a hole in the spell work and incantations that were traditionally used on the bowls to bind demons, or other methods of capturing and binding various evil creatures.

The more Michael read, the more he became convinced that this was far outside his current capacity, and that, at least at the moment, he was going to be of limited use to Jacob. But he wanted to try to help, and so he paged through the rest of the journals, following Jacob's thought process and aching at each one of the dead ends that he had meticulously documented.

Seeing demons must have given him a unique sympathy for the creatures. Michael wondered if that was, in part, what was driving him. What he planned to do with the knowledge. Whether Eleazer's trapping of mazzekin in the archive had made it so that Jacob wanted to set them all free.

A shudder went through him as he wondered what else Eleazer had trapped. Had the old man been after something more powerful than a household demon? Had he been trying to trap one of the far more powerful sheydim? A dybbuk? Had he reached too far and had that been what killed him?

It was a strange thought to have, and Michael didn't quite know where it came from. But Jacob had never said how, exactly, his grandfather had died. Just that it was after an illness—but was the illness physical, or a drive to do something that was haunting his mind?

He tucked the musing away, because he wasn't exactly going to pry. Jacob was clearly still grieving his grandfather, and he hadn't wanted to talk about the circumstances of his death. Michael owed it to him to respect that boundary. When Jacob was ready to discuss it, Michael would be there the same way Jacob had been for him.

They had nearly run out of food, and when Michael's alarm for lunch went off, he searched through the fridge and decided they needed to restock. Grabbing his coat, he headed out to the car, twirling his keys around his finger. As he settled into the driver's seat, he looked up at the Institute's façade, at the ivy that was curling up the building and the way the afternoon light played off the rose window in the building's center. He wondered what it would look like in the snow, in the summer, whether he could help restore the garden and the landscaping in the front of the building. What it would be like to turn this place into a home, instead of merely an archive. What it would feel like to honor the soul of the building, to return it to its bones as a place of community and love and togetherness, even if it was only for the two of them.

As he looked, he noticed the small row of windows right underneath the slate-gray roof tiles. Counting up, he realized that they belonged to the fourth floor, the part he hadn't explored yet. It had occurred to him that Jacob's room must be up there somewhere, unless there was a room on the third floor that he had somehow missed. Jacob had said it wasn't safe up there, but maybe he just meant for Michael—maybe he knew the building well enough that he was comfortable skirting the dangerous areas that had been affected by the water damage. The peaked roof likely meant that the fourth floor had incredible ceilings, and Michael could hardly blame Jacob for wanting to take advantage of that while simultaneously not wanting visitors to fall through the floorboards.

The sun was hitting the windows at an angle, and Michael squinted as he threw the car into reverse. He got one last glance at the top floor and found that several of the windows were cracked open on the left side. If it wasn't where Jacob was staying, he'd have to tell him that the windows were left open. With the storm a few nights ago, he didn't want any water that had seeped inside to be left to sit, not with a treasure trove of invaluable documents and objects directly below.

For a second, it looked like there was movement behind the glass, something tall and black and broad, a shadow that wasn't human-shaped and didn't make sense to his eyes. But then it vanished, and Michael decided it must have been a trick of the light—or a mazzekin playing tricks to get back at him for trapping them in the archive the night before. His stomach growled, and he put the car in drive, debating whether to grab a sandwich at the café before buying groceries. By the time he was on the road in front of the Institute, the only thing on his mind was what he and Jacob would do that evening.

Michael spent the afternoon massaging his arms, sore from lugging multiple bags of groceries to the kitchen from the car, and looking through some of the journals Jacob had kept in languages that were quicker for him to translate, like Hebrew. When he ran out of those, he started to eye the boxes of objects that were scattered around the room.

The boxes were neatly stacked, labeled in Jacob's meticulous script. Perhaps everything had looked like this before Eleazer had died, or maybe it had been a mess and Jacob had spent months cataloguing everything and sorting it away. Skimming the labels, it seemed like everything in the room was devoted to Jacob's own research. So Michael selected a box at random and hefted it up, his arms burning. He set it down on the floor, because he didn't want to take it all the way down the hall to the nearest room with a table in it.

Lifting the lid released a puff of dust and paper particles, the familiar smell of very old things that Michael wished he could bottle up and keep with him forever. The box had some notebooks at the bottom, stamped with *E.S.*, and on top rested a small wooden box. He picked it up, weighing it in his hands, and lifted the lid. Inside the velvet lining, a long chain rested in a coil. Michael lifted it out, letting the links slide through his fingers. Each one was an inch long with sharp edges, and when he squinted at them closer, he noticed writing on each of the links. He'd never seen something like this before, but as he read through the inscription, it became clear that this was the same kind of binding language that was used in the incantation bowls. It was an unusual artifact, and Michael wasn't quite sure how old it was. The metal wasn't tarnished, but then again, he had no idea what type of metal it was, just that it was roughly bronze in color.

He wound the chain around his hand, then over his wrist, trying to envision how someone might have used it.

Would it have been tied around an effigy of a demon? Would it have been placed across the threshold of a building that a spirit was said to reside in?

Whatever it was, it was something he'd have to ask Jacob about when he woke up. But as he went to put it back in the box, he realized that the chain was stuck around his wrist, holding fast even though there was no knot or lock or anything to hold it there.

When he gave a tug, trying to get loose, the chain tightened around his wrist, making him cry out. The sharp edges had pointed inward against his skin, and beads of blood were welling up from where the metal was cutting into him. The more he struggled with the chain, trying to pry it off himself with his other hand, the tighter it grew. When he flipped his hand around, he saw that the chain had somehow fused together, the links forming a bracelet around his wrist. Panic started to rise in his throat, the feeling of a hand gripping the bones of his wrist hard enough to hurt, to bruise, to crush coming back to him with sickening familiarity.

It felt like it was only getting tighter. Michael hissed as he tried to pull his hand through the loop and only succeeded in cutting a gash into his hand, which must have opened a vein because it started bleeding at a sickeningly fast rate. His heart was hammering fast with the pain and the panic, and he wanted to puke as he watched the blood flow out of his arm and onto his body, the contents of the box, the floor. He was literally watching his life drain away from him, and he was caught between being frozen to the spot with panic and frantic to get help.

He needed help with this, and he felt bad for it, but

he'd have to wake Jacob up. The sun was almost down, and Jacob would certainly be alright if Michael woke him up, because he was bleeding enough that it was possible that he'd pass out.

"Jacob?" he called as he stumbled out of the room, the chain dragging on the floor. Michael staggered as his vision blackened around the edges. He hadn't lost that much blood, had he? The only time he'd felt this way before was when he'd been lying on the pavement with a shard of rib sticking through his skin.

He made it halfway up the stairs to the fourth floor before he had to sit down, breathing hard. The edges of his vision blurred and he was nauseous, covered in blood and shaking from the pain. He tried again to pull the links away from his skin, but his fingers just slipped on the blood.

"Michael?" Jacob's voice floated through the edges of what felt like a fainting spell coming on. "What happened?"

Jacob knelt in front of him, a shadow falling over them both like Jacob was blocking out the light from overhead. And that was the last thing that Michael saw before he gave in and lost consciousness.

Michael woke up in bed, his body clear of blood and his left wrist and hand meticulously wrapped in gauze and resting elevated on a pillow. His whole hand throbbed, but the stinging pain was gone. It was dark, and there was an arm slung over his chest, Jacob pressed all along his back with his nose against the back of Michael's neck, his breath wheezing in and out.

"Jacob?" Michael turned, or tried to, but something was covering the rest of his body too, almost like the weighted blanket he used at home to help him calm down from panic attacks.

"Mmrmph?" came the mumbled answer, before Jacob's entire body jerked like he'd been electrocuted. He sat up, the weight on Michael immediately vanishing, and ran a hand through his hair, his eyes wild.

"Did you just wake up?" Jacob was staring at him, wide-eyed and ashen faced. "How long have you been awake?"

"Just now." Michael turned slowly, his entire body sluggish. "What happened?" He reached out his uninjured hand to Jacob, who took it. He couldn't tell if it was him or Jacob that was shaking.

"Oh." Jacob seemed to relax marginally. "Sorry, I must have dozed off. I didn't mean to fall asleep. Do you remember anything?"

"I remember you, and then I remember fainting." Michael sat up, his head spinning, and rested against the headboard. "You were able to get that thing off my wrist. Thank you."

Jacob let out a long, slow breath. "I'm so sorry. I should have warned you not to go through any of the boxes without me. Many of them contain Eleazer's own inventions, or artifacts that are frankly too dangerous for anyone to touch. You found one of them."

"A chain to bind demons." Michael glanced down at his wrist. "Except it seems to have latched on to me, too."

"Lucky you aren't a demon, or it wouldn't have come off without a fight." Jacob turned and leaned against the headboard too, slumping down against the pillows and resting his head on Michael's shoulder. "It's also a good thing that the counter-incantation was on the lid. Likely you weren't the first mystic to have accidentally latched those chains around your own wrists, or they wouldn't have needed to come with removal instructions. It seems like you don't remember this, but you were able to repeat the words when I read them to you. You freed yourself. I just cleaned out the lacerations so you wouldn't die of an infection. You needed a few stitches—I hope you don't mind. I like to think I'm relatively good with a needle and thread."

Michael swallowed, flushing with embarrassment that he'd been so foolish and gotten himself into enough trouble that Jacob had to rescue him and then do such extensive first aid. But he didn't seem angry or upset, just relieved, and so Michael didn't apologize like he normally would have. Instead, he decided to keep it academic. "What would they have done to a demon?"

"Bound them in service to the magician."

"Ah." That seemed distinctly unpleasant. "I guess there's a reason those aren't on display. It would probably be difficult to insure a collection that attacks the researchers who visit it."

Jacob chuckled. "I'm glad you're able to joke. You lost a lot of blood. I was worried I'd have to call 911."

"Instead, you played doctor and nurse." Michael gestured down his body, because he realized that he'd been changed into pajamas and was clean of blood. "Thank you for cleaning me up, too. You didn't need to."

It was so different than what Nate had done, hurting

him. Jacob had patched him back together instead. Cared for him and tucked him into bed instead of fracturing his ribs.

"I wanted to." Jacob kissed him on the cheek and brushed Michael's hair out of his eyes. Michael relaxed into the feeling of being cared for. "I don't get to take care of people very often. I enjoy it. Not that I enjoy you being hurt. But I do enjoy making you feel better."

"Oh?" Michael couldn't help but smirk. "And is that true of making me feel better in all sorts of ways?"

Jacob caught the hint, a wicked smile crossing his face before he slipped a hand underneath the blanket. "I can certainly think of a few ways to speed along your recovery."

And even though his hand was throbbing, and he still felt weak and dizzy, Michael lay back and let Jacob make him feel good. Jacob declined a return of the favor, instead settling on Michael's chest with his arm flung across his ribs, his fingers tracing the incision. When Michael looked down, it looked better than it had in months, no longer so red and raw.

"What do you think about me staying here for a while? I know we kind of mentioned it, but I wasn't sure—" The words tumbled out before he could lose his nerve.

He needn't have worried, because Jacob interrupted him. "Yes."

Michael looked down at him, and he was smiling. "Are you sure? I know it's really fast, like it's been a week, and I obviously can—I mean, I probably should—rent a place of my own, but I'd really like to keep seeing you, Jacob."

"Humans call it dating, Michael," Jacob replied with a

roll of his eyes. "And I'm frankly insulted that you would consider staying anywhere but here. There's plenty of room for both of us, and at this point I think Shiri might riot if you left. I've never given her as much attention as you do."

"Oh." Michael was surprised, but pleasantly so. "Thank you."

He ran his hand through Jacob's hair and wrapped his arms tighter around the other man's frame, letting the daydream of years' worth of nights exactly like this spool out in his mind's eye.

"I wish we could have met under different circumstances," Jacob whispered into his skin, his breath raising goosebumps on Michael's chest. "You deserved so much more than this."

"It's fine." Because it really was. Michael wasn't going to trade this for anything, even needing to come here as broken and sad and disgusted at himself as he'd ever been. "Right now is all that matters."

Jacob didn't reply, so Michael just held him until he drifted back to sleep in the black of night.

# Chapter 14

The next day, Michael immediately regretted his offer to help Jacob read through the books he'd sequestered from Eleazer's collection. The shelf he decided to tackle first was enormous, and as he picked three of the slimmer books off the shelf—they'd make for faster reading, and he'd feel more accomplished the more books he could check off the list—he felt like he was back in the second year of his master's degree, facing down an absurdly long reading list for his final exams.

At least Jacob probably wasn't going to test him on the contents.

He lugged the books to the sitting room, plopping them on the couch next to the laptop he'd finally fished out of his backpack. It would be easier and neater to type out his notes, since his handwriting was abysmal compared to Jacob's, and if he couldn't read what Michael wrote the effort would be for nothing.

Settling down into the cushions, he pulled the blanket off the back of the couch and draped it around his shoulders, wincing at the ache in his wrapped wrist, although it felt sore instead, like it had been sliced open. It was unusually dark outside for early afternoon, and when he checked the weather, he wasn't surprised to see that thunderstorms were predicted to start in an hour or two. It would be perfect weather for reading, if only he could motivate himself to work instead of dozing off.

Instead of reading, he indulged himself by opening an internet browser and searching for moving companies, wondering if he could just get Sarah to open his apartment for a crew and have them pack it all up and bring it here, so he didn't have to leave. The thought of going back to the place where he'd dealt with so much fear and uncertainty and pain filled him with dread, and he didn't relish the thought of having to go back and sleep in his old bed, the one he'd shared with Nate. There was nothing but bad memories there, now.

Shiri jumped onto the back of the couch and startled him by batting his head, which he took as a sign to start working, lest he admit to Jacob that he had done literally nothing all day. After wasting twenty minutes choosing the appropriate font and bullet points for his notes, he finally cracked open the first book and set about outlining the main argument.

He kept going for another thirty minutes before the lights flickered, except he didn't think it was due to a mazzekin wanting to play. The sky outside was nearly black, and as he got up to look out the window, a torrential downpour started. Shiri got up from the couch to hop onto the window seat, smacking at the glass with a paw to chase the raindrops that were cascading down the panes.

"Fuck," Michael cursed as the lights flickered again. He checked the weather on his phone, but the internet had gone out.

Wind whipped against the windowpanes, even fiercer now than in the last storm. Thunder and lightning were coming in fast, alternately shaking the archive's foundations and lighting up the sky; and the rain was so intense that Michael was not at all surprised when his phone lit up with a severe weather alert via SMS, notifying him that the National Weather Service had warned of flash floods until the morning.

He remembered, with a guilty twist in his stomach, that he'd forgotten to tell Jacob about the open windows he'd noticed the other day. "Fuck," he cursed again. But he was quite sure that Jacob would rather he wake him up while making sure the windows were secure than leave the archive to sustain yet more water damage. Plus, after where Jacob's tongue had been the night before, he figured Jacob had to be alright with Michael seeing him sleeping.

Jacob definitely slept on the top floor of the synagogue, because he'd come down the stairs from there yesterday when Michael needed help. So, he picked up his phone and started to climb, panting a bit by the second landing. Shiri trotted along after him, but when he set his foot on the bottom step to climb to the top floor, she jumped in front of him and let out a hiss.

"I know I might wake him up." Michael side-stepped her and made it to the second step before she puffed up her fur and skittered around his ankles like a crab. "But he's going to be more upset if I let his archive get soaked. It's probably not his room with open windows, not with how cold it is outside. I might be able to shut them and come back down without him even knowing I'm there."

She hissed again, and he took his life into his hands and scooped her up so that he didn't trip on her and break his neck, holding her close to his chest until she relented and stopped struggling. "I'll be quiet, I promise," he whispered into her ear.

True to his word, when he reached the door at the top of the landing, he opened it as quietly as possible and tiptoed in. It led to a foyer of sorts, with two doors on the right side and one on the left, and a massive window overlooking the back garden on the far wall. Michael put Shiri down so he could pull his phone out of his pocket and turn on the flashlight, and she promptly vanished back down the stairs. He scanned the floor to see if there were any obvious holes or roped-off areas, but the wide wooden planks that were visible along the edges of the perfectly preserved vintage Moroccan carpet in the center of the room looked pristine, perfectly shined and polished and clearly not structurally unsound. The damage must be in the individual rooms.

The left-hand door closest to him was where the open windows would be, but with the storm getting worse by the moment, he decided that waking Jacob up to at least ask him where the flashlights were was a necessity. So, he turned to the door on his right and knocked gently, not wanting to startle Jacob if he was awake somehow, maybe kept awake by the storm and the thunder still shaking the house.

When there was no response, he opened the door. It swung inward with ease, and Michael found himself in what must have been the mikveh room, since there was an immense copper tub resting in the corner, attached to a spigot with pipes climbing to the roof. Mikvehs were ritual baths that had to be fed with living water to properly purify those who were immersed, and it made sense that rainwater from the roof would be used to fill this one. It certainly rained enough, but Michael could also see how having a series of very old pipes on the top floor of a synagogue-turned-archive was a very perilous proposition.

What was more interesting, though, were the walls.

They were covered in Hebrew lettering, although it was too dark for Michael to see what they said properly without fumbling for the light switch. Lines of inch-high text wrapped around the plaster, and compared to the age of the rest of the decorations in the building, it looked fresh in the barely-there light coming in from the windows. Maybe it was just a weird way that Eleazer had decided to decorate.

Another clap of thunder rolled through the building, and Michael jumped. He made his way out of the room and to the next, knocking again and opening the door when, once again, he heard nothing. This room was expansive but felt small, crammed as it was with furniture that must have come from the synagogue's sanctuary. The jumble of pews was almost to the rafters, and while the room itself once again looked like it wasn't unsafe in the least, Michael could believe that the pews might fall over any minute and crush someone to death.

The walls were marked with the same kind of text, bands and bands of it reaching up to the ceiling on the walls that matched the outside of the building. The windows were bigger here, matching the enormous window in the foyer, and the light made it easier for Michael to squint at the lines in their totality.

It took him a few beats to realize what he was reading.

It was the same spell that a mystic would have written on an incantation bowl, except much longer. There were phrases Michael couldn't translate which must have been Aramaic, and others that detailed explicitly how a demon was to be bound, not to the will of the creator but permanently to the existence of the knowledge contained within the building.

Michael traced the words with the tip of a finger, then went back to the first room and read the beginning of the incantation by the light of his phone flashlight, even though he was loath to waste battery in case the power went out. It was definitely what it was—Michael was sure of it. It was repeated hundreds of times, and when he went back into the foyer and turned to face the door he'd come through, he realized they were painted on the back of the door too. A check behind the curtains hanging on either side of the window revealed fragmentary writing as well, the narrow strips of plaster too small to fit more than pieces of words.

He had a sinking feeling in his stomach. This didn't look or feel like decoration. Jacob's disgust at his grandfather's goal to trap demons swam to the forefront of his mind. But what had Eleazer intended to do with this?

It looked like he'd tried to turn the archive itself into

an incantation bowl. And if the walls were the sides of the bowl, then the ground he was standing on was the center.

Heart pounding, Michael knelt by the rug. Lightning flashed as he began to roll up the edge with shaking hands.

He stopped when he reached the outline of a face, the curve of a familiar brow, the shape of familiar lips.

Michael shot up from the floor like he'd been shocked, nausea roiling through him. Eleazer had drawn his own grandson where the depiction of a demon would go, and when he kicked more of the carpet back, there Jacob's hands were, bound with the same kind of chain that Michael had been trapped in the day before. There were wings and feet, also bound in chains and ending in taloned claws like a bird of prey.

It was Jacob.

Jacob, who never left the Institute. Jacob, who the café owner hadn't known about. Jacob, who hated his feet so much that he always wore two pairs of socks, even in the tub.

What if—

But no—*no.* Michael shook his head and rubbed a hand over his pounding heart. That was ridiculous, and seeing this didn't mean anything. There was a far simpler explanation, even if it was a sad one. It must have been some kind of dementia that caused Eleazer's death, and it made sense that Jacob would have moved in as a caregiver if that was the situation.

It must have been scary and sad to witness such a decline. It hurt that Jacob hadn't felt able to confide in him, but Michael knew it would come with time. It must have hurt Jacob even worse to have seen what his grandfather did, knowing that somehow, he'd come to equate his own grandson with the kind of evil that people sought to trap. And maybe if he reassured Jacob that he didn't care about all of this, that it didn't reflect poorly on him, that it wouldn't make Michael think less of an old man who was clearly in the throes of dementia or some other crisis, Jacob would feel better.

The final room on the top floor of the archive was pitch-black when he walked in without knocking.

"Jacob?" he called out, knowing this was where he'd find him. There weren't any other rooms left to search. "Are you in here?"

The windows *were* open—it was the first thing he noticed, cold air blowing in along with spurts of rain. There was a bed and a desk strewn with papers in the far corner of the room, but the rest of the room was bare. It resembled a prison cell, completely devoid of personalization. Here, too, the inscription wrapped around three walls, the only adornment.

"Michael."

Jacob's voice drew Michael's attention to the corner of the room closest to the windows, the one tucked nearly behind the open door. He could see the outlines of Jacob's face as he sat huddled in the corner, but the rest of him was wreathed in shadow.

"I told you not to come up here." Jacob sounded defeated more than anything. He scrubbed at his face, and Michael blinked because it looked like the shadows around Jacob were getting darker—although that must have been a trick of the light, or a sign that the storm outside had gotten worse. "But I guess thinking I could keep you away forever wasn't exactly realistic."

"The storm." Michael pointed at the open window, wondering why Jacob hadn't shut it despite being awake and clearly aware there was water coming into his bedroom. "I saw the open windows yesterday, and I wanted to shut them before you got more water damage on your hands. Plus, the lights have been flickering, and I wanted to see if you had flashlights before the power went out."

"Ah." Jacob tilted his head back against the corner with a sigh.

"If—If it was about what Eleazer did, I'm not going to ask you about it. You don't have to talk about it if you don't want to, Jacob." Michael bit his lip and wished that he'd thought to put the carpet back in place before he'd come in here. "I understand."

"No," Jacob said, pinching the bridge of his nose and bowing his head so that it nearly touched his curled-up legs. Michael desperately wanted to go comfort him, but Jacob didn't seem to want it. "You really don't. Fuck, Michael. It wasn't supposed to be like this."

That hit Michael like a punch to the gut. "Be like what?"

Jacob was silent for a long, long while. Michael sat down, four feet away from him, shivering in the cold. Despite everything in him that wanted to get closer, Jacob's entire posture compelled him to stay away.

"I've told you before, Eleazer Schechter was a collector. A scholar. An archivist." Jacob remained huddled in the corner, the darkness there too complete to be natural. He looked up at Michael, his green eyes practically glowing in the dark. "The collection he built here was one of the best in the country, perhaps the world. But he wasn't content with collecting books, or documents, or objects. He wanted to collect the creatures he read about too."

Michael stayed rooted in place, not sure if Jacob wanted him to come closer, or if he needed to have his space. "I know. You told me. Like the mazzekin."

"Like the mazzekin." Jacob nodded. "Like Shiri. She does enjoy the toilets, you know. I think her sense of humor is rather twisted, that she spends part of her time as a cat. Since, you know, they don't like water. It's prettier than her normal form, anyway. That one is quite scaly."

Jacob was talking about his cat like she wasn't a cat. And he was looking dead serious while doing it, the hollows of his cheeks more pronounced than ever. Michael waited for him to laugh, the way he'd laughed when he'd teased Michael in the archive about how he saw demons. But the laughter didn't come.

Michael wondered how seriously he should take all this. Was this the logical conclusion to his long-awaited breakdown, or was Jacob having a breakdown instead?

"I haven't been honest with you," Jacob said, swallowing audibly. "I didn't know how to tell you. And, well, you seem to have solved that problem for the both of us, because here you are."

"Jacob, I don't know what you mean."

Michael moved to kneel in front of Jacob, but the other man withdrew further into his corner, flinching away from Michael's touch.

"It's okay," Michael soothed, trying to be the same reassuring source of comfort that Jacob had been for him over the last few weeks. "Whatever you need to tell me, it's alright. I— You can tell me anything, and we'll be fine.

You've already seen the worst in me. Let me do the same for you." He didn't know what Jacob had to tell him, but none of it could be that bad.

Jacob looked up at him with red-rimmed eyes full of grief so deep, Michael thought he might drown in it.

"This will be the end of us," Jacob rasped, and Michael could feel the fear in it.

"No," he said with as much conviction as he could muster, reaching out to cup Jacob's cheek in a hand, thumbing across the ridge of his cheekbone. "No, it won't."

Because it had happened. Michael had fallen hard and fast and deep for this man who carried sorrow with him everywhere he went, who had helped him see his own mind in a new light while helping him past his grief, intelligent and beautiful and captivating and more solid than anything else Michael had ever encountered.

"Remember that promise," Jacob whispered, a single blood-red tear falling from his eye and onto Michael's finger, "when I tell you everything."

And then he sighed, and the air shifted, energy crackling through Michael's chest and zapping against his skin. Jacob shook his head like a dog trying to get dry, and when he looked back up his irises were a bright, crimson red. His face retained the same ethereal beauty, but somehow sharper and more inhuman, his skin as white and perfect as marble.

But the thing that shocked Michael to his core was the wings.

They shimmered into view, two towering arches that reached several feet above Jacob's shoulders, the edges covered in tiny, iridescent black scales that glistened like oil, tipped with an obsidian claw. The webbing was jet black and leathery, like the wings of a bat. They perfectly filled the space that before had looked like the darkest of shadows.

"It's not all of it." Jacob's voice was hoarse. "It's what makes sense to mortal eyes, but even this is a relief, not having to hide. Before sundown, I'm only able to blur my form, not change it completely."

He wouldn't meet Michael's eye, and when he reached down to peel off his rainbow-striped socks, he revealed feet that looked like a hawk's, covered in the same black scales, with powerful-looking talons jutting from the toes. He rubbed at the arches, the toes flexing, and sighed. "It hurts to keep them in shoes, but as you can see, I wasn't lying about them being ugly."

Jacob's laugh was tired, and sad, and Michael's overloaded brain could only compute that he was seeing something which made no sense, but that he'd been ordered to trust his own eyes, to believe his own mind.

He reached out and ran a hand over the arch of the right wing, and Jacob shuddered.

"I'm ticklish," he said, the wing flinching under Michael's fingers. The surface was hot, warm like an electric blanket, the same as Jacob's skin always had been.

"Jacob," Michael managed to get out in a moment of sharp mental clarity that hurt like a knife being slid between his vertebrae. "What are you?"

"You would call me a sheyd." Jacob licked his lips. "A demon."

Michael wasn't quite sure whether to scream or laugh or try to run away.

"Before you ask," Jacob said, raising a hand, "yes, this is real. Your brain isn't playing tricks on you. I hope that over the last few days, I've helped you see that much. I wanted you to trust me, when I gathered the courage to tell you."

Michael was kneeling two inches away from a demon, and he believed.

"Who are you?" he asked. "How did you come to be here?"

"I've had many names over many lifetimes. The first one I remember humans giving me is Bagdana. They bound my feet but gave me a weapon, because when they pulled me through the void there was another demon there, and I killed him. I was a slave and a savior both, and I was trapped until I bargained my way free. But then my name was known, and I wasn't allowed to rest. In another generation I was called back once again, the great-granddaughter of the magus who brought me to the mortal world in the first place requiring me to serve her."

Michael was rooted in place, every nerve of his body on fire, the instinct of a prey animal stopping him from moving, even as his heart jackhammered in his chest.

He believed.

He believed, and he was terrified. For the creature in front of him, and what this meant for everything he knew.

"It became a cycle, a few years of rest in my home, the middle world, followed by an excruciating trip to the mortal realm, the wear and tear on my physical form getting worse every time." Jacob ran a hand through his hair. "Sometimes it was better than others. Some of my captors became my friends. King David and his lover

Jonathan were wonderful to be around. They threw the best parties, and they kept me on a long leash, as long as I helped protect Israel from my brethren."

He gave a weak laugh. "Some humans I befriended, others I loved, some I just fucked. There were those I wanted to rip to shreds, and a few I managed to. The human world changed every time I came back. The evils that people wanted me to do altered. I've fought on battlefields and researched in weapons laboratories, overseen slavers building monuments to kings and pharaohs and tzars and emperors. I've been a spy and an assassin and a general and a never-ending pawn in the games of men. And I am so, so tired, Michael."

He closed his eyes and tipped his head back against the wall, resting against one of the lines of text written there.

"You can't see my shackles now, because Eleazer didn't need them. He bound me into this house as if it were a bowl, leaving me free to roam yet powerless at the same time. Able to do parlor tricks and speak with others like me, but unable to command any real magic. When I killed him, I had to do it with my bare hands, ripping his flesh from his bones, an ancient way of killing that I hadn't given in to for a thousand years. I consumed him. I turned his bones into dust. I thought his death would break the hold his incantation had on me, but I was wrong. He died and left me here, and now I'm trapped."

Jacob slumped even further into himself, the drooping of his wings showing defeat in every line of his body. Michael wondered at the lack of fear that Jacob's confession inspired in him, the absence of an urge to get up and bolt away from danger. Because Jacob had killed Eleazer, apparently, but Jacob had never hurt *him*. He hadn't done anything to Jacob that would warrant being hurt. Michael knew, with the rational part of his brain, that even if Jacob was dangerous to others, he wasn't dangerous to *Michael*. He wouldn't be, without cause.

And Michael wasn't about to give him cause.

"I…" Jacob sighed. "You thought you were evil because you accidentally caused a death in service of saving your own life. I've killed thousands, Michael, so many I cannot even name them. I know death prayers in dozens of languages spoken by men, because I've wrought a path of destruction through this world long before even your ancestors walked the earth. I'm no benign demon like Shiri or the mazzekin, content to cause trouble or lurk near humans but never truly causing harm. I'm a weapon. I'm a tool. I'm death become flesh. I've been the last sight of mortals for millennia."

Michael didn't know what to say, because there was real grief undergirding those words. And suddenly it all made sense, the weight of the grief that Jacob carried. Of course it wasn't about the death of one man. It never had been. Some of the fear gathering in his chest eased into a soft, sad sense of pity for this creature, who bore such a heavy burden and had no one to share it with.

"Now that you see me, now that you *really* see me, do you still consider yourself a monster?" Jacob's laugh was harsh. "Now that you know what I am, do you truly still think you're the evil one?"

"You can't help it," Michael croaked, his throat dry with pity he hadn't been able to conquer. He tried to stuff it down, because he didn't want Jacob to hear. "People made you do things. Would you have killed if you hadn't been summoned?"

"When I'm here, it's my lot. In many ways I'm condemned." Jacob hugged his chest, the spectral wings draping over his shoulders like a shroud. "I have chosen each one of those deaths. I could have defied my captors and suffered for it. It's in my nature to consume. It's in my nature to deceive. And unlike humans, the Lord our God created me to be this way. You have the potential for redemption. I do not."

"That's—" Michael was torn between being pinned in place with the horror of it all, and falling into a sick, twisting anger that was burning its way through his chest. "You don't get to claim that. You don't get to absolve yourself of your actions by saying that you're powerless to change. That's the lie you're telling yourself."

"It's not a lie," Jacob spat back, his eyes flashing. "And even if it was, it's a lie you would benefit from believing. Because when you spend your existence trying to fight against your nature, you deny your true self. And maybe that's the worst sin of all, not allowing yourself to be who you're supposed to become."

Michael couldn't help the whimper that escaped his lips. "I never wanted to be a murderer. I never wanted to kill the man I loved."

"Not even when you realized, deep down, that the man you loved would have been perfectly alright with killing *you*?" Jacob flung up his arms and snarled in frustration, causing Michael to fall back, bracing his hands on the floor. "He was beating you bloody, Michael! I can see the story written on your skin, in every way that you've tried to protect yourself from the reality since you got here. And I wish I hadn't, because if I hadn't grown to care for you, all of this would have been easier."

And the way he looked at Michael then, with so much pain and fear and rage that Michael didn't know how he was holding it all in—that look made Michael freeze.

"All of what," he whispered, "would have been easier?"

Jacob pinched the bridge of his nose and shook his head, blowing out a breath. "What I've done to try to get free. Repeating what has been done to me."

"And what is that?" Michael tried to take a step back, but his feet felt rooted to the floor.

"Gather enough power to break my bonds, assuming such a thing is possible." Jacob reached out, because they were still close enough to touch, and when his hand cupped Michael's cheek it was shaking. "It isn't easy to do, you see."

He laughed, but it was broken and wet, his eyes shining. The whites were faintly red yet again, and Michael wondered with horror whether it was because Jacob was crying actual blood. "When Eleazer summoned me here and trapped me, he did it well. The amplification of the incantation bowl, the power of the incantations—it bound me more thoroughly than I've ever been bound. It isn't my first time trapped in the mortal realm. I've been the servant of kings and queens, rich men and poor, but never before was I summoned without a mandate, for the pure purpose of being trapped and kept. I had no purpose to fulfill. I had no way to earn my freedom. And that is why I killed him, in an effort to try to break my bonds; and why, when that failed, I sought another man to break me free."

"Someone else who would believe." Michael's voice was hoarse. "Because Nate would have been fascinated. He would have listened. He would have seen it as the crowning achievement of his career to find a way to undo your bonds, even if he never got to tell another soul about it."

Because Nate had loved power over others, and setting a demon free would undoubtedly have earned him a debt. Because he had the hubris to think that he was doing the right thing, if he chose to let a creature like this go free.

Jacob's hand was still on his cheek, and Michael reached up a hand to cover it, interlacing their fingers. "You say that devastation is in your nature." Michael licked his lips. "So how can I trust that if I let you go free, you're not going to use that freedom to hurt someone?"

"You can't." Jacob pulled away, but Michael didn't let him go. It felt important, somehow, to keep him there. Like Michael's physical presence was what kept him contained, and not the words wrapping around the walls of the room. "And besides, the only way I've been able to even contemplate breaking the incantation is with a sacrifice of enormous magnitude. One which, fuck me, I no longer feel quite able to make. Not this time. Not in that way."

Michael's heart stopped entirely at the implication there.

"You see," Jacob croaked, "when you stepped across the threshold, I bound us together. I drenched my hand in the blood from your wound that first night and consumed it. After that, every moment we shared brought us closer. I was wrapping your soul around my own so that when I murdered you, I would be able to extract the most power possible from your death. Sex is one way to bind two people. So are quiet moments alone. So is shared laughter. So is caring for someone who has been hurt."

It felt like being slapped. "Was… was any of it real?"

"All of it, after that first time." Jacob's small smile was sad, the lines of his face betraying profound exhaustion. "And therein lies my problem. I realized, as I fell for you, that I was going to be unable to carry out my plan. That I would never be able to kill you, because you were one of the humans I had fallen for."

Michael's heart was pounding hard enough that he felt dizzy. He shifted on the floor so that he was sitting propped up against the wall. "What does it mean, to be bound to you?"

"That you can never leave me," Jacob admitted. "The binding will grow tighter over time. Physically, you would be able to travel, but you would always be compelled to return to my side. You will be pained if you don't. Failing to obey the will of the binding could prove too overwhelming for your mind. It would be fatal."

The floor was cool under Michael's palms as he pressed his hands to the floorboards for stability. "And it's… permanent?"

"I can try to undo the binding," Jacob said slowly. "But with the amount of power I have access to now, it would likely be the end of me. I cannot truly die, but I would be reduced to a state of immobility, unable to do much besides exist."

Michael took a moment to process what Jacob was saying; that if Michael wanted to leave, wanted to be free of Jacob, he would give him that option. But that it would come at a price which Michael found himself not actually willing to pay.

"So I'm the reason you're going to be trapped." The feeling made his heart hurt. "You're going to let me walk free and you're going to stay here, bound and miserable, and it sounds like pretty much effectively *dead*, and I'm going to be alone again, thinking about you."

"We trap the ones we love." Jacob blinked at him. "Whether that's in memories or cycles of abuse, or genuine care and devotion, it doesn't matter. Love is to capture someone. Love is letting yourself be captured. The question is whether you let those bonds anchor you, or whether they feel like chains."

Michael's heart skipped a beat for a reason entirely different from fear. "Is that a confession?"

"I believe it is." Another slow, sad smile cut across Jacob's face. "I've enjoyed this time together, Michael. Thank you."

And there it was, a dismissal wrapped in a compliment. As though once again, Michael wasn't worth holding on to. That death, or something like it, was better than being with him. The anger that flared through his chest again washed his fear away, because Jacob couldn't be evil if he was willing to let him go, no more so than Michael. Both of them had done terrible things in the name of self-preservation, but what cornered animal wouldn't?

There were two monsters in this house, and Michael was one of them; if he couldn't condemn Jacob, it meant he couldn't condemn himself, either.

Michael raised himself back up to kneeling, then leaned forward and put his hands on Jacob's knees, bracing himself. "I'm not leaving."

"You're volunteering to die?" Jacob's eyebrows shot up.

"No." Michael tightened his grip on Jacob, like he was going to vanish if he let go. "I'm going to stay here with you. I don't think I could leave if I tried. I don't want you to break the binding between us. I want it to stay. You—Jacob, you cracked something open in me. You scraped me clean. I don't know what this says about me, but no one has ever seen me the way you have. No one has ever made me feel the way you have."

Jacob let out the tiniest stutter of breath. His eyes went wide.

"I want to stay here with you." Michael swallowed. "We can think about other ways to get you free. What happens if you're broken out of this place? Does that mean someone else can summon you?"

"I— Yes, I could be summoned by someone else." Jacob laid a shaking hand atop Michael's. "As long as I'm bound here, I'm safe from that, at least. And while I'd like to go back home—staying here drains my power considerably—it wouldn't be the first time that I've stayed somewhere in the mortal realm for decades."

"So as long as we find a way to keep you, say, supported by the binding instead of being trapped by it, you can stay here. With me."

"With you holding my leash." Jacob stood, talons scratching against the wood floor, and Michael stood with him.

"No," Michael corrected, the threads of a plan forming in his mind, all the lore and folktales and bargains and stories of demons he'd collected over the years with Nate coalescing together. "You cannot deny your nature.

I've nearly killed myself trying to deny my anger. I think we can make a bargain. Neither one of us is at the mercy of the other. We're each holding the other's chains."

"What do you want me to do?" Jacob was the one who was stock-still now. "What bargain do you wish to strike?"

"You gave me back my mind." Michael reached out to grab Jacob by the back of his neck, anchoring them to one another. "I want to give you back yours. I want to work with you to figure out how to loosen your bonds but keep you free from any other summonings, so you don't have to be a servant again. I want you to stay here, with me, and I want to stay with you. I want us to protect each other. I want us to be free together. I don't care what it takes. I don't care what I would have to help you do."

"You would let me live," Jacob breathed. "You would let me be who I am, and you would stay with me. Not to use me. To let me live."

"It's the only way I can repay you." Michael swallowed past the lump in his throat. "And as you said, I cannot condemn you without condemning myself. If I accept you, I'm accepting who I am. And that finally, finally feels right."

Jacob let out a shuddering sigh, and when he leaned forward, he kissed Michael like vengeance, and like a promise sealed.

# Chapter 15

Jacob submitted to being brought downstairs, and after Michael shut the windows in his room—he claimed he didn't mind the cold as he was always hot, and that the rain was refreshing, but Michael wasn't about to sit back and watch property damage happen—he bundled Jacob out of the room and into the foyer, where he noticed that Shiri was sitting on the rug, which was suspiciously back in place.

She winked at him, and there was a brief flash of very large fangs in a blunt, scaly head. His head spun, but he mouthed *thanks* to her anyway.

The way Jacob moved made more sense now that Michael could see all of him, the slight pitching forward that he did when he walked downstairs, since his wings had to flap to counterbalance their weight. He wrapped the tips of his claws around the edges of the steps for purchase, and Michael couldn't help but marvel at the whole of him, his eyes traveling from the tips of his wings on down. Jacob twisted his head back when Michael paused on the steps.

"Yes," he said dryly, although there was still a hint of a crackle in his voice and his eyes were still red-rimmed. "I have a tail. Deal with it."

Michael was vaguely embarrassed that he'd been caught staring. Before he wondered if it was unspeakably rude—he'd have to ask about all the conventions, if there were any, for being polite to sheydim—he reached out and touched the tufted tip, the rest of it covered in the same delicate scales that Jacob's wings were.

Jacob choked and grabbed for the handrail, white-knuckled. "You do *not* know what that means. Or what that feels like."

He yanked his hand away, cheeks flaming.

"Later," Jacob promised, heat in his eyes. "But I think we're overdue for a very serious conversation first."

Michael nodded and followed Jacob down to the first floor, back to the sofa where they'd spent the last few nights together. Jacob tucked his wings in around him and sat down, gesturing for Michael to join him. He did, settling against the opposite arm to give Jacob his space.

He was surprised how calm he was, how much he trusted in his gut instinct: that Jacob was telling the truth, that Jacob wouldn't hurt him. Above all, he believed in Jacob. He hadn't once, since the revelation, truly believed that what he was seeing was a construct of his own mind.

"I'm sorry." Jacob stared into the fireplace. He whispered something, and the logs there burst into flames. "I didn't mean to deceive you. No, that's not the truth of it. I *regretted* deceiving you once I came to know you. I want you to know that everything I said, everything I did, was genuine. None of that was a lie. It was only my nature that I concealed. The bond between us hasn't warped your emotions, either. Everything you felt was a product of your own mind."

Michael was still stuck on the fact that Jacob had just performed magic. "Can we start at the beginning?"

Jacob gestured expansively. "I'm all yours. Now you know I can't leave. Ask away. I owe you complete honestly."

"Did you just light a fire with magic?" The question sounded dumb when it left Michael's mouth. "And if so, what magic can you do?"

"Ordinarily, I'm one of the most powerful magicians on this or any plane." Jacob stared into the fire. "I can kill and heal, compel and bind, raise monuments and temples and bring down plagues. Now? Binding you and me together took most of the rest of my power, everything that I had collected from the release of Eleazer's soul. I can do small magic around the house: lighting fires, heating bathwater, or healing minor injuries. If you unwrap that bandage around your wrist now, you'll find it nearly healed. That's also why your scar is looking better. I decided it was time for it to begin fading away. I can return it to the original state, though, if you like."

He brushed a hand against his ribs, and realized that, yes, he didn't feel the burn there anymore. He didn't miss it, either.

"Were you the one who did… all the stuff around here? The bathtub? The shattering lights?" Michael didn't know why that, of all of it, would feel like a betrayal. Maybe because Jacob had coached him through believing in all of it, and if it was under pretenses that he'd arranged, it would feel like deception.

"Oh, no." Jacob dragged a hand over his face. "That was all the mazzekin. In a sign of how far I've fallen, I need to treat them like children to get them to behave. I'm pretty sure that most of what they do is to try to impress me. They won't listen to reason. Maybe you'll have better luck with disciplining them once you get to know them better. Although I'm pretty sure that Shiri summoned the locusts. She likes to do that, on occasion, just for a bit of sport."

Jacob flexed his toes, propped up on the footstool, and sighed. The talons glimmered in the light.

"You always wore socks because it's the one part of you that you can't alter."

"Correct." Jacob nodded like he was a schoolteacher and Michael was acing a lesson. "The feet were very inconvenient. They always are, nowadays. Back in Israel or Babylon, or even in the medieval world, everyone was alright with me walking around like this, especially given that, most of the time, I was summoned for intimidation or to do harm. But when evil became more subtle, no one wanted their captive demon to tip the world off with his feet." Jacob grimaced. "I really don't like the way they look, though."

"I think they're captivating." Michael wanted to run his finger down the obsidian and know what it felt like against his skin.

Jacob huffed. "Didn't peg you for a foot man."

"Don't distract me." Michael jabbed Jacob in the arm with a fingertip, and Jacob looked at him with surprise. Like he couldn't believe Michael still wanted to touch him. In response, Michael twisted around until his head landed in Jacob's lap. He jerked in shock, but when Michael laid a hand on his thigh just above the knee, Jacob settled.

He thought through the last several days, all the pieces he'd missed, all the little tells he should have put together into the obvious whole. The way that Jacob had done for him.

"Oh God." His hand tightened on Jacob's thigh. "I'm so sorry. I burned you with salt." He cringed.

"Yes," Jacob said, chuckling. "You did."

"You can't touch it, but you can *eat* it?" Michael turned his head so he could look at Jacob's face. "Frozen food is so full of sodium—how are you not dead?"

Jacob pursed his lips and shrugged. "Salt doesn't stop us. It burns, sure, but I can cross a salt barrier. And don't tell me you've never eaten food that gives you heartburn?"

The surrealism of the conversation started to sink in; the fact that he was sitting here and talking to an actual sheyd about the veracity of certain ritual protective practices after spending his whole life up until this point pretending like none of this was real. "You must have thought I was an idiot when I came in here and didn't believe in all of this."

"No," Jacob said softly, brushing a hand through his hair. "I admired the way you challenged yourself to grow. The thing that would have horrified me would have been if you refused to change. Then you'd be worse off than me. You'd be a prisoner in your own mind, not in a house. And that is the worst thing of all. As long as you trust your own mind, as long as you believe in what you see, no one can truly control you. Because then, at least you'll know you're right."

Michael closed his eyes, then coughed as a weight flew onto his chest. Shiri settled there, purring, and Michael wrapped his arms around her as Jacob settled a wing over them both like a blanket.

He felt the truth in what Jacob said. It settled in his bones where the fear had been.

"I see all of you, and I don't mind," he whispered, warm and content and finally, finally free from his past. "If you still want to wear socks around me, that's fine. If you want to hide your wings or your tail or your eyes, that's fine too. But I don't want you to think that it's necessary for me. You saw all of me, and you accepted it. I see all of you, and I'm doing the same."

"No one's ever said that to me before, not quite like that." Jacob sounded choked up, and the hand in his hair tightened. He breathed in, his stomach expanding against Michael's cheek. "It is a gift. Thank you."

The moment hung between them, heavy with meaning and yet devoid of tension. The outline of a new life, an extraordinary life, was unfurling before him.

Everything that had happened—the pain, the fear, the hurt and the confusion and the doubt—had led him here. And finally, *finally*, he was right where he wanted to be.

Michael found himself out in the garden, his sneakers squelching through the mud the storm had left behind.

"Sarah."

This, he knew, was going to be the hardest call to make. He'd dialed his parents earlier to let them know that the archivist had unexpectedly offered him an apprenticeship, and that he was taking it and thinking of a career change, one that might get him out of the city. They'd sounded relieved at the development and noted that Michael sounded more settled and happier than he had in months—years—and if he didn't confess to his relationship with Jacob, that was an understandable omission. After all, he didn't need them worrying about him being able to handle both a new job and a new relationship at the same time.

But Sarah—she was sharp enough to ask questions.

"Michael." She paused. "It's been *three weeks* since I've heard from you. I'm sorry for what I said on the last call, but did I really deserve the silent treatment? Are you okay?"

Michael sighed, but he couldn't blame her for being worried. He'd just had a lot on his mind, and none of it had been updating Sarah on how he was doing.

"I'm okay." He surprised himself by feeling like yes, it actually was okay. "Look, Sarah, I have something to tell you."

She didn't skip a beat. "Don't tell me you're moving in with the hot archivist and you two are halfway to planning a wedding. God, is that why you've been incommunicado? Here I thought it was because you were pissed at me."

"Uh." Michael gaped like a fish out of water. "Well. You got the first part right."

He was busy enough wondering if demons believed in the concept of marriage that he almost missed her question. "Michael, it's… all of this is moving awfully fast, and I don't want you to fall into a relationship because it's helping you heal from what happened to you. That's— Michael, that's not a good reason to upend your life. I'm not going to deny love at first sight and all, but I want to make sure that you're doing this for the right reasons, not the wrong ones. Is he going to treat you right?"

*He should have killed me to save himself*, Michael thought, *but he didn't*.

"Yes." Michael swallowed thickly, surprising himself with the amount of emotion in the word. "We talked, a lot. He helped me realize some things about the—about the accident that I know you were trying to tell me, Sarah. And I'm sorry that I wasn't ready to listen. It's— I know this is fast, but it feels *right*."

He decided that telling her that he and Jacob were metaphysically bound together unless he was willing to let Jacob die was a bridge too far, at least for now. Something she didn't need to know. She would take it the wrong way, and she wouldn't understand.

"Oh, Michael." Her voice was like a hug. "I'm sorry. I shouldn't have pushed so hard that I ended up pushing you away. I wanted to keep you safe. But I'm glad you found a way to save yourself from your guilt, in the end."

He blinked away the tears that were clouding his vision. "You should come up here in a few weeks. You'd love it. We could help with your research and you'll get access to stuff no one else has." Just because he was bound to Jacob, it didn't mean that others couldn't come to visit. He trusted that Jacob wouldn't harm anyone he didn't want him to.

She laughed. "I'd love that. And I'd love to meet this Jacob, if he has you so captivated. Because I also need to make sure in person that he's not an asshole."

"I think you'd like him, and his research topic." He'd decided that if he was going to try to help Jacob, he was going to help himself too, and that meant at least letting some of his friends back into his life for real. Into *their* life. "I think you'll find his work fascinating."

"I'm glad you want me to meet him." Her voice was warm. "I'm proud of you, Michael. I'm going to miss you being so close to me, but if anyone deserves a fresh start, it's you."

"You'll visit," he said, and he knew she would. Jacob would like her, the vivaciousness and wit she brought to every conversation, even if he would be peeved that he'd have to go back to hiding his wings and pretending to be nearly nocturnal.

"Yes," she affirmed. "I will."

When he ended the call, he felt it in his bones that everything was going to be alright.

Michael and Jacob sat down shoulder to shoulder at the kitchen island with his laptop in front of them but angled away from Jacob, Jacob's left wing conveniently draped around Michael's body like a blanket.

"Are you sure you want to listen to this?" He swallowed.

Jacob chuckled. "I've always been curious about the human concept of therapy. But don't make me touch the computer. It shocks me."

Michael narrowed his eyes at Jacob, then grabbed his hand and touched it to the laptop. Jacob let it happen, a long-suffering look on his face, and Michael had to apologize when sparks jumped up from the keyboard.

"The telegraph was so much better," Jacob grumbled. "Wi-Fi and I don't mix."

Michael kissed his fingers in apology and opened his browser. "You sound really old when you say things like that."

"Darling, I was born almost five thousand years ago." Jacob gave a put-upon sigh, and muttered something in a language that Michael didn't recognize. "*Really old* doesn't even begin to cover it. At least this era has air conditioning."

Michael smiled as he logged into his session with Miranda. It was the last one he would need, and he wanted to tell her goodbye. He pushed Jacob's wing off his shoulder as the video turned on.

"Michael." She greeted him with a pained smile. "I'm so pleased you picked up. Our last eight sessions, you haven't logged on. It's been two months since I heard from you. Are you alright?"

"I'm better." The answer was easy, even though he felt guilty for blowing her off for so long. "Much better. I actually wanted to have this session to tell you that I don't think I need therapy anymore."

"Why?" Her brow crinkled.

"I actually met someone." Michael felt his face flush with pleasure, and he couldn't help but sneak a look at Jacob, smiling back at him contentedly, resting his head on his folded arms. "He's brilliant, and he loves me, and I think we're going to build quite the life together. He's the archivist here, so I get to stay here in the archive. With him."

"You're moving in together?" Miranda's mouth

dropped open. "Is this the archivist you met the last time we spoke?"

"Yes?" Michael didn't understand why she looked like he'd admitted to murdering kittens for fun.

"Is he—is there another person there with you?" Miranda's eyes flicked from side to side, like she could see out of the field of vision that the laptop camera provided. "Are you—do you feel safe?"

"No, and yes." The answers were both true. Jacob wasn't anyone's definition of a person.

"Michael, I have to say this is highly concerning to me." Miranda cleared her throat. "I don't like the idea that you're moving in with someone who you've only known for such a short amount of time. It sounds like you're falling into the same habits as you did with Nate, that some of the abusive patterns are playing out again, and I'm worried about you, truly."

"You don't understand," Michael said in his most reassuring voice, because she truly didn't. "This isn't like that. This is what I've been waiting for my whole life. I'm with someone who treasures me and accepts all of me."

"It's a classic tactic of the abuser," she said, her face pale and drawn. "It's colloquially called *love bombing.* Pressure to move your relationship faster, things like rushing moving in together—"

"Thank you, but that's not what this is," he said gently, cutting her off with a raised hand. "I'll make sure to pay the bill. I don't need to schedule another session. I appreciate all your help these last few months."

"Michael—" Miranda began, but he just closed out of the browser and ended the session.

She didn't believe, and it wasn't a good use of his time to try to make her see the light. Nor was it his duty.

"Are you sure about this?" Jacob leaned into him. "You heard what she said. You can still let me kill myself to free you. I know I'm dashingly handsome and exceedingly wealthy, but I am a sheyd. And if you want me to, I'll end it all." Michael was beginning to recognize the way that Jacob tried to use dry humor to detract from his anxiety, and this was clearly one of those times.

"I could ask you to do that, to free me." Michael pushed the laptop away and turned to face Jacob fully. "But I'm not going to. Because I want this. I want you. And I don't care what you are, except that you're mine. The therapist was wrong."

Jacob smiled, his contented expression reminding Michael of a cat in the sun. "You didn't believe in me when we met. You didn't believe in anything like me."

Michael swallowed, brushing a lock of hair out of Jacob's eyes, running a thumb down the bridge of his nose and then leaning forward to kiss him slowly. Tenderly.

"I didn't believe in myself when I arrived here." He drew back enough to look Jacob in the eyes, his irises still startlingly red. "I didn't even know who I was. I was drowning, and you saved me. So don't hold my prior beliefs against me. Because now, thanks to you, I believe in all the right things."

Jacob's answering grin was like the devil, and the sun, and as Michael closed the lid of the laptop with a definitive *click*, Jacob grabbed his chin and kissed him back.

# Chapter 16

Michael Stein still wasn't a good person. And if Jacob was a person, he wouldn't have qualified as good either. But now, at least, Michael felt like they were making each other better by the day.

He was happy, researching with Jacob by his side. It was better than researching with Nate ever had been.

Days melded into nights as he and Jacob sat shoulder to shoulder in the archive room, pouring over the texts that Eleazer had collected. Sometimes Michael blinked and found it was suddenly dawn, his eyes sticky with sleep and unable to focus, and he'd fall asleep on Jacob's shoulder or lap or face-forward on the desk, resting on Shiri's purring body while fur got up his nose.

They had only gone through a tenth of what was in the archive itself, and yet Michael found his anxiety growing day by day when they still hadn't found any solution to help loosen the restrictions that Eleazer had placed on Jacob. He could stay tucked away here with Jacob forever, but eventually he would die and Jacob would be alone again.

It was Michael's job to make sure he never harmed another person he loved, which meant helping Jacob be as free as possible. So, he read and read and took notes until his fingers were bleeding, only stopping when Jacob coaxed him to bed as the sun rose, or forced him to eat, or decided to distract him by doing other, more pleasurable things.

He'd taken a book to bed one morning, something so old and fragile that he shouldn't have been reading it without proper precautions, gloves and a foam cradle at the very least. But he couldn't sleep, and Jacob was out cold next to him, snoring lightly with his left wing and arm a warm, dead weight across Michael's chest.

It was a journal written by a seventeenth-century Ashkenazi mystic who claimed to have figured out how to siphon the life-force out of his enemies, storing it to fuel spells.

His heart skipped a beat as he read, mouthing over the translation, hardly trusting his eyes. *This* was what they needed.

"Jacob," Michael said, nudging him in the ribs. "Jacob, wake up."

"No," Jacob mumbled, putting his hand over Michael's mouth without even opening his eyes.

Michael moved his hand away. "*Jacob.* You need to wake up. I found it."

"Mmph," was all he got in response, and Michael cursed inwardly that Jacob was so hard to rouse once he fell asleep. He defaulted to plan B, which was patting Shiri awake where she sat on the pillow above his head. She made a small *prrp* of acknowledgment as she climbed down on top of the wing currently pinning Michael to the bed.

"Wake him up," he asked, and Shiri gave one of her far-too-toothful grins and turned to pounce right on Jacob's head with all four of her tiny feet, causing him to jerk awake with a muffled shout.

"What the fuck?" Jacob sat up, holding Shiri away from his face while Michael cradled the book to his chest to prevent it from getting in the way of Shiri's claws. Shiri wriggled free and curled up on Michael's feet. "Please tell me there's a reason you sent our cat onto my head while I was perfectly sound asleep. It better be a good one."

Jacob was never grumpier than when he was woken up early. Michael couldn't help his fond smile. "What about waking you up to show you this?"

He held the book out, a peace offering, as Jacob ran a hand through his hair and scrubbed at his eyes. Jacob squinted at the text, and it took him less time than it had taken Michael to realize what he was reading. When he looked up, his eyes were glassy. "Do you think this is real?"

"I'm seeing it with my own eyes," Michael said gently. "So yes, I believe. It's at least worth a shot."

Jacob frowned down at the text. "I'm not sure how we'd test this."

"On me," Michael said. It was simple—he was a human, and Jacob was a sheyd, so Jacob could perform the spell on Michael to see if it worked. "Duh."

Jacob cocked his head and narrowed his eyes. "You

think I'm going to let you try something potentially life-threatening when I *just* spent all that money on jewelry."

He raised an eyebrow and glanced down at the diamond-studded platinum band sitting on the fourth finger of Michael's left hand, the mirror to the one he now wore.

"Yes." Michael poked him in the chest. "I'm sure there's some kind of return policy for the engagement ring if the spell goes wrong and I drop dead. Let's do it. Now."

Jacob's jaw cracked as he yawned. "Now? Let's go back to sleep. I'm more powerful in the dark anyway."

He put the book on his nightstand and pulled Michael back down with a wing, bundling him up so effectively that he couldn't move even if he wanted to. So he settled for snuggling into Jacob's firm chest, matching the other man's breathing as Jacob's tail stroked up and down his thigh. "Fine," he sighed. "But I'm waking you up early."

He didn't get an answer. Jacob was once again fast asleep.

Ten hours later it was twilight, and Michael had gotten Jacob downstairs, fed him, and then tugged him into the archive. Jacob shushed the mazzekin as they chattered loudly enough that even Michael could hear, but Michael didn't mind—they sounded just as excited as he was. Maybe this could be used to loosen their chains, too.

Jacob dipped his finger into the bowl of ink they'd made using clay from holy ground and the ashes of holy texts. And then he inscribed the spell onto Michael's bare chest, letter by letter, as Michael held open the book.

"Alright," Jacob said, sitting back on his haunches. "Are you sure?"

His talons were tapping nervously against the carpet. Michael put a hand out to stop them from where he was lying on his back. "Yes. Absolutely."

"I'm just going to take a little bit." Jacob glared at him. "And you're going to tell me if you feel anything off."

Michael huffed a laugh. "You're sucking out my life-force. I'm *going* to feel off."

Jacob shook his head, and Michael resisted the urge to bicker with him more, because he wanted this to work, and he couldn't do it without Jacob's cooperation. "I'll tell you," Michael amended, giving Jacob what he hoped was a conciliatory and sincere look. "Promise."

Jacob stared at him as if trying to gauge whether he was telling the truth, then bowed his head and began reading the incantation.

Michael closed his eyes against the evening light filtering in through the stained-glass window, and breathed through the tugging that started at his navel, then grew to encompass his whole chest, like he couldn't breathe. It felt like he was back in the hospital, ventilated and on painkillers so strong he couldn't move his own body, the feeling of being totally and utterly helpless making his heart jackrabbit in his chest.

But then it stopped.

"I think it worked," Jacob moaned. "But the wrong way. I feel awful."

"The binding, fuck." Michael sat up and put a hand to his head. "I didn't think about that. You draining my life-force affected you too." It felt like the world was spinning and he clenched his eyes shut against the nausea rising in his throat. Every one of his muscles ached, like he'd had the flu and his fever had just broken. "I'm sorry. I didn't realize it could."

"It doesn't matter." Jacob ruffled his wings, shaking his head, then stood up shakily. "It worked."

He pointed to the glittering shard hanging between them. A tiny, tiny bit of Michael's own life.

"Go on," Michael said with a jerk of his chin, curling onto his side to fight the dizziness. "It's yours."

Because all of Michael's life was Jacob's.

Every last second.

Every single breath.

Jacob reached out, grabbing the shard in his hands. It dissipated between his palms, and his cheeks flushed with life before it faded.

"It's like a stitch was unpicked." Jacob stared at his open palms. "Like I can breathe just a little bit easier. It worked."

The look that he gave Michael, full of love and gratitude, would live in his mind rent-free forever.

Michael took the hand that was held out and let Jacob help him up, then submitted to being crushed to the other man's chest for a long minute. Jacob didn't need to say anything. Michael felt the gratitude all the way down to the marrow of his bones.

"Couch?" he asked.

"Couch," Jacob concurred. "I need to sit down."

Michael pressed a sloppy kiss to the side of Jacob's sweat-slick neck. "And then we can talk about what you're going to do with your freedom."

"You," Jacob said, turning and pressing his lips to Michael's, tilting their foreheads together. "My whole life is you."

Amongst a haze of days, during which they ordered pizza and sat around watching old movies, normal life began to resume as they grew stronger. Jacob whined the whole time as they were recovering from the spell's aftereffects, and Michael couldn't help but laugh that his ancient, all-powerful demonic lover could be laid low by something as small as a minor illness. Jacob glared at him every time, pouting, until he offered to make it better by petting his hair and getting him to drink tea, and then kissing him senseless until he forgot that he felt like shit.

They were in the kitchen for the first time since their recovery, Michael sorting through the groceries they'd had delivered from the next town over while Jacob made a salad.

"It might kill the first few people," Jacob warned. He finished dicing the radishes and threw them into the bowl with the lettuce, and then started on the dressing, his tongue between his teeth as he read over the recipe for a homemade, low-sodium Caesar. "I don't know what I'm doing, and I won't be able to feel it the way I could with you."

"I think you'll be fine," Michael said. "Or if you're not at first, you'll get better. Fuck, I think they substituted rotini for spaghetti. Oh well."

"There's more in the cabinet," Jacob said, pointing with the knife. "I put it up high, so Shiri didn't bite through the box again. I'm not sure how many people it will take, either, to get good at this. Or to have it be enough."

Michael grabbed a chair so that he could climb up and rescue the pasta from the highest shelf. Jacob could fly—he wasn't able to. Shiri, true to form, immediately appeared out of nowhere to hop up onto Michael's shoulder, begging for a piece of pasta. She had a thing for uncooked spaghetti noodles. Michael sighed, and opened the box. "Just one, Shiri baby."

The demon chittered as she took the spaghetti in her mouth and jumped down to climb onto the windowsill with her prize. "I think we're just going to have to go slow," Michael said, stealing a salad leaf as he passed by, then a squeeze of Jacob's waist. "And I know you don't want me to leave to go recruit people to come, but it's not like we can announce an official reopening. If people die while we perfect the ritual, the police will be all over us. We have to maintain *some* level of secrecy, and that means a few business trips for me to academic conferences. That's where all the young PhD students are, anyway. I'm going to pick the best and the brightest for you, darling."

"I don't want you to leave," Jacob sighed. "And I don't want people here."

"Yeah," Michael said, turning on the water and starting to fill the pot. "Neither do I. But it's temporary. And it's for a good cause, right?"

"Right," Jacob said, blinking his blood-red eyes at Michael. He smiled. "It's for us."

It was a few months before their first researcher came, given that Michael had taken a few short trips to do translation work in the meantime, at Jacob's insistence that he keep up with his career. Once they started the spell in earnest, he wanted to finish it—and he was adamant that Michael continue with his work, even if Michael would rather hide out in the Institute forever. He'd said that he was fine with Shiri and takeout sushi, and had promised to write Michael letters every day since he still shorted out each iPhone he touched, and as a result, texting was an impossibility.

The woman looked desperately eager as she stood at their front door, a backpack slung over her shoulder and a suitcase at her side. Now that Michael had long since moved into Jacob's top-floor bedroom, which had been lavishly redecorated, their subjects would stay in the guest room he'd previously occupied.

It wasn't entirely altruistic, offering to house them. The woman looked young and healthy and vital now, but she would look quite different when she left, if she left at all. They didn't need an Airbnb owner or hotel maid finding her, or noticing she was gone.

The price of knowledge would now be one's life. Nothing permanent, hopefully, not after they'd perfected the process; nothing more than twenty or thirty years off a lifespan of decades. It was only fair that if Jacob was going to give of the knowledge he was bound to, he was also allowed to take.

It would take many, many people until they gathered enough life force to allow Jacob to push the edges of his prison outward. But until then, Michael was perfectly content to be here with him, leaving for work but knowing that he would always, always have somewhere to return to. Someone and somewhere that was *home*. The two of them had all the time in the world.

"Welcome to the Schechter Institute," Michael said, looking into the woman's eyes. Jacob's hand was warm in his, the phantom ghost of a wing brushing up against his side. "May you find truth here."

# Acknowledgements

This book wouldn't have been possible without the efforts of the team at Titan. Daniel Carpenter and Rachel Vincent, my exceptional editorial team, elevated this book beyond what I thought I could ever achieve. Dan Coxon and Paul Simpson were instrumental in ensuring that the book in your hands was free of all of the errors that tried to sneak through to the finish line. Rich Mason's work as typesetter and Natasha MacKenzie's cover art made *The Way It Haunted Him* stunning both inside and out. The publicity and marketing team—Katharine Carroll, Charlotte Kelly, Caitlin Storer, Amy Hack, and Holly Clarke—have my eternal gratitude for making sure this book found its readers. And of course, thank you to Claire Schultz and Ophelia, for advocating so hard for Shiri, on behalf of all very good (and very spooky) cats everywhere.

I'd be utterly adrift in the publishing world without my agent Sophia Ramos at New Leaf Literary. You're my perfect match, and I can't wait for all the mischief we'll get up to together. And my friends in publishing keep me sane—Saint Gibson, Ben Alderson-Quinn, my one weird Canadian friend Danielle Jensen (see, I told you I'd write it), Brigid Kemmerer, Frances White, Mai Corland, K.M. Enright, Maddie Martinez, Kamilah Cole, C.G. Drews, and Amanda Woody all deserve my undying gratitude for their friendship and support.

Tory and Bertie, neither of you could catch locusts if you tried. There aren't enough thoughts in either of your heads. But I still think you're the best cats in the world anyway.

And last but not least, my family is everything to me. Mom, Dad, Allie, Mitchell—thank you for your love and support. Sacha, thank you for inspiring every romance I write, and being the complete opposite of all of the characters in this book. I could do none of this without you, and I'm thankful every day that I am yours and you are mine. And because I always like to get in the last word: I love you most.

# About the author

Laura R. Samotin and her spouse live with two enormously large felines. When she's not pursuing her academic research on military tactics, power politics, and leadership, she relishes her role as a full-time cat servant.

Find her at www.laurarsamotin.com